C000185146

SLAU

AND

FORGETTING

Josef Slonský Investigations
Book Two

Graham Brack

SAPERE
BOOKS

SLAUGHTER
AND
FORGETTING

Published by Sapere Books.

20 Windermere Drive, Leeds, England, LS17 7UZ,
United Kingdom

saperebooks.com

ISBN: 978-1-912546-71-8

Chapter 1

Holoubek was still sprightly for his age. He admired his physique in the shop window as he waited for the tram. Still slim, with barely a hint of a paunch. He looked after himself, and it showed in his appearance. His trousers had a crease, and he only needed his glasses for reading if the light was not too good, which it frequently was not in Prague at this time of year, as winter grudgingly gave way to what was laughingly called spring.

As with many men of his generation, he wore a hat, but then you would have to be silly not to do so with a wind like this one, whisking up any loose paper and driving it against the parked cars. He did not bother with gloves, though, and checked his hands for any sign of blueness. There were a few scattered liver spots, and the skin was rather papery in places, but he still had a firm grip and at least he did not shake like his old friend Miklín. Well, like Miklín used to shake, because he was long since dead. He had been quite lucky, because he had been worried about the progression of his Parkinson's disease and fortunately walked out in front of a bus while he was thinking about it. So every cloud has a silver lining, thought Holoubek, though admittedly Miklín probably would not have seen it that way.

Holoubek remembered Miklín lying there on the ground. Oddly, he had not looked frightened; just very surprised, as if a bus was the last thing he had expected to hit him as he jaywalked across the street. He had lived for a few minutes after the collision, but was unable to speak. Just as well, because his language was shocking when he was in his prime, so goodness knows what he would have said about being run over by a bus. And not even a Czech bus either; it was a German tour bus, all glass and swirling paint along the side. Miklín could see the dent in the front where his hip had made contact with the grille, and was satisfied to note that the headlight was broken. Funny how you remember those things, thought Holoubek. *I can't remember what I had for tea yesterday, and yet I can remember a road accident thirty years ago and the look on the victim's face.*

The tram was late. Only a minute or so, but what is the point of a timetable if the drivers do not keep to it? Things were slack nowadays, Holoubek told himself. People blamed the young, but Holoubek did not. It was the young who were going to have to tidy up the mess the world was in, and it was not their fault. He blamed their parents, his children's generation. Long sideburns, leather jackets, suede boots, ridiculous moustaches like Mexican bandits, and the women all flopping around with no proper underwear on and not a trace of make-up. Certainly there were some women who could do without make-up, but this lot were not among them. There was one across the street now. Must be fifty if she was a day, and she was wearing an orange tie-dye top and jeans. Jeans were all right if you had the figure for them, but her rear end looked like a badly packed rucksack.

The bell of the tram brought him back to this world. Holoubek climbed aboard and waved his pass in the air like they used to in the old days, when citizens were likely to report you if you travelled without a ticket. Not so public-spirited now, he thought. To his surprise, a young student offered him a seat, which Holoubek politely declined. Do I look that old, he wondered, looking around to see if anyone was inspecting him.

6

His son did not like him to travel around on his own, but Holoubek had lived in Prague all his life, and he knew every centimetre of it, except the new bits, of course. When he wanted to check his mind was still working properly, he would set himself the task of plotting a journey across town, recalling all the trams and buses and the best places to change. He had never really taken to the metro for some reason, unlike Cerha. Cerha was a companion he sometimes bumped into at the Red Apple, and they would compete to work out the routes. Holoubek was unsure whether Cerha was telling the truth when he said some of these journeys could be done by metro, or simply claiming to have won on the basis that Holoubek would not be able to disprove his route.

Today's journey was quite simple. Take the number 18 tram from Palouček to Národní třída, then switch to the number 17 for the rest of the journey, with a short walk at the end. Holoubek hoped that a ticket inspector might ask for proof that he was over seventy. It had happened to him once, and he had enjoyed being able to prove he was over age. He must look younger for that to happen, he thought. Admittedly it was about fifteen years ago, but it was the principle of the thing.

The principle of the thing. Exactly the reason that he was on the tram in the first place. His son had told him to let it drop, but Holoubek could not. It was the principle of the thing — but then he couldn't expect his son to understand that. He was one of the suede booted, leather jacketed, long haired near hippy generation. Authentic. That was the word he kept using. He said it was important to live an authentic life, whatever one of those was. So far as Holoubek was concerned, you were either alive or you weren't, and if you were alive, you had a life to lead, and you'd better get on with it and stop moaning. After all, there were plenty of people in the cemeteries who would tell you that you had nothing to complain about. One of them had been telling him that for a few months now. He had a complaint to make, and he needed Holoubek to make it because he could not do it himself, having been dead all these years.

Holoubek had searched a lot of rooms in his time, and there was not much you could tell him about hidey-holes. He was known for the rigour of his searches, and this despite having spent much of his career in the force at a time when every policeman had a lot of practice in searching. Barely a day went by when they were not turning someone's flat over looking for nothing in particular. As a result, Holoubek had learned a great deal about concealment. He could find a hollow wall, a concealed panel, a false skirting board, a package in a drain pipe or a recently moved floorboard that might be hiding something of importance.

However, in 1967, someone had almost got the better of him. They had been rummaging through a flat in the Old Town where they were absolutely certain there ought to be a roll of film, but despite a fairly thorough demolition of the place it had not come to light. Holoubek was dogged — some would say pathologically stubborn — so when the others had given up, he had indulged in his favourite technique of sitting in the middle of the floor, slowly scanning the room. In this way he had come to the conclusion that the film was not under or behind something, but inside it, and after some nifty work with his penknife he had found it inside the works of the record player.

He kept this information to himself, because he wanted to have somewhere private of his own in case the tables were ever turned, and over the intervening decades he had come up with a number of cunning places to keep items of various sizes and types.

The casual visitor to Holoubek's flat would have been impressed with its general tidiness, and perhaps felt a little sad that it was still mired in the seventies or eighties. There was, for example, an old-fashioned television in the corner. Holoubek could have afforded a flat screen model, but it would have had one major drawback. His confidential notes would not have snuggled inside the casing, taped to the underside of the top surface without causing a fire risk. Thus, before catching the tram, Holoubek had carefully unscrewed the back of the television, having disconnected it from the mains some time before, and had extracted a narrow manila envelope which was nestled in his inside jacket pocket. As he sat on the number 17 tram he rubbed his upper arm against the pocket to check the envelope was still there. Only a fool puts his hand in to check; you never know who might be watching. Satisfied that it was safe, he relaxed and enjoyed the journey.

Chapter 2

Captain Josef Lukas flicked through the folder one more time. Damn! There appeared to be only one way to do this. Damn! It was going to be an awkward interview, but that was what management was for. A man could not chicken out of his responsibilities.

Slonský knocked on the door, a redundant gesture since he had opened it first and begun to walk in.

'You wanted to see me, sir?'

'Yes, Slonský. You'd better sit down.'

Slonský obeyed, and adopted a facial expression of extreme innocence, as if he could not possibly have any inkling of what was coming.

'It's about retirement, Slonský.'

'I'm sorry to hear that, sir. We'll miss you.'

'Not my retirement, Slonský. Yours!'

When he had been small, Slonský had owned a dog of indeterminate breed whose response to the word 'bath' was one of profound anxiety morphing into abject terror. There was some irony in the fact that the word 'retirement' had the same effect on Slonský. He knew, of course, that it must come. He also knew that he was approaching the age when it would be laid before him, but he had hoped that if he kept solving crime they would let him stay on. He did not want to retire, because he had nothing else to do. He did not play dominoes and he had no interest in daytime television — or evening television, for that matter. He loathed gardening and his pension would not allow him to spend all day in a bar.

Lukas wore an expression of fatherly concern.

'Have you given any thought to retirement, Slonský?'

A small fire of rebellion kindled in Slonský's chest. If he was being put out to grass, he was damned if they were going to do that to him. He would preserve his self-respect by deciding that it was his choice.

'I can't deny it would be good to have some time to myself, sir.'

Lukas threw the folder on the desk. This was not going well.

'Look here, Josef. The thing is, with Němec retiring and the reorganisation going on, we can ill afford to lose you both in such a short time. I'm sorry, but I'm just not going to be able to let you go. You'll have to stay on a while longer.'

Slonský's heart turned a few flips of delight, though he tried to conceal his pleasure.

'As you wish, sir. I'm at the Department's disposal, as ever.'

He closed the door behind him and resisted the temptation to leap up and click his heels until he could not be seen through the frosted glass, behind which Lukas was grinning. He knew all along that Slonský was dreading retirement but it was so rare that he was able to get one over his lieutenant that he had been unable to resist. The puppet-master had had his own strings pulled.

'You're looking pleased,' said Officer Jan Navrátil, glancing up from a large printout of crime statistics.

'And I have reason to be, lad. I have been assured that I will be around to complete your education. The powers that be — or, more accurately, the power that is — has decided that I am indispensable to the smooth running of this department. This calls for a celebration. As soon as you've finished whatever it is you're doing, we'll decamp to a nearby hostelry and get our consciousness obliterated on Plzeň's finest product.'

'That'll be a while,' said Navrátil. 'I'm supposed to be compiling burglary statistics from the station returns for the whole of Prague.'

'Show me,' Slonský replied.

Navrátil handed over the binder of printout.

'Correct me if I'm wrong,' Slonský began, 'but this looks like a collation of burglary statistics to me. The very thing someone has asked you to put together. Allow me to point out that you already have one here.'

'Yes, but it's not right. Some of the stations misclassify crimes, and others don't use the online system properly. If you believed these figures you'd think that there was no burglary at all in Vysočany.'

'There probably isn't,' Slonský agreed. 'There'll be damn all worth nicking there.'

'I've been at it for two hours and it's no better.'

Slonský rested his hand on Navrátil's shoulder.

'Courage, lad! Fortitude! Nil desperandum but trust in Slonský. Who asked you to do this?'

'Captain Lukas.'

'And how does he know they're wrong?'

'Because they always are.'

'But does he know what the right number is? Of course not, or he wouldn't need you to work it out. Thus, it seems to me, whatever set of numbers you give him, he will accept as accurate so long as they're different to the ones he had before. Just make them up, lad.'

Navrátil was shocked. 'You can't just make up crime statistics.'

'Of course you can. We've done it for years. Not to mention economic statistics, voting figures, almost any set of numbers you care to name.'

'But we need accurate crime statistics.'

Slonský considered this novel argument for a few moments. 'Why?'

'Well, because … if we don't know where the crime is, how will we know where to concentrate our resources?'

'Crime is everywhere, therefore the police have to be everywhere. And we don't have any spare ones now so knowing we need more doesn't help us. Let me also draw your attention to the great flaw in that argument. Criminals tend to go where there aren't policemen. Thus, if we concentrate them in one area, the crime moves to a different one and we're worse off than if we'd left things alone. The only people who want to know where the crime is are the criminals. No point burgling an estate that has been cleaned out already. And accurate crime figures, which I remind you we now publish on the internet for any Tom, Dick or Harry to see, just make for economy of effort for the criminal. We're doing their research for them, Navrátil. At least, I'm not; you are.'

'That's so cynical. Our job is to prevent crime.'

'And how many crimes have you prevented sitting on your backside in this office all afternoon? Whereas if you and I had been tucking into a well-earned sausage down the road, we might have overheard criminals plotting a crime. They don't come into police stations to do it, Navrátil. Except the ones who are policemen themselves, of course.'

Navrátil chewed the end of his pencil while he tried to come to terms with the enormity of the course Slonský was setting before him.

'It's no good, sir. Making up figures is just plain wrong.'

Slonský leaned over Navrátil's shoulder.

'Not making them up is wasting time.'

A set of footsteps could be heard in the corridor. Slonský looked up in time to see a figure bearing a tray walking past the door.

'Hey, Matějka!' Slonský called.

The figure stopped walking and reversed one step. He did not attempt to turn, but nudged the door open with the back of his shoulder and turned his head to look through the resultant gap.

'What?'

'Will you answer a question for me?'

'Depends what it is.'

'Do you swear that the answer you are about to give is the truth, the whole truth and nothing but the truth?'

'Not till I know the question.'

'Fair enough. When did you last look at the crime statistics?'

'Why would I do that?' asked Matějka.

'Aha! I rest my case, Navrátil. It doesn't matter what the statistics say because nobody looks at them. Thanks, Matějka. By the way, Martinů just ran off with your ham sandwich.'

'How could … Oi! Martinů! I want a word with you.'

Navrátil still looked uneasy.

'Go on, lad,' said Slonský in his most seductive voice. 'Make one up. You know you want to.'

'I don't! I can't!'

'Of course you can. All it takes is a small movement of that little pencil of yours with the soggy top. Forty-five is a nice number. Let's have forty-five of something. Forty-five housebreakings in Kbely — or perhaps forty-five car thefts in Libuš.'

'Why not forty-five garrottings in Kunratice?'

'Don't be ridiculous, boy. We'd have put a stop to that before now.'

Navrátil pounced. 'So if I made up a report of a garrotting in Kunratice, that would be shocking, but making up forty-five car thefts is acceptable?'

'I didn't say it was acceptable. I said it was accepted. You have a lot to learn about the traditional Czech approach to statistics, lad.' Slonský sat down and stretched his legs across his desk. 'Back in the old days — don't roll your eyes like that, Navrátil, people will think you're simple — we collected statistics on crime. Because we weren't very good at policing, a lot of crime went unpunished. This damaged confidence in the police force but, more importantly, the public felt unsafe. How can you sleep if you think you may be murdered in your bed? We had three alternatives, Navrátil. We could get better at detecting crime — obviously a non-starter. We could pin the blame on a scapegoat and tell the public it was all sorted out. Scapegoats were plentiful and the government wrote the court reports so that worked quite well, all things considered. Then someone came up with the masterstroke, Plan C. Stop collecting statistics. Once we had as many murders as we could handle, we stopped collecting the data. If the bigwigs said we would have no more than ten murders in Brno, then we stopped counting once we got to ten. This improved public confidence in the police, because each year the number went down a bit. People felt safer. They were just as likely to be bludgeoned to death as before, but the point is they didn't think they were.'

'That's scandalous,' Navrátil protested.

'No doubt. But it happened. You couldn't collect a statistic without knowing why it was wanted. Look, hand me down that big book off the top of the cabinet beside you and I'll show you what I mean.'

Navrátil collected the dusty volume and brought it to Slonský, who riffled through the pages until he came to a table.

'Ah, here we are, lad. This is a table showing the number of secret police informants in Czechoslovakia in 1950 and 1952. What's the population of Prague?'

'One and a quarter million.'

'Population of Plzeň?'

'I don't know. A hundred and fifty thousand, maybe?'

'We'll go along with that. Odd, then, that in 1950 there were seventy-five informants in Prague but 1,135 in Plzeň, wouldn't you say? Even odder, look at Ústí nad Labem. In 1950, there were forty-six informants, but just two years later there were over thirteen hundred. Now tell me, son, what do you think? Are those facts, or imaginative statistics?'

'Imaginative? Don't you mean imaginary?'

An indulgent smile flickered across Slonský's lips.

'No, I mean what I say. Imaginative in the sense of creative. Imaginary statistics are something completely different. Imaginary statistics are the ones we used to make us look good.'

Navrátil's head was spinning. He grabbed his temples with both hands in a pointless effort to make the world stop.

'Suppose your police district didn't have its ten murders. People would think they'd probably happened, but you were too useless to discover them. So if you didn't make your quota, you might invent an imaginary crime or two. This was a good thing, because our success rate on clearing up imaginary crime was nearly a hundred per cent. So, instead of reporting eight murders, of which we had cleared up two, we'd report ten murders of which we had solved four. See the power of statistics, Navrátil? With the stroke of a pen, we'd gone from a twenty-five per cent success rate to a forty per cent rate. The public were happy, we were happy, everyone was happy. They were simpler times then.' Slonský emitted a nostalgic sigh. 'I'm going to get us some coffee, Navrátil. By the time I come back I want that report finished so we can get on with some proper policing. How you do that is up to you.'

The tap on his shoulder made Slonský jump.

'Do you have to do that, Mucha? I nearly wet myself.'

'That's your age,' explained the desk sergeant. 'Sudden excitement and — whoosh!'

'There's no whoosh involved,' replied Slonský. 'I meant I almost spilled these coffees.'

'Whose are those?'

'One for me, one for Navrátil. His is the smaller one.'

'Which one is that?'

'I don't know until I get them upstairs, do I? Depends how much I spill. Anyway, what do you want?'

'There's an old man at the desk asking for you.'

'Why me? He doesn't have a black cloak and a large scythe, does he?'

'No, you're safe there. He's nearer to that than you are.'

'Thank goodness for that.'

Sergeant Pavel Mucha watched Slonský's face closely for a reaction as he explained who was waiting. 'It's Holoubek. Remember him?'

'Holoubek? Is he still alive?'

'Well, he was when I came looking for you, but given the time it's taken…'

'What does he want?'

'Don't ask me. You're the detective. I'm just a lowly desk sergeant.'

'Were you around when he was here?'

'Oh, yes,' said Mucha. 'Not at the desk then, but on the force.'

'Do me a favour, then. I'll fetch him upstairs if you get a third coffee and bring them up to my office.'

Slonský forced the cups into Mucha's hands and strode off along the corridor.

'I'll get one for myself, then, shall I?' asked Mucha in a resentful tone.

'If you like. You can pay for my two while you're at it. I left my money in my coat.'

Holoubek looked around as he sat in the chair Slonský offered him.

'Could do with a lick of paint,' he offered. He took a sip of coffee. 'That's no better either,' he decided.

'What can I do for you, Mr Holoubek?'

'Call me Edvard. I saw you mentioned a lot in the papers recently over that German chap who topped himself.'

'Dr Sammler.'

'That's the one. You did a good job running him down, I thought. Obviously took the easy way out rather than go to court and prison. Can't have been a simple case for you.'

'It wasn't,' agreed Slonský, glancing at Navrátil as he answered. His assistant appeared to be fascinated by an imaginary mark on his desk top.

'And I thought "Slonský: I remember a likely lad called Slonský from my time on the force. There can't be many of that name. I've never met another one."'

'My dad had it, but I agree it's uncommon. And I was on the force in your day.'

'So I thought to myself, that's the sort of man who can help me with my problem. Someone who remembers those days but wasn't high enough up to have been involved in it all.'

'Involved in what?'

Holoubek ignored the question as he expounded his thoughts. It was unclear whether he was deaf, single-minded or just plain rude.

'I saw young Tripka downstairs. What does he do now?'

'Colonel Tripka is in the National Anti-Drug Centre.'

'Young Tripka?' Navrátil blurted out.

'His father was a policeman before him. For a while they were both on the force at the same time, hence Old Tripka and Young Tripka,' explained Slonský.

'Old Tripka was an StB liaison officer,' Holoubek added.

'Responsible for keeping us out of the way when the Secret Police were running something. In which capacity,' Slonský added, 'I'm glad to say he was completely useless.'

'Total waste of space,' Holoubek agreed. 'Of course, they didn't trust him, so they didn't share their plans with him, so it was hardly his fault. Still, good to know his boy hasn't followed in his footsteps.'

'We don't have a secret police any more,' Slonský pointed out.

'Not that we admit to,' Holoubek said, 'but you and I know that can't be true, don't we? Where would our security be without a secret police, eh?'

Slonský saw no point in trying to answer a man who so clearly had a closed mind about the StB. Slonský's own recollection was that the secret police were a pretty ineffectual bunch much of the time, and that many of the "plots" they claimed to have foiled were actually little projects of their own that had gone off at half-cock. There was, to name just one, an entertaining confusion when an StB agent had borrowed some army explosives to equip a dissident cell to blow up a railway line on the outskirts of Prague, only to be arrested himself by the "dissidents" who turned out to be StB agents to a man. However, Slonský held the view that the Czech Republic was better off without these clowns, and he did not think Holoubek was likely to agree with him.

'You mentioned a problem,' said Slonský. 'What kind of problem?'

Holoubek paused and wiped his lips with a grubby handkerchief.

'I've got something on my conscience,' he began.

'Haven't we all?' agreed Slonský. 'You couldn't be a policeman then without your conscience having a rough ride now and again.'

'I know,' said Holoubek. 'But even so…'

'Why don't you just tell me the facts? I'm not going to judge you.'

Holoubek remained silent for a few seconds, made as if to speak, and stopped. After a moment or two, he seemed to have satisfied himself that he knew how to tell the story, and he began again.

'Cast your mind back to 1976.'

'I'll do that. Navrátil, don't even attempt it.'

'I'll tell you the story as I knew it. That doesn't mean that it's right, just that it's what I heard or saw. I was working the night shift when we got a call to a house in Ruzyně. That was when the airport wasn't so big. There were some nice villas out that way, and it turned out to be one of those we were called to. When we got there we found a young girl in a blood bath. She'd been stabbed multiple times and was lying in the bathroom where it looked as if someone had tried to make a tourniquet out of a towel to staunch the flow from an artery in her forearm. We couldn't get much information because there was no-one else there. The door was wide open, the lights were blazing, and there was evidence that at least three people had been drinking and eating, but no sign of them.'

'Did a male or female ring it in?'

'A male. Didn't give a name. Didn't sound drunk or stoned, though one of the other officers reckoned he could smell something in the room when he first arrived that might have been cannabis. But remember that this was 1976. We had no DNA testing then, and drugs weren't easily come by in Prague, so he may have been mistaken.'

Holoubek took a sip of coffee, though it must have been cold by now.

'We didn't know whose villa it was, but after a bit of hunting around we found some papers. It turned out to belong to a man called Válek, who was director of a factory making kitchen goods — you know, toasters, grills, that sort of thing. Válek was out at a function with his wife and the dead girl was his daughter Jana. He came home around two in the morning before we'd managed to trace him. Bloody mess. The idiots who were supposed to be guarding the front door let him wander in on the grounds that it was his house, so I soon had them shipped off to some God-forsaken hole in Slovakia where their lack of brains wouldn't be noticed.'

'Whose case was it?' asked Slonský.

'Well, mine at first, but it turned out that Válek had connections — his wife was sister to someone in high places — and after a day and a half I had Vaněček put in charge over me.'

'I didn't know him,' Slonský said.

'Not many more brains that those numbskulls I sent to Slovakia, but a few notches up the ladder. Knew which backsides to kiss. It didn't hurt that his brother was a film director who could get you tickets for things.'

'You're spared that now, Navrátil,' Slonský interrupted. 'The people who could lay their hands on things used to get on in life, whatever their talent or lack of it.'

'Vaněček looked good on May Day. He had a chest full of medals and nobody was very clear how he'd got them until we discovered that he sat on one of the committees that decided who got them. Vain man. Had a desk the size of Austria and nothing useful ever came off it,' Holoubek continued.

'What rank?'

'I'm not sure now. A long way above me, that's for sure. But he'd never been a policeman. He'd been in the army and transferred across via the People's Militia. He had no idea how to run an investigation. To his credit, he knew that. He took me aside on the first morning and told me that although he was nominally in charge, he was going to let me get on with it. I had to brief him twice a day so he could report up the line. It sounds like good delegation but actually it was work avoidance.'

Holoubek paused for a moment. He looked confused.

'Is there a toilet somewhere near? It's that damn coffee.'

'Navrátil, would you show Mr Holoubek to the toilet and escort him back?'

While they were gone, Slonský found a few biscuits in his desk to keep his brain energy stores fuelled. He had intended to share them, but they took too long to come back and missed out.

'Where was I?'

'You were telling us that you were left in charge when Vaněček took over.'

'For a while. But it wasn't an easy inquiry. We found the man who had called us. He lived a few doors away and had seen a car driving away at speed from the villa with its lights off. He insisted he had given his name to the officer who took the call, but it had not been recorded. Anyway, he had gone down to the house to complain about the noise and found the door open. He discovered the body and used the villa's telephone to call the police.'

'Did he have an alibi?'

'His wife said he had been muttering about the noise from around nine o'clock, so finally she had told him to either go and sort it out or stop moaning about it. Off he trotted down the road, and you know the rest. We couldn't find out who was there with her. None of her friends could give us a name for either of the lads we knew must have been there. She allegedly didn't have a boyfriend.'

'Any scientific evidence?'

'I'm just coming to that. Let me keep my thoughts in order. The pathologist told us we'd read it all wrongly. His view was that she hadn't been killed in a frenzied attack. She had been stabbed a lot of times, as if the murderer was trying to see how many different places he could stab her before she died. It was a bit like that game when you have to pull out sticks and see who makes the marble drop.'

'Two killers, then, competing?'

'It looked that way. The arm wound had been the one that killed her. It severed her artery. But the pathologist said she had been conscious throughout and the loud music was probably to drown out her screams. That, and a gag that had been in her mouth and split the junction of her lips on each side.'

'Had she been interfered with?'

'She certainly had. But the pathologist thought that only one boy had raped her. I didn't really understand the test but he reckoned there was only one lot of semen there.'

Holoubek began to look weary, and Slonský hoped that he would stay awake long enough to finish his story, or at least not lose his thread and start asking where he had got to.

'After a week or so Vaněček assigned me to another case for a few days, so I lost touch with what was happening, though colleagues told me the investigation was fairly aimless. You'll have had some of those, no doubt, when nothing seems to lead to anything worthwhile and you just find yourself doing something just so nobody can say you're doing nothing.'

'One or two,' Slonský agreed. 'Or a few hundred.'

'Well, you can imagine how surprised I was when I heard that Vaněček had made an arrest and that someone had been charged with the rape and murder. Things can happen quickly, as you know, but there hadn't been a sniff of the lead at the start of that week and I couldn't find anyone working on the case who knew where Vaněček had found the evidence. The man he had charged was called Ľubomir Bartoš. He was a Slovak, around thirty years old, with a list of convictions for cat burglary. First jailed when he was about seventeen. Now, I didn't know Bartoš from Adam, but the whole thing struck me as strange.'

'Earn your crust, then, Navrátil,' Slonský interrupted. 'Why would it strike Mr Holoubek as unusual?'

'Cat burglars aren't usually violent,' Navrátil suggested. 'They travel light, so they wouldn't carry a weapon.'

Holoubek nodded approvingly.

'Not bad, son. I checked the records for Bartoš's previous arrests. Not once had he been found with a weapon on him. Of course, you can do someone some damage with a jemmy or a screwdriver, but that's different to packing a weapon that could do the sort of injury done to that poor young girl.'

Navrátil was feeling a little smug, but that was soon put right by Slonský's next comment.

'Of course, you missed the key point, which is that cat burglars, by the very nature of their calling, are usually wiry little blokes because big men aren't that agile. And pinning down a woman who isn't drugged to rape her is easier for a big man than a skinny gymnast. How big was Bartoš, Edvard?'

'Around one metre sixty-five, perhaps sixty kilos. Not much bigger than the girl herself.'

'But he had an accomplice, didn't he?' Navrátil interjected. 'You told us there had been three people there.'

'Sharp lad, this one,' Holoubek told Slonský approvingly. 'Now there's another odd thing, because the scene of crime report that I saw now only mentioned one visitor. Vaněček didn't seem to be interested in finding the other man. He'd got one, and he constructed a series of events that only required one. According to this, the girl fainted from blood loss, then Bartoš raped her.'

'Couldn't it have been that way?' asked Navrátil.

'Now there you go again, lad,' Slonský growled. 'One thing right, then one thing wrong. You heard there were three there. But in any event I'll bet the pathologist knew she struggled during the rape.'

'Extensive bruising that wouldn't have been so marked if she hadn't been able to fight,' agreed Holoubek.

'So what did young Bartoš have to say about it all?'

'It's hard to say. At first, nothing. But he was hauled into court surprisingly quickly. I didn't know it was scheduled and I wasn't there, but one of his guards said he kicked up a hell of a racket when he discovered what he was charged with, and in the end the judges had him taken back to his cell and tried him in his absence. Tried in his absence and convicted in his absence.'

'But unfortunately not hanged in his absence.'

'No. But you're leaping ahead a bit. Between the trial and the execution I had a call from the remand prison in Olomouc. That's around two hundred and eighty kilometres from Prague, you know.'

'Yes, I know. Did you know that, Navrátil?'

'I do now.'

Holoubek leaned forward as if about to impart a great secret.

'The director wanted to know whether Bartoš was coming back. I said he wasn't, but asked why he was asking me. He said "Of course I'm asking you. You signed the transfer request." Of course I hadn't, so I asked if I could have a copy. He mumbled about the fact that he'd sent someone to be hanged on what turned out to be a forgery, and in those days you knew that the kind of people who could organise that would be the ones you didn't want to mess with, so he told me it wouldn't be "convenient" to make a copy, and his photocopier was broken, he claimed. But before he rang off I got one thing out of him. I don't remember the exact dates, but one thing was crystal clear. Bartoš couldn't have done it, because when the crime was committed he was already sitting in jail in Olomouc.'

'So what did you do?'

'I tackled Vaněček about it, but he just waved me off. Said the prison director was an idiot and had got the dates wrong.

When I tried to ring the prison, the director had been reassigned and nobody was quite sure where he had gone. So I took a chance and went down to Pankrác Prison to talk to Bartoš. Unsurprisingly he wasn't keen to talk to me, because he thought I'd stitched him up. He said this fellow Holoubek had visited him in Olomouc and got him to sign something about a break-in in Prague. Bartoš couldn't actually read and write, but he didn't like to admit it. He was told if he admitted to this one he could forget the other eight cases, so as he saw it he'd get a lighter sentence for one than he would for eight. I asked him who this other Holoubek was, but I didn't recognise the description and he couldn't tell me anything useful that would help me pin it down.'

'Could it have been Vaněček?'

'No, for two reasons. One, he was too bone idle to do that and two, he hadn't the brains to come up with it. I knew Vaněček hadn't left Prague. He might have known who went though, but I never got the chance to ask him. He wouldn't talk to me about it and then he was retired about three years later when he screwed up a case. Dead within nine months in a gardening accident. They reckon he had a heart attack and fell on a fence post. Stupid way an idiot like that would die.'

'So, if not Vaněček…?'

'Good question. I've often thought about it, and I don't know. But I've got one more clue. Bartoš was a Catholic and he asked for a priest before his execution. You didn't always get one, but he did, and the priest told me that as he was being dragged from his cell Bartoš shouted "Tell Holoubek he knows Mandy."'

'Mean anything to you?'

'No, not a thing. From the context it must have been either the murderer or the policeman who came to get him, and since

I had no reason to think Bartoš knew the murderer, it must have been the policeman.'

'So we've got a miscarriage of justice and an unsolved murder. But they're nearly thirty years old.'

'I haven't finished,' Holoubek snapped. 'I got hold of Bartoš's things and drove to Slovakia to give them to his family. His mother wouldn't talk to me at first — she thought I'd been the one who'd stitched up her son — but I told her what I knew and said I'd try to clear her son's name. After a while I reached a dead end and I stopped, and there it stays to this day. But I'm not getting any younger, and it's weighing on my mind.' He fished in his pocket for the folder of papers. 'I've kept a few documents all these years. Some tell you what I've said, and some are copies of the original papers. Not many, but it's all I could get then. I don't know if the files are still around but if they are, you're the kind of man who could get them. Will you do this for me, Slonský? Will you help an old colleague's conscience?'

Slonský held his hand out for the folder.

'Out of respect for you, I'll read these. I'm not promising that we'll get anywhere. You've done this job, Edvard. You know what the chances are of picking up an inquiry successfully after thirty years.'

Holoubek nodded. 'Yes, it's a long shot. But at least I can say I've tried. And since it won't be long now before I'm going to meet up with Bartoš again, it would be good to be able to tell him I didn't forget him.' The old man picked up his coat and shook Slonský's hand. 'I'm grateful that you're even trying. Please keep me informed. I don't have a phone. Somehow when you've bugged dozens you don't want one yourself.'

'I'll get Navrátil to drop you off.'

'No point. I get free tram rides. We can't go wasting police fuel, can we?'

The faintest of smiles ran across his face fleetingly, then Holoubek turned away and tottered off along the corridor.

'Well, Navrátil, what do you think?'

'That's incredible. We hanged a man for a crime when we knew he couldn't have done it. Where was his lawyer when this was going on?'

'The chances are he got a court-appointed lawyer, who was probably told he'd confessed and who wouldn't want to oppose the State prosecutor anyway. The thought of pleading not guilty wouldn't occur to him. He'd see his job as finding some mitigating factors to reduce the sentence. Back then you didn't get too many people walking free once they were charged. It made the state look bad, you see. Can't have that.'

'But Bartoš died. It wasn't a case of eighteen months in jail then picking up where he left off. He went to the gallows.'

'He wasn't the first and he wasn't the last. Sit down and I'll tell you a bit of family history.'

Navrátil was concerned that he might be about to hear some shocking revelation, but took a seat where Holoubek had been sitting, across the desk from Slonský.

'How many Slonskýs do you know?'

'One. You.'

'Not a common name then. You heard me tell Holoubek that my dad had it. Not strictly true.'

'No?'

'No. Did you ever hear of Rudolf Slánský?'

'Yes, in history. Some kind of party bigwig just after the war.'

'Not just a bigwig. Slánský was general secretary of the Czechoslovak Communist Party. He was effectively number two in the country, second only to Gottwald. Then in 1951

Gottwald had him arrested and tried for treason, and he was hanged a year later. My dad was also called Slánský, and he decided that it wasn't a good name to have. Fortunately, his army discharge papers had been badly typed and the name was barely legible. Dad persuaded a clerk that the name was Slonský and managed to get a whole new set of papers in the Slonský name. That's why I'm a Slonský. But I was born a Slánský and that was my name until I was four or five.'

'Was it that bad?'

'It was worse than that bad. If people thought you were family of the accused, they'd shun you. You wouldn't get served in shops. A similar thing happened after the Russians came in 1968. If you'd been a progressive, some people idolised you, and others wouldn't pee on you if you were on fire. And the bit that got to me was that this wasn't foreigners doing this; this was Czechs doing this to Czechs. Or sometimes to Slovaks. Look at Holoubek. He's not a bad man at all, but you heard some of the things he had to do. And listen to the way he talks about Slovaks and Slovakia. He sent those guards there as if it was the end of the world. He said their lack of brains wouldn't be noticed there. I've met relatively educated Czechs who talk about Slovaks as if they were animals. I've never understood it. Okay, so they talk funny, but they're human beings. Most of them.'

Navrátil waited for Slonský to sit down again before speaking.

'Do you think you can help him? Won't all the files be gone by now?'

Slonský frowned in thought.

'Probably not. One thing we lead the world in is bureaucracy, and I can't imagine any clerk in the communist era deciding to throw any paperwork out unless he was specifically told to do so. In which event either the file was burned by 1977 or it'll be around now somewhere. I've no idea where, but the starting point is our own connoisseur of bureaucracy.'

'How long ago?' asked Mucha incredulously.

'Around thirty years. Nineteen seventy-six. Do you think those files will still be around?' asked Slonský.

'How should I know? And all this is to satisfy an old man's whim?'

'No, if the old man is right, it's to give a family justice. I'm up for that.'

Mucha shrugged his shoulders. 'Put that way, so am I. No point in being here if we aren't. Tell me some more, then. Where was it?'

'Ruzyně.'

'That would be here, then. Even through the reorganisations it's always been under the Prague office. Victim's name?'

'Jana Válková. Aged sixteen or so, I guess.'

'I remember that case. She was repeatedly stabbed, wasn't she? Who was the investigating officer?'

'Someone called Vaněček.'

Mucha chuckled. 'Vaněček? He was my boss for a while.'

Slonský became energised. 'What was he like?'

'Pretty useless. No, I take that back. He was completely useless. So far as I remember, he came to us from the army. He had been a staff officer responsible for planning. After the Russians came they didn't want anyone left in the Czechoslovak Army who might be able to plan a revolt, so he was moved out. If they'd had any sense they'd have left him in post, because any rebellion Vaněček organised would be doomed to failure.'

'He can't have been that bad. He got promoted several times.'

'Yes, he got promoted, but not for anything to do with military ability or policing skills. He was a grade A brown nose, always sniffing round the Presidium to see who could give him a leg up. But there was one thing he did well,' Mucha added grudgingly. 'He could certainly organise a parade.'

'A parade?'

'That was his main job. For years Vaněček organised the police element in the May Day parades. And if you wanted a bit of a show, Vaněček could lay it on for you. It didn't matter what it was, a band, a few police cars, if the price was right Vaněček could make it happen. He persuaded me to turn out as part of a guard of honour for a police officer's wedding once. We were introduced as "his men". None of us had ever clapped eyes on him before. Still, I bought my daughter her first bike on the proceeds of that.'

'Fascinating though this is, can we get back to the subject of the Válková file? How would we find out if it still exists?'

Mucha stroked his chin.

'We could look in the index. But to be honest, if there was anything controversial in the file, it wouldn't be in the general index. There is a private index but I don't have access to it. However, taking the whole thing into account, I think the best method of getting the file is just to ask for it.'

'Ask for it?'

'Yes. You know, just saying "Can I have it?"'

'Would that work?'

'Oh, yes! Gives it the appearance of normality. If you do it that way. the clerk who retrieves it probably won't even look at it, whereas if you make a big fuss about it they get very protective of their paperwork. If it doesn't exist any longer, they'll say so. Trust me, that's the way to do it.'

'I do trust you. Sort of. As much as I trust anyone.'

'That's your problem, old friend. You want to do everything yourself because you don't trust anyone else.'

Slonský waved a languid hand in the direction of a waiter, and was rewarded with a large glass of beer and a hunk of bread and cheese. He had taken a bite of it before he realised that he had actually ordered some sausage, but shrugged and carried on chewing. All around him there were the sounds of people enjoying themselves. It made you sick, he thought. All this frivolity and fun when so much is going wrong in the world.

The bar door opened and a small man with thinning hair and glasses came in. Although it was not a cold evening he was wearing a crimson scarf tied tightly at his neck, and a grey woollen overcoat. He removed both and laid them along a seat as he spotted Slonský's back.

'You look glum,' Valentin announced. 'Bad day?'

'Normal day,' replied Slonský. 'Bad is normal lately.'

'Come on,' said Valentin, 'I'll buy you a drink.'

'That's not normal,' Slonský noted. 'Are you sickening for something?'

'Fit as a fiddle, old pal. I never thought I would see having less drinking time as an improvement, but there you are. It just goes to show that you never can tell.'

Valentin was a journalist, or at least that was what he had managed to trick his editor into believing. Although quite well connected, his liking for a bottle or six had held him back. He and Slonský were long-time drinking companions, though they could go weeks without meeting up. At the moment, encounters were limited because Valentin was in demand.

At a time when Valentin's editor had been uttering dark threats about the removal of his retainer and a return to payment per story, Slonský had slipped Valentin two front page specials. The first had exposed a leading politician's liaison with a rent boy, while the second was an exclusive story that a recently dismissed government minister had been appointed to a plum job in Brussels. The fact that the minister had been sacked after Slonský wrongly arrested him for murder did not feature in Valentin's story. The result of these scoops was startling. Valentin was suddenly much in demand as a journalist and, although his retainer had been restored, he was having to work much harder because other magazines and media wanted him to work for them. This had severely restricted his drinking time, caused him to have a professional haircut rather than do it himself with a mirror and a pair of scissors, and had reacquainted him with the necktie as an everyday item of apparel. Admittedly "everyday" was a suitable description of the single tie he owned, but it was necessary if he wanted to appear on television. Valentin's television career had so far been limited to a short interview at 23:00 one Thursday evening and a recorded piece shown at breakfast time, but he lived in hope. Radio was rather kinder to him, and he had become a regular pundit on an afternoon phone-in where his characteristic blend of acerbic wit and complete failure to do any homework had won him something of a following amongst those who do not get out much.

'So what's the problem?' Valentin asked.

'Off the record?'

'Need you ask?'

'Yes. Just to be sure.'

'Then, for the avoidance of doubt, this is off the record.'

'I had a visit today from an old boy of around ninety who used to be a policeman.'

'You see, the good don't all die young.'

'No, I suppose not. His conscience is pricking him and he wants me to reopen a case from thirty years ago.'

'Don't touch it with a bargepole, that's my advice. If you fail everyone will say what a waste of time it was, and if you succeed the headlines will read "Police solve case after thirty-one years". It's not worth it.'

'Someone was hanged for something they didn't do, Valentin. That makes it worth it.'

Valentin inspected the bottom of his glass through the golden liquid for a few moments.

'Yes, I suppose it does. Who, when, why?'

'A fellow called Bartoš back in 1976. Accused of rape and murder of a girl called Jana Válková in Ruzyně. But he can't have done it because at the time the murder was committed, he was already in jail in Olomouc.'

'And his lawyer forgot to mention this in court?'

'Not a dickybird.'

'Who was his lawyer?'

'Good question. I'll have to find out.'

'It's not a unique event, Josef. A lot of people were banged up for things they didn't do, or there wouldn't be crimes today.'

'I know. But there's a difference between being banged up and strung up. I just can't see why someone would do that to a stranger.'

'Ah, the inexplicable crying out to be explained. I can sympathise with that.'

'But can we do it? How do we explain something that happened so long ago when a lot of those who were involved will be dead and gone?'

Valentin raised his glass to his lips and spoke cheerily.

'You don't know that. If you don't investigate, no-one will ever put this right. And if you can't succeed now, it isn't going to be any easier for anyone coming after you. You know you can count on my assistance.'

'Excellent,' said Slonský. 'You can have a read through the back issues from 1976 and see if there's anything in the papers I can use. Meantime, I'm going to have one more for the road. You've brightened me up, Valentin. I can see light at the end of the tunnel.'

'Careful,' Valentin replied. 'That light could be an approaching train.'

Chapter 3

Life with Slonský was full of non-sequiturs, thought Navrátil. Having been informed by his boss that they were going to do a little delving into Holoubek's case, just to see if there was enough in it to warrant asking Lukas if they could formally reopen the matter, Navrátil had quite properly asked where they were going to start.

'There's only one place to start with a case like this,' replied Slonský, before clamming up and saying no more on the subject. In the car his conversation was limited to deciding where they might grab a quick lunch and criticising Navrátil's use of the rear view mirror, though without his usual sharpness. It was as if the criticism were expected of him but his heart was not really in it.

'Pull in over there and we'll walk the rest of the way,' Slonský instructed.

The old detective flung open the car door and strode into the little cemetery, occasionally glancing at a small map he had drawn.

'She should be along this row somewhere,' he announced to nobody in particular, Navrátil having lagged a few metres behind as a result of having to lock the car up.

Navrátil felt unable to run given where they were, but was relieved when Slonský suddenly stopped and turned to face a black headstone on which some writing infilled with gold could be seen. It declared the occupant of the grave to be Jana Válková, born 23rd February 1959, died 16th July 1976, beloved daughter of Jan Válek and his wife Helena. For some minutes Slonský stood in silence as if paying his respects. He even removed his hat. Navrátil failed to see how this was advancing the inquiry but he knew better than to interrupt, so he waited patiently until Slonský squatted and picked a couple of weeds from the foot of the grave.

'What are we doing here, sir?'

'It helps. I don't know how, but being with the victim helps me. It makes me realise how important it is that we pin the blame on the person who put her there. Seventeen, Navrátil. A year older than I thought, but still it's no age. What would she be now — late forties? She should have a husband and maybe a couple of children, looking forward to being a granny. Instead of which she's been lying in this cold earth longer than you've been alive. I was twenty-eight when she was killed, lad. That's how long she's been waiting for someone to find her real murderer.'

'Bartoš is a victim too. Are we going to his grave?'

'He probably doesn't have one. More often than not they cremated criminals and scattered the ashes on the roads. If his family were lucky they may have been given an urn, but I wouldn't guarantee the right remains are in it.'

'Are her parents still alive, sir?'

'That's a good question, Navrátil. You can find me a good answer. If she's an only child born in 1959 the chances are her parents would be around seventy now, so they may still be about. The Social Security Administration in Křížová could tell you if they're drawing pensions. There can't be too many Váleks around and you've got their first names.'

'Will that be enough, sir?'

'What more do you want? Use your brain, son, if you have one. You know their surname, their first names, whom they were married to, the date of birth of their daughter — whom they will have registered — where they lived in 1976 and the

38

fact that they were probably born between 1930 and 1935. If you can't find them with that little lot give up policing and try journalism.'

Slonský stomped off towards the car, and this time Navrátil deliberately gave him a ten metre start. As he climbed in the car he braced himself for a disagreeable journey if Slonský was in one of his moods, but the temper seemed to have dissipated in moments.

'Next stop the villa, Navrátil. Try using the mirror once or twice if you can, just for form's sake. And if you see a decent bakery, pull over. I'm peckish.'

There was not much of the villa still standing. It was surrounded with security fencing on which a large notice proclaimed that it was to be replaced by a prestige development of four shoeboxes created by a local developer. However, since the sign also proclaimed that they would be ready in autumn 2004, it looked likely that the developer had run out of cash.

Slonský fished in his pocket for a penknife.

'Anyone watching, Navrátil?'

'No, sir.'

'Good.'

Slonský busied himself in some secretive manoeuvre at the fence, until a loud click announced that a padlock had come undone and they were able to part the fence panels sufficiently to slip inside.

'Come on, Navrátil, don't dawdle.'

'I'm watching for the guard dogs, sir.'

'Navrátil, the sign is at least three years old. There probably never were guard dogs. I'd like to think if I employed dogs and someone rattled the padlock chain like I just did they would at least come over to see what was happening, if only out of curiosity. But I didn't hear a bark, so I think we can assume the dogs are long since gone.'

The front door was still present, though hanging slightly open. Slonský shoved it with his shoulder and they were able to stand in the entrance hall.

'That'll be the room where she was stabbed. She'd trailed blood from there to the bathroom. The pathologist thought the boys might have carried her there, because the blood droplets and spurts didn't make sense if she had been upright.'

Slonský turned down a side corridor and pushed a door open. He pointed to a pipe sticking out of the floor.

'Bath was there. So she was stabbed repeatedly to the left of the front door and then brought across the lobby and down here to be patched up. Why? They were never going to let her live once she'd seen them.'

Slonský flicked his diary open.

'Sunset in mid-July would be around nine o'clock. The man who found the body said the lights were blazing. We need to find out when he came over. Navrátil, are you making notes of this?'

'Yes, sir.'

'It can't have been that late because the man who found her hadn't gone to bed. And I don't suppose the murderers knew when Válek would return. But Holoubek said he was on night shift.'

Slonský ambled around the building for a few minutes, then stood in the doorway scanning the houses opposite.

'Nobody directly opposite, so they probably weren't going to be observed through the window.'

'There was probably a hedge too, sir. Look at the cuttings and the stumps by the fence.'

'Well spotted, lad. Which one of these is number twenty-six?'

They turned slightly right and walked up the road. Number twenty-six was the second house they passed.

'I wonder why the folks at the first house didn't seem bothered by the music. Anyway, Navrátil, this is where the man lived who found her.'

An elderly lady was putting a bag of rubbish in a bin at the back of the house. Slonský went forward to speak to her.

'Good morning, madam. You wouldn't be Mrs Kopecká, by any chance?'

'Who's asking?'

Slonský flashed his badge in mute response.

'There's no point showing me that, young man. I don't have my glasses.'

'Lieutenant Slonský, Criminal Police. And this is Officer Navrátil. We're here about the murder of Jana Válková.'

'You took your time getting here,' the lady replied. 'We rang in 1976.'

For once Slonský was lost for words, until an impish smile on her face told him she was teasing him.

'Would you like some coffee? I'm about to make some for my husband anyway.'

'Your husband? I didn't think he'd still … didn't think to ask about him.'

She led them into the back door.

'He's not been well,' she whispered. 'He can't walk much and it gets him down. And he forgets things. He says I didn't tell him, but I did. He just forgets things.'

The man in question was sitting in a winged armchair with his feet on a small stool. His ankles looked far too large for the rest of him, but Michal Kopecký had obviously been a lean, vigorous man. His hair still showed streaks of black within the silver, and he was neatly dressed in a checked shirt and navy trousers. He wore a padded waistcoat for warmth, beneath which his chest periodically heaved in an effort to fill his lungs.

'These gentlemen are from the police,' Mrs Kopecká explained.

'What have you done?' he asked. 'Have they come to arrest you?'

'Of course not,' she told him. 'They want to ask you about poor Jana Válková.'

Kopecký waved his hand dismissively.

'That was months ago,' he said. 'And I thought they hanged someone for it.'

'We did,' said Slonský, 'but I believe you said there were two of them. And we never found the other one.'

Kopecký's eyes glowed for a moment.

'That's right. There were three dirty beer glasses. I remember now.'

'Very good,' Slonský nodded encouragingly. 'Three beer glasses. Large ones, or small?'

'Half-litre glasses. One had a handle but two didn't. One had about two centimetres of beer left in the bottom.'

'And where were they?'

'In the kitchen.'

'That's the room straight in front of you when you come in the door.'

'Yes.'

'I know you've told us before, but I'd like to hear you tell the whole story if you can, Mr Kopecký. You were disturbed by the noise. When was this?'

'It went on all evening. Válek and his wife went out about seven, and the music started around eight or half past. At least, that's when we heard it, didn't we?'

His wife was not there to agree or argue.

'But your neighbour didn't complain, although he was nearer?'

'Old Hruška? He was deaf as a post. Of course, he was very old. Over eighty.'

'You're over eighty yourself, dear,' said Mrs Kopecká, who had returned with a tray of coffee and a plate of buns which she carefully placed in front of Navrátil.

'Am I? How old am I?'

'Eighty-two, dear.'

'Well I never.' Kopecký shook his head in astonishment, and showed no sign of continuing with his account.

'So you heard music about eight o'clock or shortly after. How long did you let it go on before you complained?' asked Slonský.

'Quite a while. You can't tell young people things. But I thought if I spoke to Jana she would understand. She was a sensible girl.'

'A very sensible girl,' agreed Mrs Kopecká. 'She used to come to me to practise her sewing. Her mother didn't sew, you see.'

'Not the sort of girl to keep bad company, then?'

'Oh, no!' said Mrs Kopecká. 'She was a good girl. Of course, she was at that age when they want to show a bit of independence, and she was very aware that Daddy was somebody. I mean, that he had a position.'

'We all did,' sniffed Kopecký. 'That's how we got these villas. You had to have a certain position.'

'What was your job, Mr Kopecký?'

'I made newsreels.'

'Don't be modest, dear,' said his wife. 'These gentlemen need to know a bit more than that. My husband was responsible for making government information films. Not the political ones, of course. But he made a lot of civil defence films. That's why he was such a good witness, that's what the policeman said.'

'I don't suppose you remember that policeman's name?'

'No, sorry. It's months ago now,' Kopecký apologised. 'Some kind of bird. Holoubek! That's it — though he was too dark to be a real dove, I remember my wife saying. We laughed about that when he'd gone.'

Slonský was intrigued.

'It's Mr Holoubek who asked me to come to see you. He's retired now, you see.'

'Nice man. But it was odd that he came, because they'd already arrested that cat robber.'

'Cat burglar, dear. They call them cat burglars,' his wife interjected.

'Do they? Well, that Slovak. But Holoubek kept saying to me "You're sure there were two men?" And he asked me if I knew how the men came or went. Well, I told him I'd seen a car driving off very quickly with no lights on. I'd mentioned that when I called.'

'I'm getting a bit confused, Mr Kopecký. On the night you called, Holoubek came to see you.'

'No, Holoubek was here. I remember seeing him. He was walking around in front of the villa shouting a lot. He woke us up at two o'clock shouting at the policemen by the gate. He told them they were going to be sent to the tiniest station he could find in the Tatra mountains to see if they could learn some common sense. I remember that.'

Slonský suppressed a chuckle. He could imagine Holoubek saying that to some poor, witless officers.

'But he didn't speak to you?'

'Not then. He sent some other officer to take a statement, then we heard nothing for a while. But about a week later another policeman turned up.'

'Can you describe him?'

'Middle-aged. Stocky. He kept his hat on so I didn't see his colouring.'

'In uniform?'

'No. Overcoat and dark hat.'

'He didn't give his name?'

'No. In those days the police didn't. But he must have been police because a police car brought him. I saw it parked outside and the driver waited.'

'So, when did you speak to Holoubek?'

'Like I said, when they were just about to hang that cat robber. He said he had to get to the bottom of it quickly because they were going to hang that man and then they would never find out who the other one had been. But he said he didn't think the Slovak had done the killing anyway, so there were two murderers out there still.'

Mrs Kopecká's hand flew to her mouth in shock.

'Michal! You never told me that.'

'I didn't want to worry you, dear. And I expect they're safely under lock and key now, because I haven't heard about any more killings around here since.'

If only that were true, thought Slonský. Maybe they just didn't register. Shame Lukas didn't have the same problems with his memory.

'Let's go back to that evening when you found the bodies. Friday, sixteenth of July, 1976. It was the Friday night?'

'Yes. Definitely Friday.'

'And you were disturbed around half past eight. Holoubek tells me you were grumbling about it to your wife and she told you to go and sort it out.'

'It wasn't quite like that. I didn't like to stop their fun, but it was getting on for bedtime, and you couldn't sleep with that racket.'

'So that was — what? Eleven-thirty? Midnight?'

'Good heavens, no,' said Mrs Kopecká. 'Ten o'clock.'

'Ten?' asked Slonský, who could not remember ever going to bed at ten.

'That's right,' said her husband. 'Early to bed, early to rise. Once the sun goes down, you go to bed. When it gets up, so do you. Always lived that way. I can't understand these people who lie in. They miss the best part of the day, don't you think?'

'Yes,' agreed Slonský quickly, marking Kopecký down as a grade A nutter.

'So a bit before ten I walked down the hill to their house to ask them to turn the music down. But as I got to the street I saw two lads run to a dark car and drive off at speed with no lights on.'

'No lights on — so it was after dark?'

'It hadn't been dark long, or we'd have been in bed. But they should have put their lights on. Nobody would see a dark car in that light.'

'So you carried on to the house?'

'Well, the music still needed turning down. I got to the gate and I could see the door open, and I suddenly thought "What if they've been robbed and all that music was to cover the noise?" So I pushed the door wide open, waited in case anyone else made a run for it, then I went in. The door to my left was open and that's where the music was coming from, but there was no-one in the room. The lights were on, and the furniture had been pushed back, I think, because there was a clear space in the middle of the floor. But what alarmed me was that the carpet was stained with fresh blood.'

'A lot of blood?'

'They say it always looks a lot, but I'd say there was at least a cupful, maybe more. The shape was like a crucifix. There were blotches of blood where her arms must have been, some more round her ankles, and some in the middle, by her … well, in the middle.'

'Like she'd been sexually assaulted?'

'I suppose so. I looked in the next doorway, which was the kitchen, but that looked in quite good order except for the three beer glasses. Then there was another door that turned out to be a closet, and the one beyond that was the bathroom. She was in there.'

'I don't want to distress you, but it would help if you could describe what you saw in detail.'

Kopecký closed his eyes and concentrated.

'Pale blue tiles to my left. A tub straight in front going across the room with the taps at the right hand end. Her left arm was draped over the side of the bath and blood was dripping down the white side. You couldn't see her, just the arm. I ran to see her. I don't think she was quite dead. She didn't respond, but she was very warm. I couldn't take her pulse because her arms were slimy with blood and I didn't know then that you could do it any other way. Her slacks and underwear had been pulled down and she was bleeding down there, and it looked like there were little punctures in her tummy and breast. One breast was exposed — her right one. There was a cross cut in her nipple. She was wearing a red and navy striped top and her hair was held together with a red band to make a ponytail. Her head was turned to her left and the right side of her face was bruised and covered with a smear of blood from just above her hairline, where there was a nasty bleeding gash. Her right arm had bled a lot and the curtain had been yanked down and wrapped around it. It was sodden with blood. There was a towel in her left armpit soaked with blood from a cut in her upper arm. Her feet were close together but you could see blood running down one foot from a cut over her ankle. And there was half a footprint.'

'Half a footprint?' Slonský did not recall that appearing anywhere in Holoubek's notes.

'The front part of a left boot. Some kind of shoe with a big tread pattern. Whoever wore it must have trodden in some blood and left the mark in the middle of the bathroom floor. There was a fainter mark by the door.'

'This is really good, Mr Kopecký. You obviously have a good memory.'

'Not now. I don't remember names. But scenes — that's what I did all my working life. It's a silly thought, I know, but I remember thinking that if I'd posed the scene I'd have put her in the bath the other way round. Who sits at the plug end?'

'Was there any water in the bath?'

'No, none.'

'And no knife?'

'There was a small blood-stained knife on the floor at the end of the bath where her feet were. Just an ordinary kitchen knife like my wife uses to peel potatoes.'

'But that can't have done the damage you saw. You didn't see another knife anywhere?'

'No, not a sign of one.'

'Let's go back to the two lads. You didn't see their faces?'

'No. They were quite a distance away. The one who got in the front was broader. Not fat, just muscular. The one who got in the back was much slighter.'

'Colouring?'

'I couldn't see in that light. And neither had much hair.'

'Skinheads, I expect,' Mrs Kopecká added.

'So the chunky one was the driver?'

Kopecký looked up, his face creased in a deep frown.

'No, they both got in the passenger side. I told the policeman that at the time. Someone else drove them.'

Slonský glanced at Navrátil, who looked as astonished as he was himself.

'A third man?' Slonský muttered.

Kopecký began humming. It took Slonský a little while to recognise the tune.

'One of my favourite films,' Kopecký explained. 'Orson Welles. Paul Hörbiger. Hedwig Bleibtreu.'

Slonský interrupted before Kopecký decided to give them the whole cast.

'So the car came to collect them, or it was there all the time?'

Kopecký stopped abruptly. 'What car?'

'The car the two men got into. Outside the Váleks' house.'

'When was this, old chap?'

'You were telling us about the day you found Jana Válková.'

'Ah, yes.' There was a pause before Kopecký continued. 'What was the question again?'

'Was the car they got into outside all night?'

'I can answer that,' said Mrs Kopecká. 'It can't have been, because I took old Mr Hruška a bit of strudel. He had a sweet tooth, but once his wife died … anyway, there wasn't a car outside then. That would be about eight o'clock.'

Slonský picked up his hat.

'Thank you both. You've been very helpful. And thank you for the coffee. Navrátil, any further questions?'

Navrátil's cheeks were puffed out with the last piece of bun he had hurriedly pushed into his mouth when he realised that they were leaving. He suspected that might have been why Slonský asked him the question, because he was rarely given any chance to ask a question of his own at interviews. He chewed fast and swallowed hard.

'Do you know what happened to Mr and Mrs Válek?'

Mrs Kopecká looked apologetic.

'I don't know exactly where and when they went, I'm afraid. They stayed here for a few months, but Mrs Válková couldn't face living in that house. They eventually managed to get a flat in Prague. Whether they're still there, I don't know. Of course, if he's still alive, Mr Válek would be retired by now. They didn't keep in touch.'

The detectives said goodbye and walked back to their car.

'Damn!' Slonský repeated several times.

'What's the matter, sir?'

'If it happened now, Navrátil, it would be an open and shut case. We'd get DNA off the beer glasses, we'd have forensics on the footprints, there'd probably have been video surveillance tapes on an estate like this.'

'Surely they could have done better with what they had, though, sir, even if it was thirty years ago?'

'That's what troubles me most, Navrátil. They could have done so much better. That's what you get for putting a jumped-up circus ringmaster in charge. I could do with something to take away the taste of that coffee, lad. Pull up at the first place you see.'

'There's a burger bar at the airport, sir.'

'Okay, Navrátil. Then pull up at the second place you see.'

Lukas quickly slipped on his best jacket and straightened his tie. It was important to set a good example to young officers. He could not recall meeting Peiperová before, and was therefore surprised when he discovered that she was quite a pretty girl, which Slonský had not mentioned, with long blonde hair bundled up into a knot of some kind at the back. She was also about as tall as Lukas, and she was in uniform.

Lukas stretched forward his hand in greeting, and was met with a formal salute, which he returned rather awkwardly and hurriedly.

'Ah, yes. Jolly good. Stand easy, Officer Peiperová.'

'Thank you, sir.'

'Look, we don't go in for all that formality here. Except on formal occasions, of course, when we tend to be more … formal. Please sit down.'

Lukas introduced himself, described the criminal division to her, then invited Peiperová to tell him about herself.

'Where shall I start, sir?'

'Hm? Oh, birth, I think. I like to know all I can about the staff here.'

Peiperová launched into a description of her life and family, though Lukas was using the time to think about whom she could be attached to. It was, of course, asking too much of Slonský to babysit two young officers. On the other hand, he could not think of anyone else to whom to allocate her. With a start he realised that she had stopped speaking.

'Excellent. First class. Well now, before we assign you permanently, I thought it would be best if you spent a few days with people you already know,' he improvised. 'I believe you've worked with Lieutenant Slonský and Officer Navrátil before.'

'Yes, sir.'

She smiled, which lit up Lukas' rather forbidding office. It disconcerted him and he lost his thread.

'Where was I?'

'Lieutenant Slonský, sir.'

'Ah, yes. Good man, Slonský, with a long record of distinguished service. You'll find him honest, intelligent, observant, but also inclined to cut corners. Shocking approach to administrative tasks. Don't be infected with his lax view of record-keeping. He has done wonders with young Navrátil, who has the makings of a first class detective.'

'I'm sure I'll learn a lot, sir.'

'I'm sure you will,' agreed Lukas, hoping fervently that the things she learned from Slonský would be of a kind that he would approve. 'Unfortunately I can't introduce you just at the moment, because they're out following up a lead somewhere. That's another of Slonský's foibles. He keeps his cards close to his chest, especially when it comes to telling us where he is. But it seems to be somewhere with a poor telephone signal. Well, shall I take you to the canteen and we can have a coffee before I get Sergeant Mucha to find someone to take you over to the barracks?'

Lukas tried to sneak a peek at his watch surreptitiously. He could see it was quarter to something or other, but without pulling his sleeve back he could not quite see the hour. Where was Slonský?

Admittedly he had forgotten to remind Slonský that Officer Peiperová would be reporting for duty that day, but that was not the point. It was part of Slonský's general sloppy approach that nobody knew where he was and his mobile phone was switched off.

The object of his wrath was sitting on a stool putting himself outside a large *párek* and wincing at the disgusting muck that passed for coffee there.

'I almost wish we'd gone to the burger bar,' he muttered.

'They're not as bad as you think. Have you ever been to one?' asked Navrátil.

'Yes. That's why I only almost wish we'd gone there. I know what we've been spared.'

'Your phone is ringing.'

'No, lad, it isn't ringing because I've turned the sound off. But I'll grant that it is flashing and vibrating.'

Having spotted the name Mucha on the screen, he deigned to answer.

'Discount Funeral Parlour.'

'Slonský, Lukas is going ape here. Where are you?'

'Investigating a murder in Ruzyně.'

'Which murder in Ruzyně?'

'The one in 1976.'

'Have you just found the paperwork on your desk?'

'I'll treat that remark with the contempt it merits. I'd hang up on you if I didn't want to hear more about Lukas throwing a wobbler.'

'He's got that young woman from Kladno here and nobody to take her off his hands. He thought you'd be here to show her the ropes.'

'That arrangement might have worked better if he'd asked me about it.'

'It must have slipped his mind. Anyway, that doesn't mean you won't cop it if you don't get back here sharpish.'

'Hang on — I'll have to consult my social diary to see what I'm doing this afternoon.'

'You're free. Now get your backside over here, Batman — and best bring Robin with you. She's asked for him and if you aren't careful people will wonder how she knows him.'

'We're on our way,' announced Slonský, fearful that his brilliant ruse was about to be rumbled.

He slurped the last of his coffee on the principle that he had paid for it, however vile it proved to be.

'What did Mucha want?' asked Navrátil.

'There's a beautiful princess back at the office looking for a frog to kiss,' said Slonský. 'You'll do.'

Lukas had never been happier to see Slonský. If he had possessed a tail it would have wagged violently as the old detective eased through the doorway of Lukas' office. Springing to his feet, Lukas introduced Peiperová, then recalled that Slonský had recommended her, so they must have met already. He asked Slonský to look after Officer Peiperová for a few days until proper arrangements could be made.

'Of course, sir,' said Slonský. 'It will be my pleasure.'

This was untrue. Slonský did not want Peiperová around because she had such a profound effect on Navrátil, whose mouth dropped open when she passed by and who was prone to dribbling if she bent over to pick something off the floor. At that moment Navrátil was in the toilet examining his appearance in the mirror and wishing he had brought a spare shirt that did not look as if wrestlers had spent an hour rolling over it.

It occurred to Slonský that Lukas was so delighted to see him that there was mileage in asking for something he would not ordinarily get. The trouble was that there was nothing he particularly wanted. He hated taking holidays, his expenses were all up to date and he did not have space for a bigger desk.

Nevertheless, there were expectations of a man in his position, and he would never forgive himself if he did not take advantage of the situation.

'Will Officer Peiperová be sharing our small office, sir?' he asked.

Lukas smiled fixedly, though plainly uncomfortable with this discussion.

'That's the plan. For now.'

'Very good, sir. Then we'll need an extra chair.'

Lukas breathed a deep sigh of relief. He had anticipated a request for at least one more office, or a conference table. A chair was easily arranged.

'Of course, Lieutenant. I'll get Mucha to find you one.'

'Thank you, sir. This way, Peiperová.'

Slonský led the way to his office and held the door open, bowing his head slightly as she preceded him into the dark, utilitarian space. Navrátil performed his jack in the box impersonation, bounding out of his chair with such dispatch that his knee hit the edge of the desk and he had to bite his lip to conceal the pain.

'You know Officer Peiperová, of course.'

'Yes, sir. Good day, Officer Peiperová.'

'Good day, Officer Navrátil,' she replied.

Slonský took his seat with a broad grin.

'Well, isn't this nice?' he said. 'I love it when children play happily together. Of course, I'm aware that you two have each had one of Cupid's little arrows in your backside and that despite the formal greetings you're probably hoping I'll leave the room so you can attack each other like limpets.'

He leaned forward and fixed each in turn with a hard gaze.

'If you do anything like that on duty, I will send you, Peiperová, back to Kladno licketty-spit, and you, Navrátil, will find yourself on point duty in the busiest crossroads I can find. Is that clear?'

'Yes, sir,' they chorused.

'Outside hours, I do not care if you fornicate yourselves into a stupor and wreck half the beds of Prague, so long as I do not hear about it. Is that also clear?'

'Sir!' Navrátil began, 'Miss Peiperová and I have never…'

'No doubt!' said Slonský. 'And it's none of my business anyway. Just make sure that it stays none of my business. Whatever you do, don't do it here. And whatever you don't do, don't do that here either.'

'Yes, sir,' Peiperová replied.

'Do I have your agreement too, Officer Navrátil?'

'Yes, sir.'

'Good. Then let's not talk about that again. Peiperová, I recall that you make a good cup of coffee.'

'I make coffee too, sir. It's not just women's work,' protested Navrátil.

Slonský turned slowly towards his assistant. 'Did I say it was?' he asked quietly.

'No, but…'

'No, I didn't. Perhaps Peiperová does it better. Perhaps I want to have a man to man chat to you behind her back. Perhaps as soon as she is gone I plan to leap over the desk and strangle you with my shoelace. But if she doesn't go and make some damn coffee we'll never know, will we?' he roared.

Along the corridor Lukas looked up. It was unlike Slonský to raise his voice like that. He hoped he had done the right thing, but then contented himself with the reflection that since he had no other options, it must have been the right thing.

Chapter 4

Holoubek patted each of his pockets in turn to ensure that the contents were in order. House keys in the left pocket, handkerchief and comb in the right, bus pass in the breast pocket, identification in the inside jacket pocket over his heart, wallet in the other inside pocket. There were a few coins in the right lower jacket pocket and a small packet of sugar cubes picked up in a café in the other lower jacket pocket in case he felt tired. At 14:27 he left the house, knowing that his normal stride would take him to the tram stop without having to rush but without a long wait either. He had something to tell Slonský. It could have been done over the telephone, but Holoubek's hearing was not as sharp as it had been and he found the telephone difficult sometimes, to the point of having had it removed. Besides, if he still had the phone his son would call from time to time, but he would never see him. This way Ondřej had to show his face once in a while. He was a good boy, really. He just did not have a sense of family. That's why his wife turfed him out. That, and the incident with the gym teacher. She was a bit of all right, though. Nothing between the ears but if you wanted someone who could do a handstand in the shower, she was your girl. Of course, once he was available she went off him. Forbidden fruit and all that, thought Holoubek.

The tram arrived, and Holoubek boarded, waving his pass at nobody in particular. Fortunately no-one tried to strike up a conversation with him, and after a change of tram he arrived at police headquarters and was pleased to see the same desk sergeant was on duty.

'Holoubek, Edvard, to see Lieutenant Slonský.'

'If you'll take a seat, Mr Holoubek, I'll check he's in his office.'

Mucha rang Slonský's extension.

'Slonský.'

'Good, that's who I hoped you'd be. Mr Holoubek is back to see you.'

'He can't.'

'Why not?' hissed Mucha, who was dreading having to tell Holoubek that Slonský would not see him.

'Because I've only got three chairs and we're sitting on them. Unless, of course, he brings one up with him.'

Mucha counted to ten under his breath.

'I'll bring one with me, shall I?'

'That would work,' agreed Slonský.

A few minutes later Mucha and Holoubek arrived at Slonský's office. Holoubek now understood why Mucha was carrying a chair, which he offered Slonský with a flourish.

'Your chair, Lieutenant.'

'Thank you,' said Slonský politely. 'Just a minute.'

He fished in his pocket and gave Mucha a five-crown coin.

'God bless you, sir,' said Mucha, tugging his forelock. 'May you live for a thousand years.'

'Thank you,' said Slonský again.

'And have piles for nine hundred and ninety-nine of them,' continued Mucha.

Slonský kicked the door shut behind him.

'Now, Mr Holoubek…'

'Edvard.'

'Edvard. What can I do for you today?'

'Who is the young lady?'

'That is Officer Peiperová. She has just joined us today.'

Holoubek stood and offered his hand, which Peiperová accepted and shook firmly.

'We didn't have women officers in my day,' he said. 'Except the ones we used to trap Western diplomats, of course.'

Slonský coughed long and loud, causing Navrátil to go for some water. By the time he returned, Holoubek had forgotten the subject and had passed serenely to the question of his recent discovery.

'I went home after I saw you,' he said, 'and it occurred to me that I'd given you the copies of the official notes, but I hadn't given you these.' He pulled an old exercise book from the inside of his shirt. It was warm. 'My notes. I'm afraid they're not systematic — I just jotted things down as I discovered them. And there isn't much there you don't already know. But I tracked Válek down to his new flat in Karlín, so the address is in there. I was also suspicious about what happened to Vaněček.'

'When he died?'

'Well, that as well, though I couldn't find anything about that. But the case that he was alleged to have fouled up.'

'Why do you say "alleged"?'

'Oh, someone messed up, there's no doubt about that. Unlikely to be Vaněček, of course, because he never did anything, so how could he mess up?'

'Surely the buck stops with the man in charge?'

'Yes,' Holoubek accepted, 'but Vaněček had winkled his way out of that before. This time he couldn't do it. I was in Prague at the time, so I heard the rumours. They said that he had crossed an StB operation and unwittingly exposed an agent. Well, if he did, he wasn't the first. It was an occupational hazard, because StB didn't tell us what they were up to, so how could we keep out of their way? Like we said the other day,

Tripka was supposed to prevent it, but he was as much use as a glass hammer. Anyway, when the dust had settled I asked a few folks I thought might know, and they told me that Tripka had actually warned Vaněček off, but Vaněček pressed on because he wanted to nail an American diplomat for currency smuggling and, according to Vaněček, that was an ordinary crime such as his police should deal with.'

'He had a point,' remarked Slonský.

'If he said it. But I knew Vaněček. He'd never said anything remotely like that before. As far as he was concerned, once StB moved in, he shipped out. He warned us many times not to interfere with their "work of the highest national importance". So I found out where he was living and went to see him. He wouldn't talk to me. At least, not about that. I think he was worried that his house was bugged, because as I left he walked me up the garden path to the gate and whispered that he couldn't tell what he knew, because that was the deal he'd had to make with *them*. And a fortnight or so later he had his accident. I've often wondered if the two events were connected. Did he fall on the fence post because someone thought he'd spoken to me? If so, he was really shafted, because he didn't speak to me and they bumped him off anyway.'

'Did those things really happen then?' asked Navrátil.

'Oh, yes,' said Slonský. 'It didn't do to cross the secret police, even if you were in the business. There was a fellow I worked with called Zeman. He arrested a French embassy junior of some kind for indecency in a public place, and since he was a bright lad, he rang the StB and told them he'd got a hold over a foreigner. That was what we were meant to do. They ambled over, took the Frenchman away, told Zeman what a good job he'd done and he could expect a bit of a bonus. The bonus didn't arrive, so Zeman mentioned the incident to his boss one afternoon. Next evening, four heavies kicked the living daylights out of him in an alley not far from here. He lost the sight of an eye and was invalided out. And his boss was packed off to hold back any invading Hungarians at a customs post.'

Holoubek nodded. He knew some similar stories, but out of the corner of his eye he could see that his tram left in eight minutes.

'Are you getting anywhere?' he asked.

'We've spoken to Kopecký, who —'

'— found the body. I know who Kopecký was. He's still alive then. Must be some age.'

'Eight years younger than you, I think. But you're wearing better. The old chap's memory isn't good. But he remembers 1976 like it was yesterday.'

'Don't we all?' agreed Holoubek. 'Will his testimony be any use in court?'

Slonský considered carefully.

'I believe him. I wouldn't trust him to tell me what he had for lunch today, but take him back thirty years and his memory is sound as a bell. But a good defence lawyer would just tie him in knots and invite the judge to chuck him out. It's the perennial problem with cold cases. How much can you rely on elderly witnesses? That's my problem with these Nazi hunters. Those Nazis deserve to be punished, but how can you get a safe conviction? Anyone who was old enough to understand what they were witnessing is going to be over seventy now.'

'We're not all gaga, you know,' Holoubek bristled.

'Not all. But some are. That's why Navrátil and I have picked it up. If Jana Válková's killers aren't found now, they never will be. I don't know if Captain Lukas is going to let us take it on, but we're doing the spadework to build the best case we can to convince him.'

Holoubek pushed himself upwards with a great effort.

'Well, I wish you luck. I asked you to try, and you're trying. I can't ask for more. I should have done more myself.'

He waved a hand at Navrátil and Peiperová and headed for the door, stopping as he reached the handle.

'Keep me posted,' he ordered.

'I can't promise there'll be more to report, but if we're allowed to carry on, I'll let you know,' Slonský replied.

Holoubek nodded his appreciation, and smiled gently as he left. Navrátil followed to see him safely down to the front door.

'He seems like a nice old man,' said Peiperová.

'You think so? No better, no worse than the rest of us. You'll have to learn that those of us who have been around for a while have skeletons in our closets. The state put them there. We had to do things that we ought not to have done. Suspects beaten up, witnesses intimidated, evidence concocted, we've all done it. The generation coming to the fore now is the first one with the possibility of having clean hands. Of course, some of them haven't because they're grasping, conniving, devious, unprincipled ordinary human beings. So the torch passes to your age group. I want to live to see a police force I can be proud of from top to bottom, and I'm relying on you to give me one.'

Peiperová smiled. 'Me personally, sir?'

'Why not? Just promise me one thing. If you make it to Director, make sure you give Navrátil a hard time.'

'Why do I deserve a hard time?' asked Navrátil as he re-entered the office.

'Karma,' answered Slonský. 'And probably your Feng Shui.'

'I thought only buildings had that.'

'Look at you, lad. Full of untidy angles. Whereas Peiperová doesn't have a sharp corner on her. Altogether much more soothing to look at. Now, either come in or go and get some coffee from the canteen. Better still, let's give our new colleague a tour of the neighbourhood, starting with the bar on the corner. Peiperová, have you brought any other clothes? You're a detective now, and we only wear our uniforms on special occasions — parades, national holidays and disciplinary hearings. At least that's when I wear mine. Nip back to your room and change into civvies and meet us downstairs at the desk.'

Peiperová stood up and began to raise an arm.

'If that's a salute I'll break your elbow.'

'Just about to scratch my ear, sir.'

Peiperová looked around her and sipped the drink Navrátil had bought her without having to ask what she wanted. Slonský detected cranberry juice and ice in it, and that was enough for him to decide he wanted to know no more. At least Navrátil was still drinking beer.

'It's nice here,' Peiperová decided. 'Lively.'

'On the plus side, it's near the office,' Slonský said. 'But that brings us to the minus side, which is that it's always full of police.'

'Is that so bad?' she asked.

'I don't mind working with them,' Slonský replied, 'but that doesn't mean I want to hang around with them. There are some of them I wouldn't trust as far as I could spit them.'

Peiperová laughed. In her blouson jacket, white sleeveless top and jeans, with her blonde hair released from whatever implement of restraint held it under her hat during the day, she looked completely different. Slonský was enjoying sitting with her, once he had got over the shock of having, for the first time in his life, a colleague who wore makeup.

Navrátil had restrained himself long enough.

'Can we talk shop a moment, sir? Do you think Captain Lukas will let us investigate the Válková murder properly?'

Slonský rolled a mouthful of beer round his gums before replying.

'Not a snowball's chance in hell. And if I were in his shoes, I wouldn't either. To take up a cold case you need new evidence and a realistic chance of a conviction. Even if Kopecký told us anything new today, how credible a witness would he be?'

'He's not exactly demented, sir. Just a bit of short term memory loss. His long term memory is fine.'

'I believe you, but how would you prove it? The natural tendency is to forget things, Navrátil, and the more time passes the more we forget. Kopecký is unusual in having — apparently — been frozen in time. But it's hard to prove. Old men forget; it's what they do. So unless we find something else, we'll be told to stop wasting time and get back to the present day.'

'But an innocent man was hanged, sir.'

Slonský frowned.

'I'm not sure he was innocent, lad. None of us are. We've all done something deserving of punishment. But I grant he didn't do what they strung him up for.'

'Then we ought to clear his name. More to the point, we ought to find who really did it.'

'I admire the sentiment, son, I really do. But even if we find them, I doubt we'll get enough evidence to convict.'

Navrátil hesitated. He knew he had a convincing argument, but he was unsure that he dared to use it.

'Who cares about conviction?' he answered. 'If they know that we know they did it, that's enough for me. Conviction if we can get one, of course, but that isn't everything. We've worked on a case where we knew we wouldn't get a conviction, but we didn't let that stop us doing what we thought was right.'

Slonský looked grave.

'I didn't let it stop *me*,' he said. 'You keep yourself out of it.'

Turning to Peiperová he explained Navrátil's allusion.

'Navrátil is reminding me that we knew we couldn't get a conviction in the Sammler case. I kept the pressure on him in the hope that he would confess, but he didn't. At least, not in a way we could use.'

Navrátil was not giving in that easily.

'But you will ask Captain Lukas, sir?'

'Yes, I'll ask. I promised Holoubek I'd ask. But I also warned him that we might not be allowed to continue. And this is not a case we can pick up in our spare time, Navrátil. If you want to be useful, make me a list of loose ends we could still investigate. Now, can we talk about something else?'

'Yes, sir. What would you like to talk about?'

'Well, for a start, I'd like to know what Captain Lukas said to our new recruit here, because he's said damn all to me about what I'm meant to do with her.'

Peiperová shook her head. 'I've got no idea, sir. He said he hadn't decided exactly where I should be placed, and the people he wanted to talk to about me weren't around for a few days, so he thought I could start with you since we'd already met and you'd been the one who put my name forward. By the way, sir, thank you for that.'

'No thanks necessary, young lady. Unless I need a favour, in which event I'll remind you of my help loud and clear until it gets across. So, if the people are away that gives us two candidates straight off. Lieutenant Dvorník is on holiday in Bavaria with his chubby little wife and his rosy-cheeked little offspring. And if I remember correctly Lieutenant Doležal is on a course in Brno swotting up on character profiling or some such tosh.'

'What are they like, sir?'

'Dvorník's all right, if you don't like excitement in your life and you want endless discussions about his mother's cooking and the best types of dumpling. His wife is allegedly a good cook, which, he says, is why he married her.'

'Why didn't he just hire her as a cook?' asked Navrátil.

'Yes, we wondered that. Wives are much more expensive. On the other hand, cooks don't commonly have three children for you, especially after they've seen the first globular little horror. I've forgotten his name, but Dvorník used to bring him in to show him off, wedged in a pushchair. Doležal couldn't be more different. Mid-forties, probably sleeps in his suit, unmarried. Stamp collecting is his thing.' He leaned forward confidentially and dropped his voice. 'People say he listens to classical music. I've never caught him at it but he shuts his office door when he's working, so who knows. Peiperová, we're relying on you to discover if those rumours are true.'

'I'll do my best, sir. Do they specialize in anything?'

'Dvorník doesn't like burglaries. If he had his way he'd only do murders, but as senior lieutenant I get more of them. Doležal specializes in dullness. Even Klinger in the fraud squad says Doležal is boring company, and if Klinger says someone is boring, you'd better believe it. He isn't exactly a sparkling companion himself.'

'Do they have vacancies for an assistant, sir?'

Slonský had not considered that and it was a moment or two before he felt able to reply.

'Dvorník already has Hauzer. Doležal has an ex-academy lad like Navrátil here, but from the class before.'

'That must be Rada,' Navrátil chipped in. 'Tall, thin chap who wears a lot of black.'

'That'll be the one,' agreed Slonský. 'Looks like a professional mourner.'

Peiperová looked perturbed.

'So if they've got assistants, and you've got Officer Navrátil, maybe there isn't a place for me at all.'

It was at this point that Slonský opened his mouth without thinking. Looking back later, he had no idea why he did it, because it had got him into trouble before and was about to do so again.

'Don't you worry,' he said. 'Your Uncle Josef will take care of you.'

Peiperová jumped up and hugged him.

'Thank you!' she squealed.

Everyone turned to look at her. Those who recognised Slonský were astonished. Nobody had ever thought that an attractive young woman would be moved enough to make physical contact with him voluntarily. It was one of those moments they would describe to disbelieving colleagues for some time to come. Their memories of the incident would, no doubt, become embellished with time, because memories do that to us. They sneak in little snippets of falsehood that make the overall picture more convincing. For example, more than one observer would swear that Peiperová was visibly drunk. Another would claim that Slonský's right hand cupped her bottom. This was untrue. Slonský's hands were extended sideways like a hockey defender claiming he didn't bodycheck an opponent. Eventually he patted her gently on the back in the belief that she would not release her grip until he did so.

'I've never been embraced by a subordinate before,' he explained as Peiperová returned to her stool and he straightened his tie in a belated attempt at recapturing his dignity.

'No,' agreed Navrátil, 'I'm not one for hugging the boss.'

'Sorry, sir,' said Peiperová. 'It won't happen again.'

'Well, we needn't go that far,' Slonský answered. 'Just give me a bit of warning. I'm a trained killer, you see. It's lucky I controlled my reflexes before I broke your neck.'

'Yes, sir.'

'We'll say no more about it. Whatever that disgusting red muck is in your glass, would you like another one?'

'Thank you, sir.'

'Navrátil, wave the waiter over and tell him what it was that you bought before. I can't bring myself to say it, even if I knew what it was called.'

Navrátil glanced around him.

'I can't see one. I'll go up to the bar and organise it.'

Slonský watched Navrátil push through the crowd, then spoke rapidly to Peiperová in a low voice.

'Peiperová, I know Navrátil is fond of you. I assume you're fond of him too.'

She hesitated, unsure how to answer.

'It's not my business unless it interferes with your work. But don't insult my intelligence by pretending there's nothing going on between you unless there really is nothing going on between you. I hope it works out. You're a nice pair. But if it doesn't, please tell me so I'm not left floundering around in the dark like an idiot. Deal?'

'Deal, sir.'

'Good. He's going to be a good cop. Of course, he has the great advantage of having me to show him the ropes. But you can't make a silk purse from a sow's ear, and he's got something about him. I think you have too. Don't prove me wrong.'

'No, sir. I'll try not to, sir.'

'Trying isn't good enough, Peiperová. Make it your business to succeed. What are you gawping at, girl?'

'It's Navrátil, sir. I think he's trying to attract your attention.'

Slonský turned to look. Navrátil was fighting his way back through the thirsty masses, his arms unencumbered by drinks, but with something in his hand. As he reached them Slonský could see it was a mobile phone.

'Sergeant Mucha rang, sir. He says would I tell you to turn your bloody phone on and get yourself back to the station pronto. He emphasised the pronto.'

'Did he say anything else?'

'Yes, sir. It involved his boot and both our bottoms, only he didn't express it quite that way.'

'Right, he obviously means business. And since it is business, you two had better come too.'

Ignoring the traffic lights and the legitimate claims of drivers to unrestricted use of the road, Slonský barged across the lanes of traffic, holding his badge up like a wizard's wand, and pushed the door open without bothering about the possibility that someone might be behind it. He could see at once that whatever it was, it was important. Mucha looked unusually agitated, but he did not speak until the three detectives were close enough to be the only people who heard him.

'It's Holoubek,' he announced. 'He's been killed.'

Chapter 5

'How? When?' asked Slonský.

'Don't know,' replied Mucha, 'but the call came in and I thought you'd want it. So why don't you get yourself over to Nusle and take charge?'

'Where in Nusle?'

'At the tram stop. It sounds like a hit and run as he got off the tram after seeing you. But I only know what the City Police told us, so stop rabbiting and get over there before the duty officer wonders why I haven't given this one to him. I've logged that you were already out in a car so I diverted you there. Now go!'

Slonský came very close to running. An observer could have followed Slonský's career for a very long time without seeing the like. Certainly he had run during his army service; people shooting at him tended to encourage that activity. He had occasionally run in his younger years. But it was a long time since he had skipped down the steps in threes, and by the time he reached the car the younger officers were in their seats. Navrátil put the lights and siren on and hammered the accelerator to the floor as they headed to Nusle, while Slonský struggled to get enough breath back to allow him to speak coherently.

They screeched to a halt on Táborská in front of a stern officer holding his traffic paddle aloft.

'We're in luck,' Slonský announced. 'That looks like Štajnhauzr.' He pointed at a tall, fit-looking City Policeman who wore an entirely unofficial black bodywarmer over his black shirt. The bodywarmer was apparently crammed with useful articles, many of which other officers did not feel the need to carry. Although summer uniforms were in use, Štajnhauzr had not worn his pale blue shirt, presumably because black suited his action lifestyle rather better.

Slonský strode towards him, waving his badge to head off any other city police who might have been thinking of intercepting him.

'Štajnhauzr!'

The object of the cry turned and waved in a gesture that approached a half-hearted salute.

'Lieutenant,' he acknowledged.

'Officers Peiperová and Navrátil. What happened here?'

'There are quite a lot of witnesses, sir. I've sat them down over there on the steps of the building. Officer Krob is watching over them. Basically, they tell a similar story. The deceased stepped off the tram onto the island that separates the tram lane from the car lane. As he crossed the car lane to get to the pavement, a dark blue van raced up and smashed into him. He was knocked forward several metres and the van kept going, ran over him and sped off.'

'Anyone get the registration?'

'A good partial from a cyclist and a few other partials. I've phoned it in to traffic and they're trying to match it.'

'Good. Time?'

'Whatever time the tram came. Don't know for sure. The tram driver didn't see anything happen but the van swerved across in front of him to take a left at the junction into Pod Sokolovnou. I've got someone checking the traffic cameras to see if they can plot its course from there.'

'Why that way? If you want to get out of the city, you go straight on or you turn left a block further down at Na Květnici.'

'Could be opportunistic, sir. Maybe there was just a break in the traffic. And Pod Sokolovnou is a one way street. He wouldn't meet anyone coming towards him.'

Slonský nodded. The city boys did not investigate crime but they knew the traffic system inside out. As soon as he arrived, Štajnhauzr would have put out a message to all the traffic police to watch for a dark blue van with any match to the partial registration.

There was a crackle from Štajnhauzr's radio. He listened intently.

'Van seen heading south on Michelská near the District 4 station, sir. We've got a couple of patrols out looking for it and they're going to rig the traffic lights on Videňská to hold him up. He may not go that way, of course, but if he wants a quick route out of town, that's favourite.'

'Good work. Why did you phone the criminal police?'

'Obvious hit and run, sir, but also because I went through his pockets to establish his identity and found a piece of paper with your name on it. There was also an envelope. It makes no sense to me, but it might to you.'

He handed over a thin manila envelope. It contained a copy of Vaněček's autopsy report, apparently made with a camera. There was also a grainy black and white photograph of a small house.

'Why didn't he give us these, sir?' asked Navrátil.

'I don't know, lad. You could try asking him but I doubt you'll get anywhere. Maybe he just forgot. That's what old people do.'

'Holoubek didn't, sir. He didn't seem to forget much at all.'

'Then maybe he didn't know what to make of this and wanted to look into it a bit more.'

Peiperová interrupted excitedly. 'Sir! Isn't this an address on the back of the photo?'

'Not easy to read, but I think you're right. Zdiby.'

'Zdiby? Where's that?'

Štajnhauzr supplied the answer. 'North of the city heading towards Klecany. Not a big village. Half an hour's drive round and you'll find this place, if it still exists. It's an old photo, after all.'

'Right!' Slonský shoved the photograph in Navrátil's hand. 'Before it gets dark, get yourself over to Zdiby and see if you can find this house. Save yourself some driving — ask at the district police or council office first. Peiperová, you're not doing anything tonight that stops you staying on a while?'

She glanced quickly at Navrátil, but he was already running to the car. 'No, sir.'

'Good. Get over there and interview all the women. You'll recognise them by their lumpy fronts. Get names and addresses and the facts. We don't need formal statements just yet. Start with the ones with small children. I'll join you to tackle the men as soon as possible.'

A man with thick glasses and a neat beard was crouched over the crumpled body of Holoubek making notes and directing a photographer to take a large number of images. Slonský approached him but was stopped by a peremptory command.

'Stop! Make a wide arc and approach from the head end. I haven't checked that bit of road yet.'

'That's a bloody mess,' Slonský said.

'True, literally and figuratively. If there's a plus point in this, I suspect he was concussed by the first impact and probably didn't feel much after that.'

'That's not much of a consolation to me or him,' said Slonský, 'and it doesn't change the fact that someone ran over a man of ninety.'

'No, it doesn't,' agreed Novák.

Dr Vladimír Novák was a pathologist, and a good one at that. He and Slonský enjoyed working together, though it was a matter of professional honour to both to conceal the fact.

'Are you going to tell me it's natural causes?' asked Slonský.

'Only if you want to enhance your reputation for rank stupidity. It's a classic blow with a blunt object, in this case a dark blue Volkswagen Multivan.'

'How can you tell that?'

'Because that guy in the motorbike leathers told me it was a dark blue Volkswagen Multivan. Certainly a dark blue vehicle. There's a flake of paint on his arm where it must have flailed down the wing as it rolled him over.'

'So the van was damaged?'

'He's an old chap and he's frail, but you can't hit a human being without doing a bit of damage to the vehicle. He was dragged along under the van, so the bumper is likely to be scratched or dented. And that looks to me like a corner off a number plate. We'll do all we can here and then take him back to the mortuary. I'll work him up first thing in the morning. No point in working overnight. I don't think forensics are going to be the key to solving this one somehow. Slonský, if your colleague is going to faint, could she fall in the opposite direction so she doesn't contaminate the crime scene?'

Slonský had not noticed Peiperová's return. She looked pale and was staring at Holoubek as if fascinated by the sight of an old man dumped on the road.

'What do you want?' Slonský growled.

'Sorry, sir. I thought you'd want to speak to that lady with the brown coat on. She says the blue van had been around for an hour or so before the accident.'

'It wasn't an accident, Peiperová. Find another word for it. But thank you, I'll come now.'

Peiperová nodded and returned to her interviews.

'Looks like murder, then,' said Slonský.

'Yes, it does,' said Novák. 'But that's not a professional opinion, before you hold me to it. Now push off and annoy someone else.'

Slonský walked across the road to the small knot of people whom Officer Krob was trying to keep from wandering off. Not for the first time, Slonský wondered whether the inhabitants of Prague were different to those of other cities. Here, there were two common responses to an incident like this. Some would not want to get involved, and would try to sneak off if the opportunity arose. Krob had deployed a lot of crime scene tape to create a sort of pen for the witnesses, and, in a masterstroke of improvisation, had managed to persuade someone to bring coffee and biscuits for them. Indifference to the plight of others was something of a Prague tradition, but you can't argue with free coffee and biscuits.

The second response was to concoct evidence designed to ensure that the right person was convicted. In this case, 'right' did not mean guilty. It meant morally deserving of punishment, often as a result of some other characteristic of the accused. Being Roma was usually a good start, though many a German motorist had found himself accused of a misdemeanour once his D plate was spotted on the rear of his car. This habit was time honoured. As a very young policeman under the Communists, when cars were rationed and you had to be someone to get hold of one, Slonský had been solemnly tutored by his sergeant to understand that in any road accident involving a car and a pedestrian, it must have been the pedestrian's fault. Similarly, any collision between two cars was easily explained once you knew which car was the larger one, because its driver could not be culpable. While this was very clear to any policeman, it was difficult to maintain in the face of the united testimony of passers-by that the larger car had reversed at speed into the smaller one, a view expressed all the more vehemently by those who could not possibly have seen the incident in question.

Eva Urbanová had made no effort to slink away. A woman in her late fifties, she stood squarely facing him. Square was a good adjective for Urbanová, who was around one metre fifty tall and roughly the same across. She wore a cheap brown raincoat and flat shoes with no stockings or tights, and had the corned beef legs of a woman who likes to sit close to the fire on cold evenings.

'Good day, madam,' Slonský began.

'Are you in charge of this shambles?' she asked.

'It won't be a shambles now I've taken charge,' he replied smoothly. 'Lieutenant Slonský, Josef, Criminal Police.'

'Urbanová, Eva,' she replied, in the formal manner that had characterized the country since the days of the Austro-Hungarian Empire.

'I understand you've seen the van earlier today,' Slonský said.

'Yes. I told that young bit that. I'm pretty sure it turned up around four o'clock. The driver pulled in down the road and just sat in the cab.'

'What made you notice him?'

'I've been waiting for the landlord to send a plumber. It looked like the sort of van a plumber might have. Of course, I've been waiting a week already, so why I thought that might be him I don't know, I'm sure. Anyway, he never budged. Just sat there looking in the wing mirror.'

'You didn't see his registration number, I suppose?'

'No. I can't read it at this distance. That's my window up there.' She pointed vaguely over her left shoulder.

'Where did he park?

'Opposite side of the road in the dotted area.'

'And nobody moved him on?'

'Never a policeman around when you need one. Of course, the place is crawling with them now that old gent's been knocked over, and look at the parking now.' She gestured down the road. The parking was impeccable.

'Did you see the old gentleman being run over?'

She shook her head. 'You couldn't see because the tram was in the way. He must have got out at the middle doors. Then I heard this loud engine noise like a racing car, and the van came charging down the far lane. There was a shout and then a loud thump, and some screaming, but I didn't see anything until the van swept across the front of the tram and turned left.'

'The tram was moving by then?'

'Just started off. There wasn't a lot of space for the van to get in front, but he wasn't going to stop anyway, I reckon.'

Slonský had never had much success with young women in his life, but he was something of a charmer of women of a certain age, so he chanced his arm with Mrs Urbanová.

'My old mother wasn't very good on her feet, but she made sure she knew what went on in her street.'

'I know the type,' Mrs Urbanová said. 'Liked a chat, did she?'

'Not nosey, you understand,' said Slonský. 'Just keen to find out if she could help anyone with anything.'

'Public spirited. Not enough of that about.'

'Have you seen the old gentleman before?'

'Oh, yes!' she said, 'many times. He always got off at that stop. He must have lived in those blocks down the road.'

'Which ones are those?'

'See where this road joins the next one at an angle? If you cross to your right there there's a sort of little oblong with flats around. Then you can walk through to some more. I think he must have lived somewhere there.' A shocked look came over her face. 'You don't think his poor wife is still sitting there waiting with his tea?'

'He was a widower, I think.'

Urbanová crossed herself.

'Just as well the poor woman went first. It'll be a comfort to her, God rest her.'

'That's one way of looking at it,' agreed Slonský. 'You didn't get a good look at the van driver, I suppose?'

'What do you think I am, a ruddy eagle? I'll tell you what, though. On this side of the road, not far from where he was parked on the far side, there's a girl who does hairdressing. There's nothing much goes on that she doesn't see.' She gripped his arm and pulled down on it so he had to bend to follow it. 'Not official hairdressing, you understand, so don't say I said anything.'

'I won't mention it. I'm not interested in someone earning a bit of pin money. Would you mind walking me along a bit and pointing at the right door?'

Mrs Urbanová did just that. It was around fifty metres so she only needed to stop once to catch her breath.

'Up one flight of stairs,' she said.

Slonský climbed the stairs and knocked on the door. It was opened by a blonde woman wearing a pink polyester housecoat. He knew he had come to the right place because there was a strong smell of setting lotion.

He showed his badge.

'Can we have a word, miss?'

She looked reluctant.

'It's a bit awkward at the moment…'

'I know,' he said. 'You're in the middle of a perm and the timing is important. You carry on. We can talk while you work if that's okay.'

She nodded and he followed her in. They turned into the front room where a woman was sitting in a chair swathed in a blue plastic cape. Slonský exchanged greetings with her.

'You may have heard that an elderly man was knocked down and killed in this street this afternoon around five o'clock. It wasn't an accident. It looks as if the van that ran him over waited for him for over an hour.'

'That's awful,' gasped the woman in the chair. 'If that kind of thing can happen we could all be murdered in our beds.'

'It's my job to see you don't get murdered in your bed,' Slonský explained, 'and that will be less likely if we can put the driver away for life.'

'Better if you hanged him,' said the woman in the chair. 'You hang them once and they don't kill twice.'

'That's as may be…' began Slonský.

'And I'd castrate them first. They won't need them bits again and it means they wouldn't breed more criminals to murder us in our beds.'

'You're right there, Mrs Musilová,' said the hairdresser. 'And rapists too. They should get the chop.'

'Goes without saying,' agreed Musilová. 'And them podiatrists.'

'I think you mean paedophiles,' Slonský interrupted. 'Podiatrists look after your feet.'

'Yes, them too.'

'There's a lot of men would be less trouble to women if they didn't have hormones running through them,' continued the hairdresser.

'The law doesn't let us hang them,' Slonský explained, 'whatever our personal views on the subject. And the Czech Republic, almost uniquely, does castrate sex offenders, if they consent.'

'Fancy that. But I wouldn't worry about consent,' said Mrs Musilová.

'Well, I'd ask,' said the hairdresser, 'but if they said no I'd do it anyway.'

'That's not quite how consent works … anyway, to get back to the reason for my visit, the van that ran him over was parked opposite for about an hour from four o'clock. Did you see it there?'

'Dark blue van?' the hairdresser asked.

'That's right.'

'Yes, came just as my three o'clock left — say, around ten to four — and was there quite a while. Of course, while I'm working I have my back to the window.'

'You didn't get a good look at the driver, I suppose?'

'Yes, I eyeballed him. Black hair, not too long but not short either. Quite thick, straight, not dyed. I notice hair, you see, being a hairdresser. Parted on the left. Just lapping over his ear. He had a small earring in too. It caught the light.'

'Good. His face?'

'Didn't really see. Clean shaven. Sharpish nose. Heavy black eyebrows. I thought he could do with them plucking. Thin them out a bit. Not a bad-looking lad actually.'

'A lad? Quite young, then?'

'Younger than me,' laughed the hairdresser.

'Twenty-five?' Slonský offered.

'And the rest, love. Thirty-five to forty, I'd say. No wedding ring.'

Slonský glanced out of the window.

'You could see that from here?'

'I can see a wedding ring from a long way off, love.'

'Can't we all, dear,' agreed Mrs Musilová.

Navrátil had found the district police office in Zdiby just before the duty officer shut the door and went home for the night.

'I've got an old photo that appears to show a house here, and I was hoping you could tell me where I can find it, if it's still standing.'

'If it isn't still standing you won't find it whatever I say,' replied the district policeman, who, under direct questioning, was prepared to reveal that his name was Majer.

'That's my name, not my rank,' he expanded.

'I realised that,' Navrátil replied. 'It's unlikely that a major would be locking up a little police station.'

'We're not that little. We have a dinghy and a motor scooter.'

'I'll bear that in mind. Now, this picture. Does it mean anything to you?'

Majer frowned as he studied it.

'Yes.'

'It does?'

'I just said so, didn't I?'

'And it's still standing?'

'It was when I last looked.'

'How do I get to it?'

Majer stared into the distance as if this would help him to focus on the question in hand.

'You've got two choices,' he finally announced. 'You can carry on down this road and turn right. Alternatively, you can go back to the junction, take the main road, and turn left. It's about halfway down the road. Or up the road, depending which end you come from.'

'And it's easily recognised?'

'It should be,' Majer smiled. 'You've got a photograph.'

Each man headed for his car. Navrátil opted to take the first alternative, staying on the road and turning right. As is often the case on country roads, the inhabitants had parked at all kinds of angles, not anticipating that anyone would actually want to use the road, so Navrátil crawled along, carefully watching both wings to avoid damage to the car. After a few minutes he saw a house on the left that was a possible candidate, so he pulled in and stepped out of the car to get a better look.

It could have been the one, but then so could the next one or the one after that. Three very similar houses differed only in the decoration applied to them. Looking closely at the photograph, Navrátil ruled out the centre house, whose front path curved rather than following a straight line between gate and front door, and had finally decided the third house was the likeliest candidate when a police car came to a halt beside him and Majer climbed out.

'Hello again,' said Navrátil. 'Come to tell me which one it is?'

'No,' said Majer, looking as if the idea of further assistance had not occurred to him. 'I live here.'

'You live here? Why didn't you say?'

Majer shrugged. 'You didn't ask.'

'But weren't you curious about why I'm walking about with a picture of your house?'

'That's not my house. I live in the middle one. It has a curved front path, do you see?'

Navrátil counted to five before replying. 'Yes, I noticed that.'

'Your picture is the house next door.'

'I'd worked that out too. Who lives there?'

'My neighbour, Mrs Grigarová.'

Navrátil was losing patience. It would soon be dusk and he was keen to get out of the village before night fell. He had seen too many films in which people like Majer became zombies and feasted on the flesh of visitors once darkness arrived.

'Look, I don't suppose you ever met him, but we think this is the house where a policeman called Vaněček lived. Can you think of anyone who lived here around 1979 and might be able to confirm that for us?'

'Yes. My dad.'

'Great. Where will I find him?'

'Here. He lives with us. Come in and I'll introduce you.'

Navrátil followed Majer into the centre house, and was surprised to see that the hall was covered with photographs of people in police uniforms. He paused to look at them, which Majer took as an invitation to describe them all.

'That's me, obviously. That's Uncle Viktor. So is that. That's Uncle Ivo — he's on my mum's side. That's Mum in her first uniform. That's Ivo again, receiving his medal for rescuing a little kid who fell in the river. Now this one is unusual, because both my uncles are in it. You can't tell because of the riot shields, but the third from the left is Ivo and Viktor is the one putting his helmet back on after someone lobbed a brick at it. And that's Dad when he first came here.'

'So he was in the police then?'

'Man and boy his whole life. Until he retired, of course.'

Majer motioned Navrátil through to the front room where Mr Majer senior was reading a magazine about sporting guns. Introductions having been made, Navrátil decided to get to the point and avoid anything approaching small talk.

'Mr Majer, we're investigating a death this afternoon in Nusle. An ex-policeman was the victim of a hit and run.'

'Call me Benedikt. It'll be confusing otherwise. What was his name?'

'Holoubek. Edvard Holoubek.'

Benedikt looked pained.

'Did you know him, sir?'

'Only slightly. But a hit and run is a bad way to die, and it's doubly bad at his age. Holoubek was a good policeman. One of the few you could trust to be completely straight with you. Of course, I'll do whatever I can to help.'

'When he was killed he had this photograph in his pocket.'

'That's the house next door. Why did he have that with him?'

'We can't be sure, sir…'

'Benedikt.'

'Benedikt. But it seems likely that it was connected with a case from the past that he worked on. We believe the house in the photograph may have been that of another policeman called Vaněček.'

'No doubt about it. Though it's stretching the truth a bit to call him a policeman.'

'That seems to have been Holoubek's opinion too, sir.'

'It would be. Vaněček was a deadweight. He minced around in his dress uniform any chance he got — hang on, I'll show you what I mean.'

Before Navrátil could stop him, Benedikt had pushed himself out of the chair and could be heard rummaging in a cupboard. He returned after a couple of minutes with a dog-eared paperback book with a slate blue cover.

'Police handbook from the seventies.' He flicked through the first few pages. 'There you are. Nineteen seventy-two. There's Vaněček.'

Navrátil found himself looking at a passport-sized photograph posed in the classical Communist portrait position, with the left shoulder nearer the camera, the head turned slightly to the subject's left as if looking beyond the photographer's right shoulder. The cheap paper made the photograph look slightly blurred, but Vaněček proved to be a rather portly man with plenty of space on his chest for his many medals.

'What did he get all those awards for?' asked Navrátil.

'God knows. Shutting up and keeping out of the way would come high on the list. How he managed to stand upright with that lot dangling off his front I don't know. They had specially stiffened uniforms, you know, to take the weight of the metal without tearing.'

'And he lived next door.'

'Not while he was in the service. He was retired before he came here, and not voluntarily either. Some kind of cock-up on his watch, it was said. Of course, Vaněček was very keen to give me his side of it, and I was just as keen not to hear it. I knew his sort. They'd put good men at risk by their carelessness. It didn't surprise me if the stories were true and he'd done the same. He said he hadn't.'

Benedikt rubbed his chin thoughtfully.

'One funny thing, though. He didn't seem to care much what the other villagers thought, but he was very concerned that I should believe him. At the time, I didn't.'

'And now?'

Benedikt looked at his hands, inspecting the backs of his knuckles carefully as he thought.

'It's not evidence, of course, but his death was very peculiar.'

'That's what we're really interested in. The autopsy report said he fell on a fence and penetrated his chest.'

Benedikt laughed out loud and stood up, causing Navrátil to follow suit.

'Follow me, young man.'

They walked together to the back door, which Benedikt flung open. He stepped into the garden and invited Navrátil to do likewise.

'Tell me — where in these gardens can you see any fence you could fall on? It's barely changed these thirty years. The only fence I can see next door has wooden rails running horizontally across the posts. It's as smooth as a baby's bottom. I don't doubt for a minute that Vaněček fell on a fence somewhere — it's too daft a story not to be true — but it wasn't in his garden.'

'Did you know the StB had come for him?'

'Officially, no. They wouldn't tell a district policeman like me. The first I heard was when one of my men came tearing into the office to see if I was still there. He'd seen the car going down this street and he couldn't think of anyone else the StB would want to talk to. I, on the other hand, was concerned about my wife and son. Those swine weren't above getting to a man by arresting his family, so I got myself over here as quickly as I could. They were helping Vaněček into the car. Odd, isn't it, how police put a man into a car? They push gently down on his head so that he won't bang it on the roof, then they take him away and kick him to death, hang him or throw him onto a stake. He looked at me very briefly, and I've never seen a man look so terrified. I didn't see him again. But it's the fact that the StB came for him when he'd been retired for a while that made me wonder if there was something in his story.'

'Which was?'

'I didn't pay it much attention, because in those days the truth was irrelevant. If those above you disciplined you, it was pointless spending time on proving yourself innocent. It only annoyed them. I thought Vaněček should just get on with his life and stop trying to change his history. But, for what it's worth, and bear in mind that I know none of this first hand, he claimed that he had been tipped off that a group of students were producing pornography. He raided a clandestine press and it turned out that they weren't producing pornography, but political pamphlets, and one of those he arrested was an StB operative who had to blow his cover to get out of the cells. Some of those involved were foreign students. Now, normally anything involving foreigners would go straight to StB, but he said nobody told him foreigners were involved. Vaněček protested his innocence but Tripka produced a memo that he said should have alerted Vaněček. Do you know Tripka?'

'I've heard of him. StB liaison, I believe.'

'At the time, yes. He came back into the mainstream and was a deputy director of police when he retired. Well, the memo was a turgid thing, but it was the usual story — a line at the bottom of page nine that might have been relevant. Vaněček wasn't convinced and argued that the sentence referred to something quite different. He wouldn't let it drop, and after a few months they came for him. He was writing letters to the Party hierarchy, talking to journalists and so on. Stupid of him, because the journalists were all good Party members too. That's all I know.'

'Is his wife still alive?'

'I don't think so. She only stayed on here for a month or so, then the house was reallocated. After all, he qualified for it, not her.'

'Any other family?'

'Never heard of any. Certainly no children.'

Navrátil inspected the photograph again.

'I'd love to know why Holoubek thought that looking into Vaněček's death was worthwhile. They barely knew each other, according to his account.'

'Why do we do anything? To revisit our past. To set the record straight. You see, you young people think that history is fixed but your future can be changed. Actually, those of us who lived through Communism know that the past can be rewritten any number of times but your future depends on things you can't change. And because the past may change, it's important to learn how to forget. As I get older, I find it becomes easier. Nowadays I forget all sorts of things.' Benedikt smiled with a touch of resignation. 'Sometimes it's good to forget,' he added.

Chapter 6

Štajnhauzr was an impressive sight, waving his arms energetically to direct other policemen, pedestrians, onlookers and the television crew which had just arrived. He saw Slonský returning and marched across to him.

'Do you want the good news or the bad news first, Lieutenant?' he enquired.

'Let's get the bad news out of the way.'

'It won't make any sense unless I tell you the good news,' Štajnhauzr replied. 'The good news is they've found the van. The bad news is that it's in flames. However, there is potentially some *very* good news.'

'Has anyone ever told you you're an aggravating little sod?' asked Slonský.

'Yes, quite a few, but I ignore them. One of the officers who arrived first decided he couldn't put the fire out, but he might be able to preserve some evidence, so he used his toolkit to get the steering wheel out of the van.'

Slonský was astonished. 'It could have exploded at any time,' he gasped.

'Yes, but that's Officer Trousil for you; full of guts, or no brains at all, depending on how you want to look at it. Anyway, he's bringing the wheel over to give to the forensics team.'

'Team? What team? There's Novák, but I haven't seen any others.'

'I assumed there'd be more coming.'

'I don't think there are any more. And if there were, I bet Novák wouldn't pay them overtime.'

Peiperová coughed gently.

'I've got names and addresses, sir, but there's not much useful from them, and the officer is asking if he can get them more coffee.'

Slonský glanced across at the makeshift pen where Krob was dealing manfully with the small crowd he had enclosed with his tape. The old detective motioned to Peiperová to follow and walked slowly across to see Krob.

'Officer Krob? A word, please. Peiperová will look after these people for a few minutes.'

Krob looked hugely relieved.

'Sir?'

'A job well done, lad. Very resourceful of you. Did you pay for the coffees yourself?'

'I got the coffee free, but I bought the cookies.'

'Got the receipt?'

Krob produced a sliver of paper from his notebook. Slonský took it, glanced at the total and repaid Krob for the biscuits.

'I'll get my expenses quicker than you, and with less argument.'

Slonský tried to address the witnesses, but they were too busy haranguing Peiperová. Some wanted to go, whereas others were happy to stay if further coffee was likely to be forthcoming.

'Quiet!' yelled Slonský. 'Thank you all for your assistance. The ladies can all go. Officer Peiperová and I will talk to each of the men as quickly as possible. Please give your names and addresses to Officer Krob while you're waiting.'

Krob wondered whether this meant he had been involuntarily transferred to the criminal police, but the truth was much more prosaic. Slonský had merely taken his assistance for granted.

The crowd was dispersing. They had been questioned, and it was getting too dark for them to see what was going on in the road, so there was no point in staying. Novák had completed his work and had supervised the removal of Holoubek's body. Despite Slonský's scepticism a trio of scenes of crime technicians had appeared and were combing the road surface. The traffic diversion was working as smoothly as could be hoped so Štajnhauzr was ready to leave the scene and belatedly end his shift.

'Štajnhauzr,' Slonský called. 'Could you do me a favour?'

'If I can, Lieutenant.'

'Could you drop Officer Peiperová back at her barracks? She'll give you the address.'

Štajnhauzr agreed readily, and Peiperová thanked Slonský. Although exhilarated by her first real case, she was dead on her feet.

'I'll see you at seven,' said Slonský. 'Wear civvies. We're going to find Holoubek's flat and search it, so dress appropriately.'

'Yes, sir.'

Peiperová was about to salute, but recognised just in time that saluting when you are in plain clothes looks silly. She followed Štajnhauzr to his car and left Slonský to have a few words with Novák.

'Anything useful on the wheel?'

'Yes, a plastic bag, and it's staying that way until I can get it back to the lab.'

'Come on, Novák. It wouldn't be hard to do a quick test for fingerprints.'

'No, it wouldn't,' Novák conceded, 'but it might ruin other trace evidence, spoil the evidence trail, introduce contamination and make me even later for my supper than I already am.'

'Do you want to pack up and join me for a beer and sausage somewhere?'

Novák looked Slonský in the eye. 'Do I look like the sort of person who is devoted to beer and sausage?'

'No,' said Slonský, 'but you could slum it for once. We don't all sip kabinett Riesling and suck anchovies for fun.'

Novák looked at his watch.

'All right. Just the one. You can have what you like, but we're going somewhere that does a decent glass of red, and you're paying.'

Slonský draped an arm round Novák's shoulders.

'Of course, old friend. You'll enjoy it, trust me.'

'Trust?' stammered Novák. 'You?'

'I thought I might find you here,' said Navrátil, who could not help noticing a number of beer glasses on the table, along with Novák's head. 'What happened to Novák?'

'He's tired,' Slonský explained. 'It's lifting all those heavy glasses.'

'Novák drank this much?'

'No, Novák drank two glasses. With a teeny-weeny double schnapps in each.'

'You spiked his drink?'

'Of course not, Navrátil. What do you take me for? I ordered and he said "I'll have what you're having", so he only has himself to blame.'

'I thought Novák only drank wine.'

'And from now on he probably will. But it's been educational for him. He now knows what a beer tastes like.'

'No, he doesn't,' said Navrátil. 'He knows what a beer tastes like after it's been spiked with a double schnapps.'

'Good point,' agreed Slonský. 'Now, are we going to engage in Jesuitical debate all night or have you got something for me?'

'It was Vaněček's house. He told his neighbour — a policeman called Majer — that he had been stitched up for crossing an StB operation.'

'Holoubek said that.'

'So he did. But the story Holoubek had isn't the same as Majer tells. Holoubek said it was to do with currency offences, whereas Majer says it was an underground publishing press.'

Slonský shrugged his shoulders expansively. 'Does it matter? And do we have any reason to favour one story over the other?'

'Majer has a more detailed story.'

'Maybe Majer just has a better imagination. Anything else?'

'Majer doesn't think Vaněček died in his garden. There's no fence he could have fallen on.'

'Isn't now or wasn't then?'

'Both.'

Slonský gulped a large, satisfying mouthful.

'I knew it. So who came for Vaněček?'

'Probably StB. Majer knew nothing about it beforehand, so it's unlikely to have been ordinary police.'

'Hang fire, young Navrátil. We'd tell them now, but it didn't always happen then. It's suggestive, but not conclusive.'

'Fair enough. But they came for him after he'd been retired a few months. He was telling everyone he'd been hard done by.'

'Are you going to sit down? If you are, I'll give you a hand to shift Novák.'

'It's all right, sir. I'll get a stool.'

A waiter glided alongside the table.

'A large glass for my young friend. Novák says he has had enough. And if you can persuade the horse to give another sample, you can refill that.'

Navrátil had his notebook open.

'I wasn't going to have a drink, sir.'

'Nonsense. You can't watch me drinking. I'll feel lonely. And, as you know because I've told you so, beer is the essential lubricant that moves the cogs of the Slonský brain. Even that example of farmyard urine. Now, exercise your own brain. What could have provoked the StB to come back for Vaněček after he had retired? For some reason, they wanted him removed. They'd be pushing on an open door with the police force then, because that's what most police seem to have wanted too. But they'd achieved that. Why do they need to beat him up and kill him?'

'Was the killing an accident, or deliberate?'

Slonský mulled it over.

'Holoubek didn't voice any suspicions, and he knew more than we do. Maybe it was just an interrogation that went wrong.'

'And the suspect ended up dead?'

'Oh, it happened all the time, lad. You didn't know he had a dicky heart, or sometimes they did themselves in for fear of further pain.'

'How could they do that? Weren't they searched for anything that could harm them?'

'Yes, but I've known one throw himself down a stairwell. Mucha will recall that one; if I remember rightly he was at the foot of the stairs when the fellow landed. Do we know where Vaněček was buried?'

'No, sir.'

'Find out first thing tomorrow. If it's a grand affair it was probably an accident. When it's deliberate they don't care what people think of the headstone.'

Navrátil noted the order on his pad.

'So they remove him,' Slonský continued, 'but they give him a smart house in the country outside Prague. That looks to me like an endgame. That's saying to Vaněček "This is where it stops, so make the most of your new home, because you're history now." Then two or three months later they're back to give him a hard time.'

'Majer says he'd been writing letters and mouthing off trying to get himself reinstated.'

'Then he really was as big an idiot as Holoubek said. But they could have ignored that. In those days he wouldn't get an audience if they didn't want him to. So we're drawn to the conclusion that Vaněček knew something and was threatening to reveal it. And that might be about the Válková case, or it might not. We'll have to see what Vaněček was up to during that time that could account for it. First thing tomorrow see if his personnel file is still in existence. I doubt it, but these things get overlooked.'

'I thought I was looking for his grave first thing tomorrow?'

'You are. And you're looking for his personnel record. You'll have to learn to multitask if you're going to make it to the top, lad.'

'Can you multitask then, sir?'

'Yes. I can drink coffee and write out your dismissal notice at the same time. Now, drink up your beer and then you can help me get Novák to your car. You can drop him off on your way home.'

'Where does he live, sir?'

'I don't know, Navrátil. You'll have to find out. That's what being a detective is all about.'

Chapter 7

It was ten to seven, and Peiperová was standing in front of Slonský's desk.

'Sit down, girl, and stop making the place look untidy. Untidier than it actually is, anyway.'

'Thank you, sir. Where, sir?'

'Have Navrátil's chair. He's going to be a few minutes late today. It seems one of his drinking companions spent the night on his sofa and he has to take him home first.'

Peiperová's face betrayed her thoughts.

'It's all right, Peiperová. Navrátil was the essence of sobriety. I was with them myself.'

Peiperová relaxed.

'Sober, assuming Navrátil went straight home, that is. Now, young lass, we have to find Holoubek's flat, get the key, and search it. Navrátil has his own list of jobs but will doubtless want to come and play with us later.'

'Do we have any leads, sir?'

'No, Peiperová, because this is not a dog-walking club. You've been watching too many detective shows on television. In real life you have to go out and find your own leads, because nobody gives them to you. We know the tram stop he normally gets off at, so we can assume it's easier to get to that one than any other. We also, thanks to the little woman shaped like an outdoor privy that you found, know which direction he walked in after he left the tram. But our best clue is that he was a policeman, and therefore probably drew a policeman's pension, which, pitiful as it is, is still enough to keep his old body and soul together. Until they were separated by a dark blue Volkswagen Multivan.'

'Were there any clues in the van, sir?'

'A very good question, Peiperová, and one I shall be pursuing with Novák when he sobers up. In the meantime, here's a telephone number. Do you have a mobile phone?'

'Yes, sir.'

'Good. Then let's exchange numbers. I'll get you a police issue mobile as soon as Captain Lukas signs it off. The police pensions office won't be open yet, so you can call in a little while. When you get the address off them, give me a call. We'll see if the local council have a name for the landlord.'

'Couldn't he own it himself, sir?'

'Peiperová, where's your sense of history? When Holoubek was earning, private property was a no-no in the Czech Republic, remember? And when it became possible to buy flats again, I doubt if anyone would give a mortgage to a retired man living on a pension.' Slonský shook his head sadly. 'How soon they forget,' he murmured.

Whatever he was about to say to Peiperová, he was interrupted by the sound of his telephone ringing.

'Slonský,' he answered.

'Bastard,' said the caller before hanging up.

Slonský replaced the receiver carefully.

'Sounds like Novák has made it to his office,' he said.

Peiperová had departed, and Slonský had managed to catch Lukas as the latter was hanging his coat up.

'All going well?' he asked.

'Not really,' replied Slonský. 'An old man has been run over deliberately, perhaps because he was trying to reopen a dodgy police enquiry from thirty years ago, the van that did it has gone up in smoke, a second death from the past appears to be very suspicious though the police didn't think so at the time, perhaps because they did it, I'm baby-sitting two officers with a combined age of about eighteen who keep looking at each other like rabbits, and Novák is abusing me down the phone because he lost count of his drinks last night. Apart from that, everything's fine.'

'Good, good,' said Lukas. 'I can't do much about Peiperová, but she's a bright girl and no doubt she'll be a considerable help to you.'

'Actually, she already is,' agreed Slonský, 'and she'd be even more help if she had a mobile phone so I can find her.'

Lukas opened his drawer and signed a chit.

'I can trust you to fill in the details, I hope?'

'Of course, sir.'

'But I've taken the precaution of specifying a single mobile phone in case you were planning to take a market stall this weekend.'

'Very wise of you, sir. My police salary doesn't go very far.'

'Join the club. And you don't even have daughters.'

'Yes, sir. How are … they?' asked Slonský, who had utterly forgotten their names.

'Both well, thank you. Eva has completed her teacher training now, and Eliška is studying the viola at the conservatory. Of course, neither has an income, so they both depend on their poor father.'

'It's just as well you're a captain, then, sir. On a lieutenant's salary, one of them would starve.'

'I was a lieutenant once, Slonský. You can manage if you're prudent.'

There was a gentle rap on the half-open door, and Navrátil poked his face into the office.

'Just letting you know I've delivered Dr Novák, sir, so I'm here now.'

'Well, why are you here, Navrátil? Aren't you supposed to be finding Vaněček's grave and his personnel record?' asked Slonský.

'Yes, sir. I'll set off now.'

'Just a minute, Navrátil,' Lukas exclaimed.

'Sir?'

'I just wanted to congratulate you on those burglary statistics. A first class piece of work. Of course, it bore out my contention that things are getting better in the face of some ill-informed comments from local politicians, but it's good to have hard facts to back up one's argument. Well done, young man.'

Navrátil blushed, which Lukas interpreted as embarrassment at being praised, rather than sheepish acknowledgement of the fact that they were the fruit of his imagination, as Slonský was quick to remind him obliquely.

'Yes, well done, Navrátil. I don't know how he did it so quickly, sir.'

'A keen head for figures, no doubt,' chuckled Lukas. 'We'd better watch you closely, Navrátil. If you're this good with statistics Klinger will have another try to seduce you into joining the fraud squad.'

Navrátil forced a smile as he left. Klinger had, indeed, made a previous attempt to persuade Navrátil to join him upstairs, but the young detective, while flattered to be asked, found Klinger's obsession with order and detail too wearing to contemplate working there. Klinger was a man who folded sheets of paper precisely in half with the care of an origami adept before shredding them, and Navrátil found that just a little spooky. Well, quite a bit spooky actually.

'Did you know an officer called Vaněček, sir?' Slonský asked.

'I didn't really know him. Knew of him, of course. Came to a sticky end.'

'Allegedly impaled on his garden fence, sir.'

Lukas winced.

'I meant his career, actually. I didn't know about his death.'

'The snag with the police report from 1979 is that he apparently died on a fence that wasn't there.'

'Some mistake, surely.'

'A fairly elaborate mistake, if you ask me. We'll try to retrieve the file, if it still exists. I'll add that to Navrátil's list. What do you know about the incident that led to his dismissal, sir?'

Lukas paused to collect his thoughts before speaking.

'He had been having a bit of difficulty with the StB for some time. Vaněček had his deficiencies as a policeman, but he was quite clear that we couldn't do our jobs if the security forces didn't keep us informed. He had complained a couple of times that Tripka was too much in the StB's pocket. That was Colonel Tripka's father, of course.'

'And Major Tripka, as he then was, was the StB liaison officer for the police.'

'That's right. But that's the point. He was supposed to be "for the police"; our man in their camp. There were suspicions that he was more like their man in our camp. Anyway, there was a crime reported by a hotel. I think a guest's briefcase had been forced open and important papers taken. Vaněček launched an inquiry, only for Tripka to announce that the case had been opened during an StB raid. Vaněček was livid. He complained to his superiors that his men had wasted valuable time, and — more to the point — the guest was a foreigner who would go home with a poor impression of the Czech police if they didn't make a real effort to restore his property.

101

The interior ministry ordered the StB to return the papers so that Vaněček could give them back to the foreigner, but Vaněček was instructed to say that they had been stolen by an opportunist who didn't speak English and didn't realise what he'd taken. I remember that case quite well, because I was one of the policemen who had to interview all the hotel staff. I wasn't around when the StB got their own back, but none of us was in any doubt that that was exactly what they had done. It was several months later, and they claimed that Vaněček had fouled up one of their operations. He was removed and forced to retire.'

'According to his ex-neighbour, who was also a policeman, Vaněček refused to go quietly and that's why the StB came back for him a few months after retirement.'

Lukas said nothing for a few moments, and Slonský had no intention of filling the silence, believing that there may be more to tell.

'If he did,' said Lukas, 'he was stupid. The StB wouldn't let him tell his story. The snag is that we don't really know what that story was — or do we? Are you keeping something up your sleeve?'

'No, I'm not. I genuinely don't know what to think. Even if Vaněček was hard done by, I don't see why he needed to be eliminated. They could have ignored him. Unless, of course, he had hard evidence. But if he did, I don't know what it could be or where he kept it. I'll bet the StB took that house at Zdiby to pieces looking for it.'

'So where do you start?'

'My head tells me to start with Holoubek. He's the most recent one by thirty years, and we've got forensics to help. But my heart says it all starts with Válková. She's the innocent one in all this. You can argue that Vaněček brought it on himself, and that Holoubek did the same by trying to reopen the case.'

'He was ninety years old, for goodness' sake, Slonský. Whatever he knew, he didn't deserve to end his days under a truck.'

Slonský smacked his fist into his cupped hand.

'No, you're right, sir. He didn't. No-one does.'

Lukas rose from his seat and walked round to perch on the corner of the desk.

'I would back you to find the killer of Jana Válková if anyone can. You're an obstinate, insubordinate, disorganised nuisance and the bane of my life much of the time, but you're also the best detective I've got. Now, get your chin up and tell me how you're going to do it. Who is doing what?'

'Novák is doing the forensics. Peiperová is looking for Holoubek's flat so we can search it. Mucha is trying to find the original file on the Válková killing. I'll ask him to try to find Vaněček's too. Navrátil is hunting out Vaněček's grave and his personnel record.'

'Why his grave?'

Slonský shrugged. 'It helps me.'

'Fair enough. It sounds like a good plan. But I need hardly remind you to be careful. Someone who would kill a ninety-year-old won't baulk at further violence.'

'You needn't worry about me, sir.'

'I wasn't. I was reminding you to worry about Navrátil and Peiperová.'

'Oh. I do, sir, I do.'

When Slonský set out to join Peiperová he found Mucha at the front desk hanging his coat up.

'Got something for you.'

'Two plane tickets to Jamaica? The keys to a new BMW?'

'Better than that.'

Mucha offered a dog-eared dusky red folder. A paper label gummed to the top right hand corner described its contents.

'I can't read this here. Let's go to my office.'

Slonský could hardly contain his excitement and bounded up the stairs in pairs, while Mucha ran along behind, vainly trying to get his second boot off. The first was behind the front desk.

'Now, what have we here?'

Mucha pointed to the first page.

'List of contents.'

Slonský leafed through the sheets, skimming each briefly before moving on. After a few moments he paused, frowned, and began again. Without commenting he unlocked his desk drawer and took Holoubek's folder out, reading from each of the folders in turn.

'This is odd. Holoubek has copies of pages that aren't here.'

'Do you know when he made them?'

'Shortly after the sentence was passed. Do you know the file history?'

'Yes, I checked that while I was up at records. The file was taken into permanent store on 8th September, 1976.'

'That's less than eight weeks after the crime. The investigation and trial whizzed along.'

'It's the day after Bartoš was executed. See the last page for a copy of the warrant.'

'Has it been taken out since?'

'Who knows? We've got records since 1990, and it hasn't left the building, though that doesn't preclude someone consulting it at the library desk. But here's an odd thing. Count the pages.'

Slonský hurried to obey.

'Fifty-three.'

'Now look at the 1990 cataloguing docket on the front.'

'"Number of pages: fifty-nine." Someone's had six since 1990.'

'Apparently without taking it out, and right under the eyes of the library staff.'

Slonský pushed the files to one side so he could get his feet on the corner of the desk.

'Curiouser and curiouser. The only people who could go to records and get their hands on this file are police officers. If anyone took six pages out, it has to be a police officer. But why?'

'I was sort of hoping you'd want to know who.'

'Well, who and why, I suppose. Find out why and we'll know who.'

'Find out who and you might know why.'

'I'll have to read this closely and see if I can work out where the pages have been taken from.'

'I found one. The account of the first interview with Bartoš in prison is missing page five. The pages are numbered in the bottom corner.'

Slonský checked for himself.

'Not only that, old friend, this front page is either a ringer or there was a fib in the original papers. This is described as the first police interview with Bartoš, but it says it took place in Prague, whereas we know that Bartoš was first interviewed in the remand prison in Olomouc. And that interview isn't here at all. How did you get this?'

'I tried the truth. Honesty is always the best policy, my old mother used to tell me.'

'I'm surprised you've got on in this police force, with an attitude like that.'

'It's obviously held me back, because I'm just a sergeant and you're a mighty lieutenant.'

'I think that has more to do with your legendary refusal to apply for promotions.'

'I applied while I was getting them,' Mucha objected. 'It's just that once they turned me down I didn't want to face that disappointment again by reapplying.'

'Three of the pages Holoubek copied aren't here. Then we know page five of the prison interview is missing. So that leaves two more we don't know about. Not yet, anyway.'

'Why not just take the whole file?'

'You're checked for files when you leave, aren't you? It wouldn't have been easy to get a whole folder out. Besides, if it was missing altogether it might have provoked comment one day. With the incriminating pages removed, it's less of a threat, and there's just a chance we'd flick through it, not notice the editing and put it back.'

'Bit daft leaving the label on the front, then.'

'Who would count the pages?' asked Slonský.

'Well, me for a start,' replied Mucha. 'And Klinger would.'

'That's true,' admitted Slonský. 'Klinger would count them, line them up and straighten the edges. But we knew it had been edited because we had pages that weren't here and should have been. Our murderer doesn't know what Holoubek gave us.'

'Then why kill Holoubek?'

'Ah, good point. Though he might kill Holoubek because he feared Holoubek knew more than he actually did. The truth is unimportant. It's what the murderer *thought* Holoubek knew that caused his actions.'

Mucha picked up his boot.

'Too deep for me. I'm going back to vegetate at the front desk.'

'So we've signed this out for use in an investigation?'

'I said you needed it because the case was being reviewed for reopening.'

'That's good. So I can keep it as long as I need.'

'Yes. But even if I hadn't said that, you would have kept it as long you wanted anyway, wouldn't you?'

Left alone, Slonský concentrated on the file Mucha had brought him. Naturally indolent, Slonský rarely exerted himself, but these were precisely the circumstances that triggered his fastest work. Within a few minutes he had compared the watermarks in the paper and concluded that page one of the Bartoš interview report had been retyped after the other pages. The paper was old, but it was made by a different factory. That was not quite conclusive, because he knew that officers like himself might grab fresh paper from other people's shelves in a hurry, which might be a different batch, but it was a hint that someone might have removed something of importance. There was nothing in the file to indicate that Bartoš had ever been in prison in Olomouc, but then Slonský realised belatedly that he only had Holoubek's word that he had been there, so he made a note to get Navrátil to check that too. A few sums led him to conclude that Bartoš might yet have family living somewhere. His mother would be in her early eighties, if not older, but it would be worth tracking her down if she were still alive. He allocated that job to Peiperová, then decided that Navrátil would do it better. On the other hand, Peiperová had to start somewhere.

No sooner had he thought of her again than his telephone rang and he found that she was calling him.

'I wondered when you expected to get here, sir.'

'Where is here?'

'Holoubek's flat, sir.'

'When you tell me where it is, Peiperová,' Slonský replied testily.

'I left a message on your answerphone about an hour ago, sir.'

'I don't have an answerphone.'

'Yes, you do, sir. Is there a little red light flashing at the top of your phone?'

'Yes.'

'That's to tell you I've left you a message.'

'The flaw in this plan, Peiperová, is that I have no idea how to retrieve it.'

'When I hang up, sir, just press the message key. It'll ask for your PIN number. Put that in, and it will play my message back.'

'But I don't have a PIN.'

'Then it's probably the factory default, sir. It might be 0000, but Sergeant Tomáš's phone was 2512.'

'I've got a better idea, Peiperová. Why don't you just tell me what the message was?'

'Very well, sir. I've found his flat. If you come to the end of Táborská where we found him, I'll show you where it is.'

'That's better, officer. I'm on my way. Meanwhile, you can do something very important for me.'

'Sir?'

'Find me a coffee and a pastry and keep them warm.'

Peiperová was waiting patiently by the front door with a small carrier bag in her hand.

'Didn't you want one?' asked Slonský.

'I didn't see any point in letting it go cold, sir.'

Slonský tried the coffee. It was still warm.

'Got the key?'

Peiperová held it up.

'You can do it. I've got my hands full. Nice pastry, this. You made a good choice.'

Peiperová placed the key in the lock, stepped outside the door frame, and turned it.

'And what was the point of the little sidestep, pray?' Slonský enquired.

'In case it was booby-trapped, sir.'

'I see. So if it exploded you would only lose a hand instead of being killed.'

'I suppose so, sir.'

'Whereas I would be decorating the passageway because you didn't think to tell me of your precaution.'

'Sorry, sir. I thought you would know what I was doing.'

'I never know what anyone else is doing, Peiperová. Always assume that I'm completely ignorant, then make it your job to ensure that I'm not ignorant.'

'Yes, sir. Shall we go in? Watch the rug on the polished floor.'

Slonský followed her into the flat, and watched with approval as Peiperová donned evidence gloves before touching the door handles. He closed the front door by nudging it with his rear end.

'Nice flat. Small, but neat. Let's treat this as a training opportunity, Peiperová. What do you deduce?'

'About what, sir?'

'About Holoubek.'

Peiperová looked around slowly.

'He's been widowed a long time. There's no sign of a female touch. No flowers or bright colours. But his clothes are all hung up and there are shoes in the cupboard in pairs. He took a pride in his appearance. There's very little dust, so he must have had a cleaner.'

'I doubt it. A policeman's pension doesn't run to a cleaner. And cleaners don't organise your pantry like that.' He pointed to a series of jars with large handwritten labels.

'Everything is well looked after. The radio is old but still working and I haven't seen a television like that for years.'

Slonský knelt behind the television with his pastry jammed in his mouth to free a hand. When he stood up, he had a broad smile.

'The crafty old codger,' he said admiringly.

'Sir?'

'Come along, girl. You've got eyes. What do you see?'

'An old television.'

'And?'

'Is it broken? It isn't plugged in like the radio was.'

Slonský plugged it in and turned it on.

'Evidently not broken, then.'

He turned the television back off and removed the plug from the socket.

'I'm sorry, sir. I don't know what you're hinting at.'

'The television works, but is unplugged. There could be lots of reasons for that. But when I see a screwdriver on the shelf behind the television — and the television has been moved forward to let someone as big as me get behind it — coupled with my knowledge that Holoubek was a policeman who must have searched hundreds of houses, I draw a definite conclusion. He unplugged the television so as not to kill himself, because he used the screwdriver to take the back off it, and he did that because he used it as a hiding place for something he didn't want anyone to find. What more natural than to guess that this is where those copies he gave us have been kept? He retrieved them just before he came out and if he'd made it back home he'd have put his room back in good order.'

'Why hide them, sir?'

'Habit? Fear? A belief that they're still being looked for by others? Who knows? Now, it would be a dereliction of duty if we didn't take the back off and look for ourselves.'

Suiting action to the word, he swallowed the last bite of pastry, took a slurp of coffee and knelt behind the television.

'Adhesive tape residue on the inside of the upper surface, but no more papers. Now then, Peiperová, we have to take this place to bits. And in view of our discovery, that means taking bits to bits too.'

People told Peiperová that Slonský was idle, but his assiduous searching gave the lie to that. They had found nothing to do with the case, but Peiperová found an address for Holoubek's son.

'We'd best stop and tell him the sad news. It's not too far away. No need to take your car.'

'Just as well, sir. I haven't got a car.'

'So how did you get here?'

'By tram, sir, the same way Holoubek got to our office.'

'So how do you plan to get back?'

'In your car, sir.'

'I haven't got a car either. Or, more accurately, I haven't brought one with me. You can never park the thing anyway. Come on, we'll walk.'

They were still on their way when Slonský's mobile phone rang. He glanced at the screen.

'Novák. Must be important. He never rings me.'

Slonský ducked into a doorway to answer the call.

'Have you rung to swear at me again?'

'No, business before pleasure, Slonský. I thought you'd like to know that the steering wheel came up trumps. We've got a lot of prints including a nice clear set from the right hand and some partials from the left.'

'Excellent. Have we got a match—'

'Yes. It goes on getting better and better. They belong to a man called Roman Pluskal.'

'What's on his record?'

'Everything apart from murder and riding a bike without lights. He was a rent collector for some local bad boys. It'll probably mean more to you than to me, but he sounds like just the sort of person who would do a bit of driving for someone.'

'Good work, Novák. I owe you a drink.'

'No, thank you,' replied Novák primly, and hung up.

Ondřej Holoubek was at work, but a neighbour knew the school where he taught. The principal sent for Ondřej and lent the detectives his office so they could speak undisturbed.

'Dead? How?'

'He was run over by a van driver, I'm afraid. The doctor says he didn't suffer.'

'Poor Dad. To make it to his age and then…'

'Are you all right, sir? Can I get you anything?' asked Peiperová.

'I'm fine, thank you. But poor Dad. Poor, poor Dad.'

'Did you know he'd been to see us twice recently?'

'I knew he'd been once. He told me he went the other day. I didn't know he'd been back.'

'Yes, sir, yesterday. He was killed as he returned home. I'm afraid it wasn't an accident.'

Ondřej sat up as if an electric shock had been passed through him.

'Not an accident? You mean it was deliberate? Someone murdered him?'

'Yes, sir. We're working on the basis that the motive for killing him was connected to his visit to us. Do you know what he wanted to tell us?'

'Yes. At least, I know the general story, but not the detail. He was obsessed with a case from thirty years ago. He believed an innocent man was hanged and he wanted to put that right.'

'There's not much you can do for someone who's been hanged, sir.'

'You can restore their good name, Lieutenant.'

'What more did you know, sir? Did he discuss his plans with you?'

'No, he didn't. To be honest, I'd have tried to discourage him. I'd probably have failed, because he was a stubborn old devil, but I'd have tried.'

Slonský gave Ondřej a card.

'If you come across anything that could help us, I'd be grateful for a call.'

'Of course. Thank you for coming to tell me in person. Where is he now?'

'He's at the mortuary. I'm afraid we have to conduct a post-mortem on him, but as soon as we can we'll release him to you.'

'Can I see him?'

'I'll make a call to see where we stand on that, sir. Will you excuse me a moment?'

Slonský retired to the corridor to ring Novák, who said that the body would be ready to view by the time Ondřej got there. Slonský rang for a car to pick them up and take Ondřej to the mortuary and then home again.

Slonský was impatient to ask questions but Novák was determined to take Ondřej into the viewing room personally. However, as he ushered Ondřej through the door, Novák handed a printout to Slonský.

'This is interesting,' said Slonský. 'Pluskal has a varied record. Assault, drunk and disorderly, assault again, assault when drunk and disorderly, possession of narcotics with intent to supply, assault, obtaining money with menaces and another assault. Connected with the Griba gang.'

'Who or what is Griba?' Peiperová asked.

'Good question. Griba runs a mob who do all sorts of naughty things, chiefly involving drugs, illegal gambling and prostitution. They also run a little protection racket.'

'So if we know all this, why haven't we stopped them?'

'Well, there you are. The courts keep asking for evidence. I've complained about it, but I get nowhere. And the evidence we get never quite stands up. Witnesses change their minds, exhibits get lost or damaged, people unexpectedly emigrate — you know the sort of thing. You stay here and see young Holoubek gets home. I'll call you with instructions in half an hour or so.'

'Where are you going, sir?'

'I'm off to see a hairdresser.'

Armed with confirmation from the hairdresser that the person she had seen in the van was Pluskal, Slonský called Mucha to arrange for all officers to be alerted to watch for him.

'Tell them not to try tackling him single-handed,' said Slonský. 'It could be dangerous.'

'Don't worry,' Mucha told him. 'As soon as they see the word dangerous the risk that they'll try to arrest him will drop to zero.'

'Any ideas where he might be?'

'I'd be surprised if the drugs squad weren't well informed on Griba and his men. I'll ask Tripka.'

'You do that. Has Navrátil returned yet?'

'Yes, a couple of hours ago. I looked in on him and I'm pleased to report he isn't sitting in your chair, even though you aren't there.'

'Is he doing anything useful or is he gazing at a photo of Peiperová?'

'Are they an item, then?'

'Heading that way. He's young. He'll learn.'

'Isn't young love wonderful?'

'Not just wonderful, but nauseating. Don't let him leave till I get there. Use reasonable force or hide his shoes, whichever works better. What about Peiperová?'

'No sign of her.'

Slonský rang Peiperová and directed her back to Holoubek's flat to continue the search. Since time was of the essence during a murder enquiry he restricted his coffee break to twenty minutes, during which he fortified the inner man with a *párek*, having been bewitched by the smell of sausage when attempting to walk past the stall.

Navrátil was on his knees on the floor of the office. The contents of a folder were strewn around him, and he was busy affixing sticky notes to several of the pages.

'Anything of interest, Navrátil?'

'It seems that Vaněček was cremated and his ashes were scattered because no family could be traced.'

'But Majer said that Mrs Vančková moved out after Vaněček's death, so why didn't she try to claim the body?'

'Is it possible the record is wrong, sir? Wouldn't she have kicked up a stink if we hadn't given the body back?'

'Privately, but she wouldn't have any mechanism to do so under the old regime. If the StB didn't return a body, who could you complain to?'

Navrátil digested the information and pondered over it for a few moments.

'Sir, didn't Vaněček have friends in high places?'

'He must have done at one time. But it's amazing how quickly they forget you when the StB reels you in.'

'But wasn't there anyone among them who wouldn't be scared of the StB? Wouldn't anyone speak up for him?'

'Not a snowball's chance, lad. In a Czech popularity list he would have come just below Heydrich once he was in custody. But where did you get your information?'

'His personnel file, sir. I've marked the relevant pages. He left the service in May 1977. It says that he was disciplined for interference in a security operation, demoted to Major and retired with a pension. That sounds harsh to me.'

'It sounds bloody generous to me. A lot of people wouldn't have stayed out of jail, kept any rank or got a pension.'

'He moved to Zdiby and then it records that his pension ceased after he was arrested for disseminating anti-State propaganda, whatever that means.'

'It means moaning, lad. Any date for that?'

'Pension ceased 24th May 1979.'

'Anything else useful?'

'Two things, sir. He died at Pankrác Prison, so he may be in the records there. And between the end of the Bartoš case and his demotion he was working on a profiteering enquiry.'

'No more details?'

'No, sir. It just says it was bourgeois anti-social profiteering.'

'Aha!' Slonský cried, causing Navrátil to jump a little. 'You don't speak the lingo, Navrátil, but that's a sort of code for anti-corruption work. He was tracking down people who counted who had lined their pockets. That won't have made him popular either. We need to find out if anyone was prosecuted as a result of that investigation. A lot of the old StB files are still around and we'll have to check whether any of them mention him. That's a big job, so get the address and a pass from Mucha and stay there till you've checked it out.'

'Yes, sir. Do you think I'll find anything, sir?'

'I don't know. That's why you need to look. Generally speaking, Navrátil, I don't ask you to do things when I already know the answer. Unless you've annoyed me with stupid questions and I feel like wasting your time, of course.'

'Yes, sir. Sorry, sir.'

Slonský flopped into his chair.

'No, I'm sorry, lad. It wasn't as daft as I made out. Besides, I'm going to spoil your plans for a day or two. I'm going to take Peiperová on a long trip.'

'I thought I was your assistant, sir.'

'So you are, and it's a compliment to you that I think I can leave you to look through the StB archives without having to hold your hand. Peiperová is coming because I'm planning to look for Bartoš' family and I may need a female officer. I

117

suppose the Slovaks might give us one, but it's safer to take my own. I'm planning to go tomorrow, spend a day or two on it and come back at the weekend. Don't worry, I'll make sure Peiperová has her own room in the hotel.'

'I'm sure I can trust you, sir.'

'Yes, that's the sad thing. You can. Twenty years ago … who knows?'

Lukas looked doubtful.

'I hope this is an efficient use of our resources, Slonský.'

'So do I, sir.'

'I can understand the need to speak to Mrs Bartošová if she is still alive…'

'I've checked with the local council, sir, and she is. She still lives in the same house as she did when Bartoš was hanged, in the country to the north of Dolný Kubín.'

'Couldn't we ask the local police to go?'

'They don't have enough background, sir. Besides, I like to see the whites of a witness's eyes when I question them.'

'Well, is it necessary to take Peiperová? That means two hotel rooms.'

'We could always share, sir, but she may snore.'

'Slonský! There is no question of your sharing a room, under any circumstances. Do I make myself clear?'

'Perfectly, sir. Thank you — she's a fit young woman and I'm not sure I'd be able to fight her off if she jumped on me.'

A tiny smile flickered on Lukas' face.

'I think the expression I'm looking for is "in your dreams", Slonský.'

'You may be right, sir, though I don't have those dreams anymore.'

Lukas scrawled a signature.

'Very well. But tell the Slovaks what you're up to, do it all by the book, don't upset anyone and come straight home afterwards. How is it going?'

'Peiperová is searching Holoubek's flat now, sir. I'm going to join her. Navrátil has Vaněček's personnel file. We know he was investigating corruption when he was sacked.'

'That's suggestive. Do we know whom he had in his sights?'

'Not yet, sir. While we're away, Navrátil will check the StB archives, but it's a long shot. The chances are that the villain was one of us, but we might strike lucky. And we know Vaněček's ashes were scattered, allegedly because he had no family, though we know his wife was still alive.'

'You know what that means, Slonský. The body was so badly damaged they couldn't risk letting his wife see it.'

'That explains the cremation, sir. It doesn't explain the scattering. A convicted criminal might be scattered, but Vaněček wasn't convicted. And as Navrátil points out, he must have had powerful friends. The StB can't have known how powerful. Surely they wouldn't want to risk upsetting anyone in high places.'

'I doubt if they cared. They were almost untouchable. And they'd have gauged the reaction to his arrest. I assume they'd have held him for a few days. Firm intervention might have saved him, but I'd hazard a guess that nobody lifted a finger. And when nobody made a fuss, they proceeded to maltreat him.'

'It would be interesting to know who Válek called to get Vaněček brought in, sir.'

'So it would, but you'd have to find Válek first.'

'I've got his address, sir. Holoubek found him.'

Lukas glanced at his watch.

'You've just got time to go and see him this afternoon.'

Navrátil was a little surprised to be told to leave Vaněček's personnel folder and fetch the car, but Slonský disliked driving around Prague if he could persuade someone else to do it.

'Shouldn't we ring first, sir?'

'No, Navrátil. We want to surprise him so he doesn't have time to make up a story.'

'It'll certainly be a surprise, sir. It's been thirty years since his daughter died.'

'I think we need to approach this interview with the maximum of tact, lad. Leave all the talking to me.'

Navrátil managed to stifle his response, but the keen observer would have seen his mouth drop open.

'Eyes on the road, lad. Bear right here and then left at the next junction.'

They found the apartment block and Slonský led the way up to the third floor. They knocked on a door that had once been cream but now looked slightly yellow. After a few moments and a lot of noisy shuffling the door was opened by a large old man walking with a crutch attached to his right elbow.

'Mr Válek?'

'Yes.'

'Lieutenant Slonský and Officer Navrátil.'

'Come in. The neighbours will have a field day if they see policemen here.'

'Are they inquisitive, then, sir?'

'Nosey bitches. Especially her across the corridor. Old cow.'

Válek sank into an armchair and indicated a similar chair and the sofa. Slonský took the chair.

'I'm sorry to bring this up after all this time, sir…'

'Jana. You've come to talk about Jana. Have you found the other man?'

'It's more complicated than that, sir. You'll recall that a man called Bartoš was hanged for killing her.'

'Yes, I remember. How could I ever forget? He took my precious girl from me.'

'That's the problem, sir. He didn't.'

Válek reddened and glowered at them.

'Don't talk nonsense. He was convicted and hanged. He did it.'

'I'm afraid he can't have done, sir. He was in prison for something else at the time.'

Now Válek blanched.

'In prison? But surely you knew that?'

'We did, sir. I'm trying to find out why we ignored the fact. But, more to the point, we've reopened your daughter's case and I've been assigned to finding her real killer.'

'Killers, Lieutenant. There were two of them.'

'That's my first question, sir. Why did they stop looking when they charged Bartoš? You knew there were two, and they must have known there were two as well. Didn't you press them to keep looking?'

'I certainly did. That fat pompous officer — what was his name? — the one my wife persuaded them to appoint.'

'Vaněček.'

'Vaněček! That's him. Bloody useless. We'd have been better off keeping that stringy one who was on it at first. At least he was a proper detective. Vaněček couldn't find his own backside with a map.'

'May I ask, sir, how your wife had Vaněček appointed?'

Válek rubbed his hands together as if he were washing them.

'Her sister was married to an army general. My wife rang her sister to tell her what had happened, and my sister-in-law said her husband would make sure the best man was put on the job.

He'd served with Vaněček in the army, so he rang him for suggestions, and Vaněček said he would take it on himself. At the time we thought that was the best possible arrangement. It soon became clear that he was a clueless imbecile.'

'Are your sister-in-law and her husband still alive, sir?'

'No, neither of them. General Mikula died ten years ago, and my sister-in-law followed last year.'

'I'm sorry to hear that, sir. You were going to explain why the search was stopped.'

'It was Vaněček. He told us he'd got a confession from this man Bartoš, but Bartoš had given a statement that didn't mention an accomplice. It was therefore clear that Kopecký must have been mistaken. He advised us not to mention the second man because if the court thought the confession was wrong about that the judges might throw it out altogether and then Bartoš would go free.'

'Did you believe that, sir?'

'I'm not a lawyer, Lieutenant. I can't argue with people who know how the courts work. But I have to admit that I didn't think Kopecký would be wrong. He was an interfering busybody but he had eyes like a hawk.'

'In what way was he interfering, sir?'

'He wanted the street kept exclusive. He started a residents' association and we had all kinds of rules about when the garbage had to go out and where it could be put. All that sort of thing. But he was an honest man and his wife was lovely with Jana. Are they still around?'

'Yes, sir. We met them a few days ago.'

'I should give them a call,' muttered Válek. 'They were good neighbours.' He raised his voice. 'Not like that interfering woman across the hall.' He mopped his face with a large white handkerchief. 'Sorry. I'm all alone in the world now, you see.

No-one to fight my battles for me. Wife's dead, poor Jana's dead, I've got nobody. The Kopeckýs were good friends. I just didn't appreciate that at the time. I'd like to talk to them again.'

'If you want to give me your details, I'll ask them if they want to make touch, sir.'

Válek nodded his thanks.

'If it's not too painful, sir, it would help us if you would talk us through the night your daughter was killed. I know it's a long time ago, but…'

'I'll never forget it, don't you worry. You can't forget a minute of a day like that. Memories don't work that way. My wedding day went past in a blur, but the 16th of July, 1976 is in my head forever.'

Válek closed his eyes for a moment while he decided where to start.

'I was manager of a kitchen electricals factory. We were close to sealing a deal to provide irons and toasters to Hungary. They were paying for them with hi-fi equipment, of all things. Goodness knows how I was meant to sell those, but that's what the ministry had agreed. The Hungarians were in town and the ministry threw a dinner for them. All of us who were negotiating deals were told to go. I didn't like going out on a Friday, but I didn't have a choice.'

'And you left Jana alone?'

'She sometimes went to a youth club on Friday nights, but I told her I didn't want her walking back home from the tram stop on her own. To be frank, I wasn't convinced that she would come home at the normal time if she knew we were out. She wasn't a bad girl, you understand, but you know what teenagers can be like. So I confined her to the house. She complained and asked if she could have some friends round.

My wife agreed, thinking she meant the girls she used to hang around with.'

'But in fact she invited boys.'

'She must have done. She let them in and they had some beer together. The boys must have brought that. It wasn't mine. I didn't know Jana ever drank. She was only just seventeen.'

Válek's eyes were glistening as tears filmed them over. He paused to wipe them away with a thumb.

'We didn't know that she was friendly with any boys. Of course, we asked her best friends, but they swore they didn't know of any boyfriends either. There were one or two who lived nearby, but they didn't fit the description Kopecký gave. They all had longish hair. It was the fashion then.'

'So you have no idea who they were?'

'No, none at all.'

'Surely you didn't believe that Jana would have let Bartoš in and shared a beer with him?'

Válek nibbled his thumb in agitation.

'I couldn't see how they could possibly have known one another. They just wouldn't move in the same circles. And he was a dozen years older than her at least. But Vaněček was very persuasive. He told us we obviously knew very little about our daughter's private life so how could we say that she didn't know Bartoš?'

Slonský checked that Navrátil was making notes of the conversation.

'So you went out, sir, and you came in — when?'

'About half past one, I think. We were brought back by car because I'd been drinking so many toasts to those damn Hungarians. When we turned in to the road we saw the police cars and noticed that our front door was open. I ran in — a couple of police tried to stop me, but I pushed them off and told them I lived there — and I heard talking in the bathroom. When I ran in there I found Jana. It was horrible. That skinny policeman pushed me outside and sat me down in the lounge with my wife. He told me what had happened. That's it, I think. I remember the policeman went outside and yelled at the pair by the front door. Something about sending them to the tiniest police station in the Tatra mountains. After a while they let us go in to see her. They had put her on a trolley and covered her with a sheet so only her face was showing.'

'Did you go to the court hearing, sir?'

Válek nodded.

'I wanted to see the murderous monster who took my baby. He looked such an insignificant little squirt. But he was only there for a few minutes. When they read out the charge he went berserk. I didn't catch what he shouted — he had quite a strong Slovak accent — but it was something about the police having tricked him into confessing. The judges ordered him taken away and they carried on without him.'

'Didn't his lawyer object to that?'

'His lawyer barely said a word. Mind you, he only looked like a kid himself. I don't know where they got him.'

'He doesn't seem to have known that Bartoš was in prison when the crime was committed. And when he was told, he doesn't seem to have made a fuss about it.'

'That figures. I don't think he would have known how. He was a novice.'

'You don't recall his name, by any chance?'

Válek hoisted himself out of the armchair without a word, and limped out of the room. When he returned, he had a large black loose-leaf folder.

'My scrapbook of the trial.'

Slonský and Navrátil goggled at each other.

'You've got a scrapbook? May we read it?'

'Be my guests, but I'd rather you didn't take it off me. I'll go and put the kettle on.'

Slonský flipped the cover over. There was a newspaper article and a photograph of Bartoš being bundled into court. The witnesses were right; he was very slightly built, almost like a jockey. There was a large man in uniform a couple of steps behind him.

'Isn't that Vaněček?' asked Navrátil.

'I think so.'

Slonský scanned the preamble rapidly. Suddenly he prodded the paper with his forefinger.

'There, Navrátil! Look who was lawyer for the defence.'

Navrátil gawped at the page.

'Here we go again,' he said.

Chapter 8

Lukas spat his coffee across the room.

'You need to interview whom?'

'The Minister of the Interior, sir.'

'Slonský, are you going to make a habit of this? Need I remind you that you arrested a Minister of the Interior and charged him, quite incorrectly, with murder?'

'That was the last one, sir. I'm not planning to charge this one.'

'I'm delighted to hear it. By the way, why are you still here?'

'Why are any of us here, sir? It's puzzled better minds than mine.'

'It's not a philosophical enquiry, Slonský. I thought you were going to Slovakia.'

Slonský had the grace to look embarrassed.

'It's Peiperová, sir. She needs some time to get herself ready.'

'Well, I'm very surprised. I thought she would be an organised young woman.'

'Yes, sir.'

'So why isn't she ready to go?'

'She's sleeping, sir. I may have overlooked telling her to knock off last night.'

'You left her searching Holoubek's flat all night?'

'It never occurred to me that she wouldn't stop when she'd done a full day, sir.'

'She's under your command, damn it! Of course she won't stop until you say.'

'She could have called me to remind me, sir.'

'She shouldn't need to.'

'And it wasn't all night, sir. She caught the night bus back to the barracks.'

'The night bus doesn't go to the barracks, man. She must have walked quite a distance, alone, at night. I'm surprised the guards let her in.'

'They didn't at first, sir. She doesn't have a Prague identity card yet and they wouldn't let her in with the one issued in Kladno. Fortunately Navrátil was able to vouch for her.'

'And I suppose he was just passing?'

'I believe she rang him, sir.'

'I'm very close to speechless, Slonský. I trust there will be no repetition of this shocking episode.'

'I'll certainly try my best, sir.'

'No, Slonský, you will not try. You will succeed.'

Slonský adopted his most innocent expression, as if to convey his extreme willingness to please.

'Don't do that, Slonský. You look like an illustration from *The Good Soldier Švejk.*'

'Yes, sir. Sorry, sir.'

'So explain to me why you want to interview the minister.'

'Dr Pilik was the defence lawyer when Bartoš was on trial, sir. He doesn't seem to have made much effort to keep him from the noose, and I'm curious to know why.'

'We need more than curiosity, Slonský. Are you alleging corruption?'

'Do you think I should, sir?'

'You don't have any evidence, Slonský,' yelled Lukas in exasperation. 'I grant it looks bad, but his client had confessed.'

'His client had allegedly confessed, sir, but since said client could not read or write, you'd have thought a lawyer might have questioned the confession. Not to mention asking about the missing accomplice, or what Bartoš was shouting about when he was manhandled out of the court, since he is said to have claimed that he had been induced to sign a false confession following promises made by a police officer.'

'Vaněček?'

'No, and that's another thing I want to ask him about. The statement was taken in Olomouc by another officer. Vaněček processed it, but who gave it to him, because he didn't go to Olomouc, and the statement arrived here before Bartoš did? The statement in the file is alleged to have been made in Prague, but I suspect it's the Olomouc one retyped.'

Lukas threw his pen petulantly onto his blotter.

'I suppose there are sufficient irregularities there to warrant an interview. We will go together. I'll clear it with the Director of Police and make an appointment. You'd best stay in Prague until we know when that will be. In the meantime, give the girl the day off. It's Friday and she'll probably want to go home to see her family for the weekend.'

'Yes, sir.'

Slonský made for the door.

'One last thing, Slonský. The last time you persuaded me to see a minister with you, you came close to wrecking both our careers. If you do anything untoward this time, I will leave you to sink on your own. In fact I'll hide the lifebelts. Is that clear?'

'It certainly is, sir. No lifebelts.'

Slonský telephoned Peiperová, apologising for waking her and telling her she could have the day off since she had worked seventeen hours on the day before. He told her he would collect her from the barracks at 07.00 on Monday morning, when she should be ready to go to Slovakia. If plans changed he would call her. Peiperová thanked him and rang Navrátil, which explained why it was that Navrátil was both well-informed and grumpy when Slonský told him about the plans for the day.

'What shall I do, if you have to stay here, sir?'

'You can get yourself across to the National Archives and look out anything in the StB records that looks useful. I only have to stay in Prague. And I suppose I'd better put my mobile phone on. It's been a tense morning, Navrátil. I could do with a beer.'

'It's only half past eight, sir.'

'Is it? It seems later than that. I suppose we'd better settle for a coffee. Come along, lad. I'll pay.'

Slonský left the room, leaving Navrátil checking his hearing by placing a finger in each earhole. No, he couldn't hear any voices. It must have been real.

Lukas rang to tell Slonský that Pilik would see them briefly at eleven o'clock, by which time Slonský would no doubt have polished his shoes, ironed his shirt and generally smartened himself up.

'Have I got time to book into a clinic for a facelift, sir?'

'Don't be facetious, Slonský. We must make a good impression on the new minister.'

'If he's done anything corrupt I could ensure he's impressed by how quickly I get his carcass into a cell.'

'He's not a suspect, Slonský. He is an involved party, that is all. Don't annoy him.'

'Don't worry, sir. I won't. Unless he's done something, of course. Then I'll annoy him a lot.'

As Slonský and Lukas were shown in Slonský found himself wondering if the office would have changed at all since Dr Banda occupied it just three or four months before. He soon discovered that the changes were minimal. The computer and telephone had been moved to the other side of the chair because Pilik was right-handed, so the visitors' chairs had been inched sideways a little to keep both in sight. The same snooty secretary showed them in, offered them the same execrable coffee and once again bypassed Slonský to serve Lukas first.

'I understand you wish to speak to me about an early case of mine,' Pilik began.

'Yes, minister,' agreed Lukas. 'The defence of a man named Bartoš.'

Pilik nodded in recognition.

'Not a case I like to remember.'

'I'm not surprised,' said Slonský, earning himself a stamp on the instep from Lukas.

'You'll realise it was a long time ago. One of my very first cases, in fact, and the only client I've ever had executed. And, of course, since the Czech Republic no longer has capital punishment, the only one I will ever have.'

'I suppose as Minister of the Interior you could bring it back, sir.'

'I could try — if I had the inclination, which I haven't. I haven't had it since Bartoš hanged, in fact.'

Lukas did not like the turn the conversation was taking, and intervened to bring it back to safer territory.

'May I ask how you were appointed to the case, minister?'

'I'd been in practice only a few months. I had a telephone call saying that Bartoš needed a court-appointed lawyer, and I was next on the list of possibles.'

'Surely a more experienced advocate should have been selected for a murder trial, sir?'

'But it wasn't a murder trial,' Pilik explained. 'When I was appointed it was about a series of burglaries. Bartoš was living in Olomouc, but it seemed that he had come to Prague and conducted a string of break-ins. He admitted some but of course he had no real idea where he had robbed. He just walked around the streets looking for likely targets. The police tried to get him to confess to a list of places. Bartoš was sent over to Prague and I went to see him. I think I was allowed about fifteen minutes with him.'

'That's not very long, sir.'

'No, it isn't, Captain. He agreed that he had confessed to burglaries in a couple of places and he hoped I could get him some allowance for having pleaded guilty. I said I would try, but that wasn't guaranteed — some judges would inflate the sentence so that they could take off the allowance and it would make no real difference. Then I had a message to say the trial would start in two days and that Bartoš had been charged with murder because a young woman had been killed at one of the houses he'd confessed to burgling.'

Slonský pulled his chair forward to get nearer to his prey.

'How could he confess, sir? He couldn't read and write.'

The minister looked acutely uncomfortable.

'I didn't know that then. I'd never had a client who couldn't read before. And he didn't say anything about that. It was only after he had been sentenced that one of the policemen asked me why I hadn't questioned the confession.'

'That policeman wasn't a man called Holoubek, was it?'

'I don't know. It may have been. The name rings a bell.'

'The newspaper accounts of the trial say that Bartoš kicked up when he heard the charges. Was that the first he knew of them?'

'Probably. I hadn't been allowed to see him again. Bartoš can't have known that I'd tried. He shouted one or two very unpleasant things at me.'

'I'm not surprised, sir. The prospect of getting your neck stretched tends to put social graces out of your mind.'

'I did the best I could, Lieutenant. I'm not saying I wouldn't do better now, but given the poor hand I was dealt, I tried hard to shake the police case. But the judges kept coming back to the confession. The verdict was inevitable. In those days it was often decided before you got into court anyway.'

'And when Holoubek told you about the confession, what did you do?'

'Well, of course I went straight to the President of the Court. He was a monster. He said it would be an unnecessary embarrassment to socialist justice if the verdict were shaken in any way, and that for the sake of my career I should let things lie. In any event, he said, it was futile because he happened to know the execution had been carried out. I protested that the date set was still a few days away, but he said that the date was "an administrative decision" that the governor of the jail could vary. Pankrác needed the space so the governor had cleared the cell.'

'"Cleared the cell"? Is that what they called hanging an innocent man then?'

Pilik was now acutely uncomfortable.

'It's not my choice of words. And while he may not have signed the confession, we don't know that he didn't do it.'

'Yes, we do,' Slonský snapped. 'He had the best possible alibi. He was already in jail when the murder happened.'

Pilik went pale. Lukas wondered whether he was about to faint and looked around for a bottle of brandy.

'In jail?'

'In Olomouc.'

'But surely the police must have known that?'

'They did. Why didn't you?'

'Nobody told me,' wailed Pilik. 'They just told me he'd been arrested there and returned for questioning. They didn't tell me he had an alibi.'

'Well, they wouldn't, would they, sir? Even a complete beginner like you might have got him off if they had.'

Pilik winced involuntarily.

'I recognise that this incident doesn't show me in the best possible light,' he began.

'No, you're right there, sir,' Slonský confirmed.

'But it was a long time ago. Things have changed here since. You're old enough to remember what it was like. If someone wanted him convicted there wasn't a lot I could have done.'

'No,' agreed Slonský, 'but you could at least have tried.'

Lukas was starting to feel a little wan himself, and he still could not see any brandy. He ran a finger inside his collar which felt rather tight.

'The thing is, sir,' Slonský continued, 'the case has been reopened and is likely to be quite a sensation in the press. Whatever we think of what happened, you should prepare yourself for some awkward questions from the media.' He stood abruptly, causing Lukas to follow suit. 'Thank you for your time, sir. We'll see ourselves out.'

As they walked back to Lukas's car Slonský strode out forcefully, causing Lukas to trot at intervals to keep up.

'Do you really think the press might get hold of this?' Lukas enquired.

'I'm sure of it, sir. You know how they like embarrassing people in power.'

'Of course, we must not fetter the press,' Lukas mumbled. Slonský knew what was coming next. 'But the police don't come out of this too favourably either. How will we handle that?'

Slonský stopped. 'I could brief the press first, before they hear somewhere else.'

'Out of the question! We can't draw attention to this. Most embarrassing.'

'How about I prepare a briefing sheet that throws all the blame on the StB? Just in case.'

'Do you think we could?'

'Well, they get the blame for everything else. They'll be used to it by now, sir.'

'But do the facts bear that interpretation?'

'Oh, I think they could, sir.'

'Well, Slonský, let's hope that the press show no interest. We'll have to keep our fingers crossed.'

'Yes, sir. Fingers crossed.'

'This is good stuff,' agreed Valentin. 'Minister of the Interior lets a client hang because he forgets to ask if he can read and write. I can see the headlines now — "What kind of nincompoop do we have running Law and Order?"'

'That's good. I like that,' said Slonský. 'Another?'

'Go on then, if you're paying.'

'I thought you were taking your earnings to the bank twice a day in a wheelbarrow now.'

'Things are better, there's no denying it. But the big money is in television. I do all right. And this little beauty should snag me a bit extra.'

'Just hang on until after Monday so I get to Bartoš' mother first. I want her to hear from me before she reads anything in the papers.'

'It's a deal. Though if he couldn't read, what's the chances that his mother will be able to?'

'Fair point.'

'How are your little turtle doves?' Valentin asked.

'I'm keeping them apart. Navrátil is at the Archives wading through mountains of StB papers. That should occupy him for a day or two. Peiperová has gone home for the weekend. I try to keep her out of the office. That way I don't have to look at Navrátil's bushbaby impersonation. Plus she doesn't actually have a desk.'

'Cunning,' said Valentin approvingly.

'I like to think so,' Slonský smiled.

Chapter 9

The Slovak police were fascinated to hear from Slonský. In no time at all he was put through to the chief of the City Police, who was polite and keen to be helpful, qualities that would have rendered him utterly unsuitable for employment in Prague.

Slonský asked whether they could ascertain if Mrs Bartošová were still alive and still lived at the address Slonský had. Within moments both had been confirmed. Slonský was impressed with their filing system, until the chief explained that the Bartoš family were well known to the police, having been what are euphemistically called 'service users' for many years past. Every policeman in Dolný Kubín knew where the various Bartoš family members lived. They actually lived a little way out of the main part of town, which was a blessing because there was only one route they could reasonably take to get home with their swag. The chief had heard of the hanging but it did not seem to have changed the family's ways.

'I need to interview Mrs Bartošová about her son's conviction. Would you be able to send an officer to ensure everything is done properly?'

'Of course. Drop in at the police station as you go through and I'll send someone to guide you and interpret.'

'Don't they speak Slovak?'

'Yes, they speak Slovak, but they'll probably pretend they don't understand Czech. And their dialect is a little difficult to follow sometimes. If you shake hands with them, count your fingers afterwards.'

'Thanks for the tip. I'm bringing a young policewoman with me, Officer Peiperová.'

'Tell her to wear trousers. The Bartoš house is no place to wear a skirt.'

'Then I'll change my wardrobe plans. See you on Monday afternoon.'

Navrátil had expected his search of the StB archive to be achingly boring and unproductive, and he was not disappointed. For a few hours he found nothing but dead ends. It was clear that Vaněček and the StB were not on each other's' Christmas card lists, because the files held a number of vituperative and pompous memoranda from the former and some frosty replies from the latter. There were also some notes from various StB personnel to Tripka asking him why he could not control Vaněček better. Tripka replied to one that he was in a dilemma, because Vaněček was a superior officer but he did not always appreciate the wider importance of StB work, so he had consciously withheld some operational material from him for fear that he would impede the investigation. When Vaněček found this out, there had been a very difficult interview with Tripka being threatened with a transfer to the border police. Another exchange caused Navrátil more concern. It looked as if the StB had flooded an area of Prague with prostitutes in order to trap Western businessmen attending a large conference, but Tripka had not told Vaněček. There had been a sharp increase in pickpocketing and Vaněček, who was looking after security for the conference, had ordered the area cleared. The prostitutes were rounded up and taken into custody. The StB had protested and Vaněček, instead of answering them, had taken his complaint directly to the minister, arguing that these tactics would give the

Communist system unwanted bad publicity in the West and should be outlawed. To the StB's surprise the minister, who — as Vaněček knew well — was something of a puritan, had agreed and had instructed them that this sort of provocative action must cease at once. However, his letter had been annotated 'Be more careful!' by some StB hand and there was no sign that the security police had paid any heed to it.

It was not until late afternoon that Navrátil finally located a file that related to the arrest and interrogation of Vaněček in 1979. It was surprisingly thin, but that proved to be due to substantial editing over the years that had removed some of the pages. Nevertheless, he settled down to read it and make some notes.

The top of Navrátil's pencil was soggy, always a sign of deep cogitation. He had scoured the files and kept coming to the same conclusion. There was no reason in those files for anyone to arrest Vaněček. Certainly that had changed. There were a number of file notes concerning 'Statements made by the witness Vaněček' which later became 'Statements made by the prisoner Vaněček', but those were things he had said after he was detained. Navrátil could find no reason why he might have been arrested in the first place. There was no warrant, no preparatory papers, and indeed the matter did not seem to have been discussed beforehand.

'So they just pulled him in?' said Slonský.

'It looks that way.'

'Well, there's a conundrum, then. Even in those days just arresting people at random and beating them to death in custody was frowned upon a bit.'

'Sir, was he arrested? This bit about "the witness Vaněček" puzzles me. Did he come in voluntarily as a witness?'

Slonský considered for a few moments.

'He'd have had to come in voluntarily a few times, wouldn't he? He doesn't become "the prisoner Vaněček" until the fourth or fifth statement. But I suppose he might have made a complaint that was turned against him. What are the statements about?'

'In the later ones, it looks like Vaněček is defending himself against a suggestion that he has deliberately fouled up StB operations. He keeps saying that he didn't do A, B or C. But in the first couple it's about what he was told and when. There's a piece here where he's arguing that these allegations have already been investigated and he was exonerated.'

'And was he?'

'Nobody seems to have checked.'

'But is there ever a specific charge mentioned — any hint that they planned to take him to trial?'

'Not a thing.'

'And no report on his death?'

'Just a file note to say that it happened. 24th May, 1979.'

Showing an unaccustomed display of energy, Slonský picked up the phone and dialled a number he must have known by heart.

'Novák.'

'You certainly are. You know you're my favourite state pathologist and I've often said you are a pivotal figure in our fight against crime?'

'What do you want?'

'Your inestimable assistance once more. A policeman called Vaněček died on 24th May, 1979. He allegedly had an accident in his garden, which know can't have happened. Presumably an unexpected death would have triggered an autopsy?'

'I know where you're going. It would only have triggered an autopsy if he was found in his garden. If something happened to him in custody they wouldn't have called us, would they?'

'No, I grant that. But why come up with the garden story — which, incidentally anyone with half a brain would know was untrue; even Navrátil spotted that — unless they intended him to be found well away from StB headquarters in some safe place like, say, his garden?'

'Then the local police would have taken a look at it, and called your lot if they were suspicious.'

'And if they were too thick to be suspicious?'

'They'd have called us, I suppose. Or, conceivably, just sent for an ambulance to shift the body and the hospital he was taken to would have called us.'

'Then, just possibly, somewhere in your archive…'

'Slonský! Do you have any idea how many files there are in our archives?'

'No,' said the detective. 'I bet you haven't either. Let me guess — a hundred and two?'

'More than that.'

'Two hundred and sixty-eight?'

'Stop playing games. It'll take an age.'

'You've got a name and a date. Presumably there's an index. And young Navrátil is sitting here looking bored and would be very happy to come down and help you find it.'

There was the deepest of sighs at the end of the line.

'I'll see what I can find. I'll call you back.'

'Wonderful. Don't forget Navrátil goes home at five.'

Slonský dropped the receiver and beamed at Navrátil.

'When do I ever get to go home at five?'

'Poetic licence. And I didn't say whether it was p.m. or a.m.'

'Are you going to make me work all night like you did…'

'Enough. That was a mistake. And the girl has a tongue in her head, as I suspect you're set fair to discover for the rest of your life.'

'Nothing like that is planned. We're still getting to know each other.'

'Can she cook?'

Navrátil was nonplussed.

'I don't know.'

'You don't know? The single most important fact about a future wife and you don't know?'

'It's not been high on my list of priorities.'

'Then bump it up, lad. Looks don't last, but cookery skills do. When everything is beginning to sag and she's covered in crow's feet you'll be able to content yourself with the thought that she can still turn out a good *svíčková*.'

'She's a long way from sagging yet, sir.'

'Ah, you think that, but it creeps up on you, son. That's the odd thing about Czech women. For years they're tall and blonde and good-looking, then you go out for a beer and when you come back they've dropped ten centimetres and developed a backside like a carthorse.'

'Sir, you can teach me about a lot of things, but I'm not sure you're an authority on Czech women. After all, you've been divorced a long time.'

'I haven't played hockey for thirty years but I still know what a goal looks like. Look out of that window and show me a single good-looking older Czech woman.'

Navrátil accepted the challenge. He watched patiently for a while before triumphantly pointing along the street to his left.

'There! The woman in the wine-coloured coat.'

Slonský took a brief look and sniffed.

'Obviously a foreigner, Navrátil.'

He left the room before Navrátil could argue.

Slonský was in a quandary. The canteen had run out of anything containing meat. There was an egg roll, and several types of salad, some of which contained bits of meat, but he risked inadvertently eating something green in trying to pick them out. Not only that, but the lady behind the counter advised them not to touch the pastries, which were two days old.

'The salad is very fresh,' she said.

'I went straight from breast milk to meat,' said Slonský.

'Well, I'm not giving you breast milk and we're out of meat,' came the reply.

The queue was growing restless. There was only Navrátil in it, but he was restless enough for any number of others.

'Out of meat? What sort of canteen runs out of meat?' whined Slonský.

'Wait here,' said the assistant, and returned in a few moments with a hunk of salami and a bread roll.

'Bless you, Anna,' Slonský whispered. 'I was just telling Navrátil that a good Czech woman looks after her man's stomach.'

Anna smiled.

'You also said that Czech women sag — ouch!'

'I'm sorry, Navrátil. Was that your shin? Don't hold the queue up, lad. Grab your coffee and pay up.'

No sooner had they taken their seats than Mucha beckoned from the doorway. Slonský beckoned him in return. This continued until Mucha gave in.

'Novák says you're to come and get it.'

'The little devil. Usually he plays hard to get.'

'He also says he can't take it out of the building so get your backside in gear and get over there before he goes home at five.'

'Clock watcher. Navrátil, ask Anna to put these coffees in a takeaway cup. I'll eat my sandwich while you're driving.'

'And what will I do with this?' asked Navrátil, indicating his half-eaten egg roll.

'If you've got any sense you'll heave it in a bin and get something edible. Come along, lad, we can't keep Novák waiting.'

Novák peered at them over his glasses.

'There's more to this than meets the eye.'

'I'm the detective,' said Slonský. 'You're not trained for it.'

'True. But if I'm signing stuff out of the archive that has a bad smell about it I want to know what it's all about before I hand it over. And I have the upper hand because I have the file.'

Slonský reached inside his coat and pointed his gun at Novák.

'And I have this.'

'You wouldn't pull the trigger,' Novák scoffed.

Before Navrátil could stop him, Slonský pulled the trigger.

There was a loud click.

'You complete idiot!' yelled Novák. 'It's just as well I've got iron bowel control. That could have been loaded.'

'It is loaded,' said Slonský. 'But the safety catch is on.'

Novák snatched the gun.

'Slonský, the safety on this model disengages when you grip hard and pull the trigger.'

'Does it? I forgot that. Just as well that I also forgot to load it, then.'

Novák held it sideways to remove the magazine, and was rewarded by seeing Navrátil dive towards the ground.

'Navrátil? What are you doing?'

'Saying a Hail Mary,' was the reply.

'I've been shot,' Slonský announced, 'and it's not so bad.'

'You have? Where?'

'In a warehouse,' said Slonský. 'And I was not running away from the enemy, whatever anyone tells you. It was a ricochet.'

Novák handed the disarmed gun back.

'It wouldn't be a great feat of marksmanship to hit your backside, Slonský.'

'No,' agreed Slonský, 'but it was round a corner. I wouldn't have minded, but it was a police bullet. And they wanted to charge me for a new pair of trousers.'

Novák opened the dog-eared file.

'First things first. He didn't die on 24th May. It was the 28th.'

'But his police file says he died on the 24th.'

'No doubt it does. But the local police at Zdiby found him in his garden on the 28th.'

'Couldn't they tell he'd been dead four days?' asked Navrátil.

'Apparently not. They remarked on the absence of rigor mortis, but that had passed off by the time he was found. The photographs of the body are monochrome, but you can clearly see that his face is livid. There's simply no way he could have died in the posture in which he was found, propped up on a loose fence post, which, incidentally, doesn't match any of the others in the garden. He died lying face down. I'd guess he was injured and thrown on a cot with his head hanging over the edge. The actual cause of death was a series of blows to the chest. The fifth to seventh ribs on the left side were all broken and the skin was pierced. But you can see from this picture that the skin was pierced from the inside by a piece of rib, rather than from the outside by a fence stake. It looks as if he suffered from a flail chest. The ribs broke in two places so that whole segment of ribcage wouldn't move when he breathed. There's a pleural tear as well.'

'Is that bad?'

'The pleura is the sac inside the chest. If the broken rib rips it, the lung on that side has trouble filling and air can enter the chest cavity. It's painful and it's life threatening. Without serious medical care he'd have less than a fifty-fifty chance of surviving.'

'And the cover story is nonsense?'

'Unless the fence wore boots, complete bunkum. I'd say Vaněček was kicked repeatedly while he was lying on the ground, then dumped on his bed to die.'

'And the pathologist said that too?'

'That's the interesting bit. He obviously knew the truth, but he didn't dare tell it, so he was crafty. He wrote what he was told to write, but he left plenty of clues to those of us who know these things so we could see plainly that he knew what really happened. Look here, for example. He measured the top of the fence post and notes that it was eighty-three millimetres in diameter. But he puts that in table 5 and immediately below he notes that the wound he labelled C measures 117mm across. He's telling us that the post can't have made that wound. Again here, he notes that the body was found on 28th May and that death must have been a little before that, but he says he knows this because there were only early signs of skin blistering. But skin blistering happens around day five after death. He knows the death occurred on the 23rd or 24th.'

'Wasn't that a risky thing to do, sir?' asked Navrátil.

'Very risky,' Novák replied. 'He must have known that his work could be reviewed by a second pathologist who could have shopped him. But if it was, nothing seems to have been said. The file was put away, and until today that's where it has been.'

Slonský was leafing through the file slowly.

'Bastards,' he said finally. 'This wasn't an interrogation. This was a punishment killing. I thought they'd accidentally killed him, but it's clear they didn't expect him ever to leave alive. They wanted it to look like an accident, but you can't accidentally kick a man to death. They didn't want him to go to trial, so they didn't need to charge him, because a charge would be irrelevant anyway. Whatever Vaněček was saying, they weren't going to let him go on saying it.'

'Who are "they"?' demanded Novák.

'Good question. But we've got some names.'

'Have we, sir?' asked Navrátil.

'We know who signed the witness statements. That's your next job, lad. Decipher the signatures and see if they're still alive. The pensions office may help again.'

'Surely you'll never get a conviction after all this time, Slonský,' said Novák.

'Perhaps not. But when I look them in the eye, they'll know that I'll know, and I'll make sure they never forget I know. I want them to toss and turn every night for the rest of their lives.'

Slonský marched through the door and indicated the clock over Mucha's counter.

'Time you went home, lad. Have the weekend off. On Monday, find those StB hoodlums. And have a look through that file Mucha gave me. You may spot something I've missed.'

'Thanks, sir. Have a good weekend.'

'I won't. Remind Peiperová I'll see her at seven to drive to Slovakia.'

'I will if I see her, sir.'

'"If I see her"? Of course you'll see her. Around six o'clock on Sunday evening, I'd guess.'

'How…?'

'Because she won't be able to escape from her family until late on Sunday afternoon, but her mother will accept that she wants to get back to Prague before dark. Then all you need is a knowledge of the train times from Kladno and it's pretty elementary, really.'

Mucha coughed loudly.

'Sorry, Navrátil, one of the servants is trying to attract my attention. What is it, Mucha?'

Mucha adopted the fawning posture of a peasant addressing his lord, his eyes fixed on the floor and his head bowed.

'Begging your pardon, sir, but there's somebody waiting here to see you.'

'Who is he?'

'It's a lady,' said Mucha, tipping his head to one side to indicate a woman in a cheap raincoat sitting on the bench against the wall.

Slonský scrutinised her closely.

'That's not a lady. That's my wife.'

Chapter 10

Věra Slonská stirred her coffee slowly. It contained more sugar than was good for her.

'Still got your sweet tooth, then?'

'I suppose so. It's my only vice.'

'Apart from running off with second rate poets, that is.'

'Keep your voice down. No need to tell everyone.'

'Really?' Slonský boomed. 'Don't you want people to know you dumped your husband to shag some greasy slimeball?'

'All right, I can understand you're upset.'

'Upset? I lost two years of my life to the bottle. I finished up in a one-room flat on my own for thirty-five years so I think I'm entitled to be upset.'

'You could have found someone else. Someone better than me.'

'That's true. There's no shortage of women better than you, but I didn't realise that at the time. I was heartbroken and you didn't care.'

'I didn't mean to hurt you.'

'You mean you were dancing in the nude and accidentally fell onto his penis?'

Věra pulled a handkerchief from the cuff of her blouse and dabbed her eyes.

'I know I did wrong. I'm sorry. This isn't easy for me. Can't we be a bit more civilised about it?'

Slonský bit his lip.

'I'll try. Why hunt me out now after all these years?'

Věra sipped her coffee and replaced it delicately on her saucer before speaking.

'I haven't been entirely honest with you.'

'You mean it wasn't just one out of work poet but an entire writers' workshop?'

'No.'

'You were always a lesbian?'

'Of course not.'

'I give up.'

She took a deep breath. The canteen was a very public place for this sort of discussion but Slonský had refused to go anywhere more private, claiming that she would pretend to have been attacked if there were no witnesses.

'My relationship with Petr didn't last long.'

'How long?'

'A bit less than a year.'

'And after that?'

'After that? Nothing.'

'Nothing? Nobody else?'

'I was wounded. I understand what I did to you because he did it to me. He took me skiing in the Tatras and walked out. I had to find the money for the hotel bill. I sold my wedding ring.'

'Some justice in that, I suppose.'

'Josef, I was miserable. Have some compassion. I knew you wouldn't have me back and I knew I'd been incredibly stupid and ruined it all.'

Slonský pushed a crumb round his plate with his fingertip.

'You don't know that because you didn't ask.'

'I didn't need to ask. You made it very clear what you thought of me when I was packing. As I recall words like slut, whore and scumbag were used.'

'Nothing personal. I say that to all the wives who leave me.'

'I got a job as a filing clerk and tried to start again. But I never found a man to settle down with. They just wanted a fling. I wanted to put down roots.'

'Was this in Prague?'

'Not at first. I worked in Slovakia for a while, but my mother was ill, so I came home to Prague. I thought I might go to one of the places we used to go to see if I could bump into you, but then I remembered how angry you'd been and it didn't seem like a good idea. After Mum died, I moved out of town and got a flat.'

'So what made you come back now?'

'I saw an article in the newspaper about you and that German banker. There was a photograph of you. You haven't changed much.'

'Of course I have. I'm around fifteen kilos heavier for a start.'

'Twenty-five, probably. But your eyes are the same. And while I said some spiteful things about you, I knew you were one of the few honest policemen in town. I never doubted that, Josef.'

'Thank you. I appreciate your endorsement. But it still doesn't explain why you came to find me.'

'I have a confession to make. There's something I didn't tell you that you have a right to know.'

'You're not going to tell me I've got children?'

'No, of course not. The thing is, we're still married.'

'What?'

The small number of diners in the canteen turned instinctively to see what had happened.

'What do you mean, we're still married?'

'Simple statement of fact, Josef. When Petr deserted me, our divorce had not come through, and I never completed it.

Actually, I never got round to asking for one. I told you I had, but I hadn't. You can check if you want.'

'Don't worry, I will. And you're not getting half my pension.'

'The only way I'd get anything is if you were killed in service, and then it wouldn't matter to you.'

'I'd rise from the grave to put a stop to it. Just because I'd be dead doesn't mean I wouldn't be bloody furious.'

'I don't want your money. I wanted to tell you where we stood in case you'd found someone else and had inadvertently been a bigamist. I'd have put things right for you if I could. Then I'd get out of your life again. Josef, I'm sorry for what happened and I know I can't put it right now. I'd like us to be friends if we can, but I understand if that's too difficult for you.'

'Difficult? I wish it was impossible.'

'You loved me once, Josef.'

'I loved bootleg Barry Manilow recordings once, but I've grown up.'

'Well, I've tried...'

Věra picked up her handbag and turned to say goodbye, but Slonský was running to the door.

'Stay there,' he barked. 'I'll be back soon.'

Slonský was gone about twenty minutes, and when he returned he was flushed with excitement.

'Sorry. Just needed to check something. Look, I need to get back to work. I really don't know where we are. This has all come as a big shock to me. Leave me your address or phone number and I'll give you a call in a few days. I've got a big case on and this isn't the time to be making important decisions. Once it's over, I'll give you a call.'

'Promise?'

'Promise.'

Věra wrote her telephone number on a paper napkin, then put her coat on and picked up her handbag.

'It's good to see you. I thought you might hit me.'

'I've never hit you. I don't hit women and I despise men who do.'

'I know. But nobody ever provoked you like I did.'

'True. But that still doesn't justify hitting a woman. You know what I always used to say. A gentleman wouldn't hit a lady, so any man who does can't be a gentleman, therefore...'

'He doesn't deserve to keep his gentleman's parts. See, I do remember. Goodbye, Josef. Don't forget to call.'

'Goodbye, Věra.'

He walked her to the door, waved one last time, and walked back to his office, lobbing the crumpled napkin into a waste bin as he did so.

Personnel would have a lot to answer for if Slonský were in charge. Fancy leaving a door unlocked. Well, not unlocked exactly. Just locked with a lock that was so basic a passing stranger with a picklock could open it really easily.

Slonský had been here a few times on disciplinary matters, so he knew his way round quite well. The filing cabinets filled a wall in the back office. Although all new records were kept electronically, they had never quite got round to entering all the old paper records into the computer system. Slonský's own record was still partly on paper, but he resisted the urge to edit it. However you looked at it, his presence in the personnel department after hours with the lights off would take some explaining. He would come up with something — he always did — but it was not easy to think what that might be.

He found the folder he wanted and scanned the postings its subject had held. From 1972 to 1974 he had been at a listening station keeping an eye on the Americans. It was obvious, once you knew what to look for.

He returned the folder to its drawer, switched off his flashlight, and opened the office door just enough to slip outside, shutting it with a gentle click as he did so. He finally exhaled, turned, and found himself face to face with Navrátil.

'Jesus Mary! You made me jump. What are you doing here?'

'Wondering what you're doing creeping around personnel with the lights off.'

Slonský drew himself up to his full height and his chin jutted out defiantly.

'There is a perfectly good reason but I decline to give it.'

Navrátil shrugged.

'Fair enough. It's not my place to question your actions. But if anyone saw you, what are you going to tell them?'

'Who saw me?'

'Nobody. I stayed here to keep a lookout.'

'So did you follow me?'

'Follow is too strong a word. I came to talk to you but you were so preoccupied you ignored me.'

'Then I must compliment you on your shadowing technique. I had no idea I was being followed.'

'From the look on your face you wouldn't have noticed if the Presidential Guard and its band had followed you. So what have you found out?'

'I don't know just yet. A germ of an idea is forming in my head but I can't quite see how it all fits.'

'And what did your ex-wife want?'

'Private business.'

'It was private till you bellowed at her in the canteen, sir. After that it was all a bit public.'

'We've got something to work out, that's all.'

'If you want any advice about handling women…'

'I'll ask someone other than you, thank you. Now, go home, Navrátil, as I am about to do.'

Slonský strode off along the corridor, leaving Navrátil musing about the events of the evening as he smoothed out a crumpled paper napkin.

Chapter 11

It was a chilly morning so Peiperová was wearing a winter coat and boots. She almost walked past the blue Octavia that Slonský was occupying, but he wound down the window and called her.

'Sorry, sir, I thought we were meeting inside.'

'And waste five minutes going in just to come back out? Get your seat belt on and make yourself comfortable. It's a long way to Dolný Kubín.'

Peiperová began unbuttoning her coat.

'I wouldn't bother with that, lass. You'll be glad of it when you get out to fetch us some breakfast when we're out of town.'

Slonský drove at his usual speed, around five kilometres per hour over the speed limit. They drove through the city and headed south-east on the road to Brno.

'Good weekend?' Slonský suddenly asked.

'Yes, thank you, sir. Yours?'

'You already know about mine, don't you?'

'Yes, sir. Some of it anyway.'

'How much did Navrátil tell you?'

'That your wife turned up and there was a bit of a scene.'

'"A bit of a scene"? If you think that was a bit of a scene you should have been there when she said she was leaving.'

'I'm really sorry, sir. It must have been difficult for you.'

Slonský looked confused as if the idea that it might have been difficult had not occurred to him before.

'Thank you, Peiperová. It's good to know someone appreciates my position.'

'So what will you do now, sir?'

'Now? I think I'll pull over by that bakery so you can get us some breakfast.'

Peiperová was driving as they entered Dolný Kubín and looked for the police station.

'There it is,' said Slonský. 'Pull in at the side of the road.'

They entered the station and effected introductions. A young man in motorcycle gear was detailed to lead them to the Bartoš house. He introduced himself as Officer Jakubko.

'I'll ride ahead, sir. It's not too far. Just so I know, am I going to have to arrest them?'

'Not that I know of. They haven't done anything in the Czech Republic.'

'Very good, sir. They don't have a good name around here, I'm afraid.'

A few minutes later Jakubko signalled a right turn and pulled into a small yard. There was a long, low building on one side that had seen better days, a hen house and a fenced compound containing some unpleasant-looking dogs. Jakubko put his motorbike on its stand and smoothed out his uniform, stowing the helmet in a pannier and donning his uniform cap.

'Shall we go in, sir?'

They walked towards the door, which opened to reveal a scruffy man in a tattered vest who was chewing on a corn cob.

'Whatever it is, we ain't done it.'

'Nobody is accusing anyone of anything, Viktor. These officers are Czechs. They've come all the way from Prague to see your mother.'

'Why should she want to talk to them?'

Slonský intervened. 'Because we want to get justice for your brother Ľubomir.'

Viktor considered this as he chewed.

'Bit late. You hanged the poor bugger.'

'Yes, and I don't know why. But if I could talk to you all inside, we might get some clues.'

Viktor turned and held the door open behind him with his foot.

'Ma, these folk are from Prague. They want to talk to you about Ľubo.'

An old woman was sitting by a potbelly stove peeling potatoes.

'What about Ľubo? You can't pick on him anymore.'

'I know, Mrs Bartošová,' Slonský replied. 'I want to find out why he was hanged.'

'There's no reason. They just did it.'

'Mind if we sit down?'

'If you like. It'll make a change to have someone to talk to other than Viktor. I don't get out now, what with my legs.'

She indicated the limbs in question. There was no obvious problem with them.

'Who's the maid?' she asked.

'This is Officer Peiperová.'

'Married? My Viktor's going spare.'

'I'm spoken for, I'm afraid,' said Peiperová, causing Slonský to do a double take.

'Shame. You look like you wouldn't take any lip from a man. He can be a bit mouthy, our Viktor. Gets him into trouble sometimes, don't it, Jako?'

Officer Jakubko agreed that it did.

'That, and the vodka,' the old lady expanded.

'I had the impression you had a big family,' Slonský began.

'I have, but they're all married and away now, except Viktor. And Ľubo of course.'

'I'm Lieutenant Josef Slonský. I was visited a little while ago by a retired policeman called Holoubek. He was involved in investigating the murder your son was convicted of. Holoubek told me he had discovered too late that your boy was already in jail in Olomouc when the crime was committed.'

'That's right. He came over to see me. It was too soon after. I sent him packing. It does you no good to hear your boy's innocent when they've just hanged him.'

'Holoubek was murdered himself a few days ago. I think he was killed because he was trying to get your son's case reopened.'

The old lady stopped peeling for a moment.

'That's a shame. He was a decent man, for a policeman.'

'What I don't understand is why someone in the police came to Olomouc to get your son. Why pick him out? He must have known him already, but I can't see how. I mean, your son had been run in any number of times around here, but I can't work out why the villain thought he was the best person to frame. Tell me what your son did after he left here.'

She resumed peeling.

'He'd been banged up too many times here. I thought if it happened again he'd get a long sentence. He wasn't a bad lad, just not very bright. He couldn't read, you know. They thought he was thick, but one of my grandsons is just like him. I don't know what they call it, when they can't make out letters to spell words.'

'Dyslexia?'

'That's it. That's what the school said. Dyslexic. The grandson gets special help, but poor Ľubo didn't. He just got written off as an idiot. Couldn't get a job, so he did odd bits here for me, then he discovered he could climb. That's when he took to cat burgling. He got himself a bike and he used to go off places to burgle for a few days, then he'd come back here. But he couldn't get shot of the stuff, so he said he'd have to move. He went up to Bratislava, then when that got too hot for him, he crossed into the Czech bit of the country to live in Olomouc. It was all one country then, you remember.'

'But how did he come to the attention of a policeman in Prague? I can't find anyone connected with the case who had ever worked in Olomouc.'

'Just before they hanged him, he said he'd try his luck in Prague. Bratislava was a poor place then, but he thought people were better off in Prague. They'd have stuff worth nicking. So that's what he did.'

'Why did he get caught?'

Mrs Bartošová sighed.

'He couldn't read, could he? He broke into a few houses. At one of them, he stole a medal. He didn't realise it was some special Russian thing they'd given a bigwig. Shouldn't be accepting medals off Russians anyhow. But he got caught trying to flog it in Olomouc. They picked him up and charged him with burglary. He co-operated, mind. When they took him back to Prague he showed them where he'd been. He didn't know they were important people's houses. He just thought they looked posh.'

Slonský thought for a moment.

'You don't know anyone else he burgled? Did the owners get their property back?'

'I don't know. He'd spent the money, of course.'

'What money was that?'

'He found some money in one of the houses. Quite a stash by all accounts. But it wasn't crowns. It was some other sort of money. He had to find someone to swap it with. I think they ripped him off, because he said he only got about a tenth of

160

what it was worth, but he couldn't argue because he didn't know where else to trade it and he didn't want to be found with it on him. They didn't charge him over the money, because he didn't have it any longer when he was taken in. I think it was just the eight burglaries. He pleaded guilty, but then they said he'd killed a girl doing one of the robberies and next thing we knew he'd been strung up.'

'Jana Válková.'

'Was that her name? Well, I'm sorry for her parents, but I knew my Ľubo. He wouldn't hurt a girl. Might chance his arm with her, see if she was interested, but he wouldn't force her.'

'The odd thing is that Mr Válek didn't report a robbery, so Jana can't have been killed during one.'

Peiperová had her index finger raised as if wishing to discreetly catch Slonský's eye. He nodded to her to continue.

'May I ask if your son always worked alone? Could anyone have known of his plans?'

'Always alone so far as I know. What kind of help could anyone give a cat burglar?'

'But it sounds as if you knew his plans.'

'Only the gist of them. He kept himself to himself. He said he didn't trust others not to blab. He told one of his brothers once that he was planning to rob a place nearby and it got out. He didn't half give his brother a hiding. After that, he got even more tight-lipped. He only told me so I would know where to start looking for him if he didn't come back. He said if he fell, he'd probably wind up unconscious in hospital somewhere and they wouldn't know who he was, so we needed to come looking for him.'

Slonský picked up his hat and stood to indicate they had asked all their questions.

'Thank you, Mrs Bartošová, Mr Bartoš. You've been a big help.'

'Are you actually going to do anything or was this just for show?' asked Viktor.

Slonský's eyes blazed for a moment, and Peiperová held her breath in anticipation of the angry riposte, but Slonský recovered himself.

'No, I want to find out who framed your brother, who really killed Jana Válková, and who killed Edvard Holoubek.'

Mrs Bartošová resumed her peeling.

'Mr Detective, if you do find out who it was,' she said, 'I hope you'll tell us so Viktor and his brothers can take a trip to Prague and beat the living daylights out of him.'

'Unfortunately,' Slonský responded, 'we're expected to guard our prisoners so that doesn't happen to them. Weird, isn't it?'

'It's not that weird,' she added. 'You gave Ľubo a medical to check he was fit before you hanged him.'

Jakubko was torn between two conflicting instructions. He was under orders to facilitate the Czech guests' visit in every way so that they would finish and go home as quickly as possible, and he had been told to do all he could to make them welcome, so when Slonský asked for a recommendation for a café, the young police officer had to decide whether to tell them there were better coffee places elsewhere, or take them to his aunt's little place which, while small and something of a sixties time warp, did a really good coffee and a nut and poppyseed cake to die for. The conflict did not take long to resolve, and soon the motorbike was propped against the decaying plasterwork of a café while Jakubko, Slonský and Peiperová tackled a large piece of cake each.

'Is it good?' he asked.

'Yes, very good,' said Slonský. 'Are there any vacancies for an experienced detective in your force?'

Jakubko laughed.

'We don't have one. We have to send to Žilina if we want help.'

'Does it happen often?'

Jakubko pondered.

'Not since we've had all these cameras in the town. We had a bicycle stolen a while ago, but we solved that ourselves.'

Peiperová delicately replaced her coffee cup on her saucer.

'Sir, did that really get us anywhere?'

'Not really. I mean, it probably solved the crime for us, but apart from that, it was a bit of a waste of time.'

Peiperová and Jakubko gazed at him in surprise.

'Solved the crime? How? Who?'

'I'm saying nothing till I've checked it, but I now have a hypothesis to test. And that's one more than I had when we came. Now, shut up and enjoy your cake. Actually, I might just have another piece, seeing as Jako's aunt went to all the trouble of cooking it.'

'What time will we get back, sir?'

'That depends on how fast you drive, Peiperová. If you press on that pedal under your right foot, the car goes faster.'

'I know, sir. I just don't know the roads very well.'

'Like the Slovaks themselves, lass, they're often dark and twisted.'

'Sir! That's really prejudiced of you!'

'Joke, girl, joke. It doesn't represent my real view of Slovaks. Given that they don't have our advantages and the beer is maiden's water, I admire their sturdy independence. Jakubko was a nice lad.'

'Yes, he was, sir.'

'I hope Officer Navrátil isn't the jealous type. I don't want him driving up here and challenging Jakubko to an inter-force duel.'

'He has no reason to be, sir. You're just stirring things.'

'You know, you're very wise for one so young.'

'Thank you, sir. To return to my original question, when will we get back?'

'If we drive non-stop, a little before nine o'clock. However, that nice Captain Lukas has approved an evening meal for us, so we could stop somewhere and eat at public expense at a reasonable time, rather than grabbing some fast food just before bedtime.'

'Sounds like a plan, sir. I'd be happy with that.'

'Good, because the alternative was that you sat in the car until I'd eaten mine, and I might have felt slightly guilty about that. If I ever felt guilty, which I generally don't. Now, I'm going to snatch forty winks. Wake me up just before you hit anything.'

Instructed to find somewhere to eat around halfway, Peiperová spotted an inn about forty kilometres east of Brno and pulled off the road. It turned out to be an excellent choice, and by the time Slonský had filled himself with home-made venison sausages, dumplings of various kinds and a litre of the local brew, he was feeling benign. Peiperová had expected to switch seats, but Slonský had other plans.

'You'll be nicely rested after that break, so you may as well carry on driving for a bit.'

As they drove along they chatted about police life, promotion prospects, Prague, promotion prospects, inside information on other officers that they might not want made public, and promotion prospects. Slonský found himself experiencing an unexpected feeling. Having regarded Peiperová as a supplementary nuisance, over and above his existing necessary nuisance, he now found himself thinking that keeping her around would make life more interesting. This was strange, because it was only a little over three months before that his arm had been twisted to take Navrátil under his wing. Officers assigned to work with Slonský seemed to have an above average sickness rate, and eventually Lukas had run out of options. However, the academy was sending Navrátil to him for further in-post development, and someone had to supervise him. While the idea that Slonský could supervise anyone made the average senior officer gulp, Lukas was in a position to exert pressure. It was Navrátil, or work on your own, so Slonský took Navrátil, having been assured that he could work a kettle. As Lukas had suspected, Slonský enjoyed having a captive audience. Navrátil laughed at his jokes, was impressed by his successful deductions, made or fetched coffee on demand and was happy to do some of the tedious grunt work that Slonský detested. Lukas also suspected that Navrátil might have been doing some of Slonský's paperwork, the quality of which had improved markedly in the last three months. Tackled on this point, Slonský claimed that it was because he felt an increased responsibility to do it well. Lukas noted waspishly that this increased responsibility seemed to run to numbering his list entries consecutively, indenting his paragraphs in a consistent way and no longer typing random headings in a completely different font.

Thus the partnership between Slonský and Navrátil had flourished, and now Peiperová had come along. By skilfully keeping them apart, Slonský had avoided the worst of Navrátil's impersonations of love's young dream, and there was no doubting the fact that Peiperová was clever, conscientious and very, very ambitious. It was undeniably true that three people could do more work than two, and nowadays Navrátil needed much less supervision. In fact, Slonský belatedly realised, Navrátil was the best policeman he had worked with for a long time, despite his youth, and one day this pair of puppies would become top dogs in the Czech police. He only hoped he had retired by then so he never had to work for them.

Slonský suddenly realised that Peiperová was talking to him.

'I'm sorry, Peiperová. What did you say?'

'I asked if the link you found earlier was that Bartoš had robbed someone important who got their own back by framing him.'

'Well done, girl. It seems very petty for people in high places, but the obvious one was whoever had the dollars or marks. They probably shouldn't have had them, so they couldn't report them missing, so they had suffered a real loss. Alternatively, perhaps they were entitled to have them, but it was government money and they'd have to describe how they lost it, which would have been difficult. Either way, they'd be cheesed off with Bartoš.'

'Annoyed enough to have a man killed?' There was genuine wonder in Peiperová's voice.

'I've known people killed for less. And I've known people who thought nothing of settling scores with a bit of murder. If there's one thing that I learned from living for forty years under Communism, it's that you should never underestimate the sheer pettiness of people in high places.'

'But even if we allow that he would want to do it, how could he actually effect it?'

'Well, we're entering into the realms of supposition here, and that's a very bad thing for a detective to do. After all, we're meant to work out our solutions from the data. If we start working out our solutions, then looking for the data, we might bias our investigation. I'm surprised at you for even suggesting it, Peiperová.'

'I'm sorr—'

'However, I can envisage a world in which the murderer takes advantage of the fact that the investigation has been left in the hands of a complete nincompoop like Vaněček, under which it would soon grind to a halt. The murderer knows by now that Bartoš is under lock and key. He goes to see him, gets the signed confession — worthless because Bartoš can't read it anyway — and drops it into Vaněček's lap. Vaněček breathes a sigh of relief. Just to make sure, our man has had Bartoš brought to Prague, signing the paperwork in Holoubek's name to cover his trail. If Vaněček sees the signature, he'll think Holoubek has given him a discreet hand, or maybe it was a line of inquiry Holoubek started before he was removed from the case.'

'So taking Bartoš round Prague looking for the houses he burgled was a charade?'

'It may have been. Or maybe the murderer wanted to check he'd got the right man. After all, there wouldn't be much satisfaction in getting Bartoš hanged if you discovered afterwards that the real villain was still out there.'

Peiperová suddenly pulled in to the side of the road.

'What are you doing?' snapped Slonský.

'Sorry, sir. I can't drive and argue at the same time. We haven't asked a key question. Just who took Bartoš around? It's our murderer who has most to gain from it, and from what we hear about Vaněček, he's unlikely to have come up with the idea. If he did, the murderer must have prompted it. If we can find that out, perhaps we'll have our man.'

'Yes,' agreed Slonský, 'and if Navrátil has been reading the investigation files properly, perhaps he'll tell us tomorrow.'

Chapter 12

Navrátil was already at work when Slonský breezed in one minute late.

'Productive day yesterday?'

'Not very, sir. I've got some possibilities. How was your day?'

'Very good. I think we may be slowly knitting together a case.'

'I tried deciphering the signatures but without names to start with, it's almost impossible. They've faded anyway. Personnel found me an internal handbook from around 1979 that lists some of the staff in the StB, and they're busy trying to compile a catalogue of those known to have been with the StB in Prague then, but they say it will be incomplete because the StB deliberately destroyed some files.'

'The StB destroyed a lot of files about informers, but it's difficult to destroy pay records. They've just got to look in the right place. You'd think a police personnel department would know how to conduct an inquiry, lad. Of course, if they were any good at running inquiries they wouldn't have been sent to personnel, I suppose.'

'Did the Slovaks give you anything useful?'

'Yes, I think so. It seems that Bartoš robbed some big houses in Prague and got off with some foreign currency. Now, what sort of person would have been able to amass a stash of foreign currency in those days?'

'A black marketeer? Organised crime?'

'Our crime was strictly disorganised in those days, son. There were currency speculators, and there were black market traders, it's true, but none of them could have known that Bartoš was in jail in Olomouc and none of them could have arranged for him to be taken round Prague pointing out the houses he'd burgled in exchange for a supposed reduction in his sentence. I'd like to know who suggested that to our friend Vaněček, because I'll bet he didn't come up with it himself.'

'Anything else, sir?'

'Yes, but it's probably going to involve some more work in the archives for you. You'll be getting a taste for it now.'

'I hate it, sir, but if it has to be done to find the murderer —'

'Murderers, lad, plural.'

'We know that?'

'Perhaps "know" is a bit too strong, but it's highly likely. After all, we're looking at murders spanning thirty years. There can't be too many men who have been active all that time.'

'You have been, sir.'

'Yes, Navrátil, but I'm not a murderer, am I? Despite extreme provocation.'

'I only meant, sir, that someone of your age would fit the bill.'

'Don't go getting ideas, Officer. If I go down, I'm taking you with me.'

'What do you need me to do, sir?'

'I've just changed my mind. You've spent enough time in the archives. Let's give this one to Peiperová.'

Slonský glanced at his watch.

'If she ever turns up, that is. Six minutes late. When she gets here, she can have a look for Czechs who received Soviet honours. Somebody had a Soviet medal stolen, but I don't remember seeing that mentioned in the papers anywhere? Do you?'

'No, sir. Why would a Czech get a Soviet medal?'

'International solidarity, the joint struggle against capitalism, stitching up other Czechs, the list of possibilities is endless. But there can't be that many Czechs who got one, and whoever it was got burgled, because it was when he tried to sell the medal that Bartoš got picked up. Whoever got the Order of Lenin or whatever it was would be the sort of man who had the clout to get a Slovak cat burglar hanged, evidence or no evidence. As for you, I want you to follow up on Roman Pluskal. Nobody has turned him in, and no officer has clapped eyes on him. I wonder why? Let's see if he has a credit card or mobile phone, where he's using them, what state his flat is in, all the usual things we do when we really haven't got a clue what else to do. Meanwhile, I'll do the really important bit, and get us some coffee.'

Slonský had just reached the door when his phone rang. Since he had never quite mastered the black art of transferring a call to Navrátil's extension, he picked it up himself.

'Slonský.'

'If you want to see your niece again, drop the Holoubek enquiry,' said a male voice.

'Who is this?' asked Slonský, before realising that he was talking to a disconnected line.

'What is it, sir?' asked Navrátil.

'Someone threatening my niece, but I haven't got a niece,' replied Slonský, feeling more than usually confused. It took him moments to realise that Navrátil was quicker on the uptake. The young detective was sprinting down the hall.

'I'll try her room, sir.'

Slonský realised that someone must think Peiperová was his niece, though he was unclear why. On the other hand, they did not apparently realise she was a policewoman, perhaps because she did not wear uniform and had spent very little time in the office since she arrived. He was also perplexed by the fact that someone apparently knew it was worth ringing his desk at 07:07, rather earlier than some of his colleagues would have been there. Through the bafflement he could see one important step he had to take, so he walked to Navrátil's extension and dialled a number.

'Technician First Class Spehar.'

'Slonský. I'm glad you're there. I need a phone call tracing urgently. Who do I call?'

'You just called him. I'll get Ricka on it straight away.'

'Is he good?'

'Well, he's better than me and you've only got two of us to choose from at this time of the morning. Now please tell me the number that was called and leave us to it.'

Slonský's mobile phone tinkled quietly, evidence that he had either changed the ringing volume by accident again, or had forgotten to charge it.

'Yes?'

'She hasn't slept here, sir. Her bed is made and it's cold, and nobody I've met yet recalls seeing her this morning. When did you last see her?'

'I dropped her off at the car pound last night about half past nine. She said she wanted to walk back.'

'I'll plot the street cameras and see if there are any on her route.'

'No, Navrátil, you come back and get on with finding Pluskal.'

'But sir —'

'You're too close to it, lad. Trust me and your other colleagues to do all we can for her. Meanwhile, we've got a

172

murderer to find, and that's what you'll do. I'll go and ask Lukas for some extra manpower to find Peiperová.'

'I want to help, sir.'

'I'm sure you do. But your emotions are involved, and emotions make for bad policing.'

'Don't you have emotions, sir?'

'Of course I do. I want her back safe and well. But I can control mine better than you'll control yours. Now stop yapping and get on with finding Pluskal. And that's an order.'

Ricka proved to be a snowman-shaped lump with thin, straight hair cut like a moth-eaten mop. His fingers flew across the keyboard as he scrutinised four monitors in front of him. So far as Slonský could make out, one was filled with zeros and ones, while another had a green bar that lit up lines in turn and travelled up and down the screen. Ricka did not seem interested in these. His attention was focused on another that had pop-up boxes appearing and vanishing in quick succession.

'Have you got anywhere?' Slonský asked.

'The mobile number you gave us isn't helping. It's switched off now and no calls have been made from it since last night. Your call came from a public phone booth at the main train station. Did you recognise the voice?'

'He said so little. No obvious accent.'

'Our phone system here has been improved a lot recently. Who knows your extension?'

'I don't know. Who knows yours?'

'Not many. But your caller didn't get switched by switchboard. He dialled your extension directly.'

'That figures. He also knew I was leading on the Holoubek case.'

'But that was in the papers and on the television. He went to a public call box, and he dialled directly to you. I think you know him.'

'I don't hang around with criminals.'

'Yes, you do, it's your job. You have to spend time with them to arrest them.'

'Tell me, why didn't they accept you in the diplomatic service?'

Ricka frowned.

'Why would I apply to the diplomatic service?'

'Never mind. My mistake. Can you identify the exact box?'

Ricka passed him a slip of paper.

'That's the number. The station master should know. It would be good if there was a camera looking at it.'

'It would be good if there was a camera looking at it,' said the station master, 'but we don't have enough of them to cover everything.'

'Is there a camera anywhere near it?' asked an increasingly exasperated Slonský.

'This one covers the nearest corner, but the actual boxes are out of sight.'

'Never mind. Wind it back to 07:00 this morning and let's see if anyone heads towards those boxes.'

They sat tensely, watching the milling crowds. It was impossible to track where everyone went, but nobody walked purposefully towards the phone booth.

'Okay,' said Slonský. 'If they didn't go to the booth on the way out from the trains, maybe they went on the way in. Where's the nearest entrance?'

The station master found the appropriate recording and played it. Slonský threw his hat on the ground in annoyance.

'What earthly use is that? All you can see is the top of a lot of heads.'

'Well, we only need it to watch for blockages. We don't need to know who the people are, just that they can get to the trains.'

Slonský could feel the rushing sound in his ears again. The doctor had told him that was a bad sign. When it happened, he was supposed to calm down. In fact, he found it helped more if he let rip.

'Is there no way of finding out who used that damn phone at 07:07?' he snarled.

The station master relaxed. If that was all they wanted to know, why hadn't they said?

'There's Jiří.'

'Jiří?'

'The guy who sells the papers at the entrance.'

Slonský bounded down the steps and strode through the station hall. As he passed the phone booth he could see a trestle table laden with newspapers and magazines.

'Jiří?' he asked.

An upright bundle of rags stirred and a face poked out.

'Who wants to know?'

'Slonský, Josef, Lieutenant in the Criminal Police. Just past seven o'clock this morning, someone made a short phone call from that booth.'

'I know.'

'You know?'

'Yes. I wondered what anyone could possibly say in so short a time.'

'Can you describe him?'

Jiří stroked his chin.

'Any chance of a drink out of this?'

175

'Help me find the guy and there's a bottle in it. Not to mention you won't get your fingernails pulled out like he might.'

'Like that, is it? Important to you.'

'Very. A young woman has been abducted and he was involved.'

'Oh, so it was a ransom demand? That makes sense.'

'Can we get on? What was he like?'

'Black hair, plenty of it, jeans, dark jacket over a navy t-shirt or jumper. And he had a mobile phone.'

'A mobile?'

'Yes, that's what I thought was odd. He'd got a phone, so why use a public call box? But of course if he was up to no good, he wouldn't want the call traced to his phone.'

'No, he wouldn't. So someone called him?'

'That's right. He stood there smoking for about ten minutes, waiting for a call. I mean, he had the mobile in his hand all along. Then it came, he just listened, put the mobile away, and walked over to the booth. Then he made his call and in no time he was gone.'

Slonský had a bad habit of not emptying his pockets very often, but it came in handy now and again. He suddenly recalled something in his jacket pocket and paid it on Jiří's table. Jiří inspected the photograph cursorily.

'That's him. Well, if you know who he is, why are you wasting my time asking me all these questions?'

Slonský dropped a banknote as he retrieved the photograph.

'That should cover your time, unless you're an off-duty lawyer.'

Jiří indicated his threadbare coat and scuffed shoes.

'Do I look like a lawyer?'

'Not really,' agreed Slonský. 'Not slimy enough.'

Lukas cornered Slonský on the stairs.

'Why didn't you tell me about Peiperová?'

'I was going to once I knew for sure what had happened. I thought the most important thing was to get the search under way.'

'Have we any clues?'

'An identification of the man who phoned me. Roman Pluskal, the same thug who ran Holoubek down.'

'The link was already there, I suppose. It's natural that he would want the inquiry halted.'

'Wouldn't all criminals? May I ask how you know about this, sir?'

'Navrátil came to ask me to overrule you.'

'I see. And did you?'

Lukas sighed and draped a heavy arm round Slonský's shoulders.

'Josef, there is no danger that I would do that to my best detective. Unless, of course, this gets too much for you. I don't have a lot of spare manpower but I'll see who I can borrow. When it's one of our own...'

'Thank you, sir, but I can cope.'

'You've lost Peiperová and you excluded Navrátil from this case. That leaves you precisely one person, yourself.'

'Not quite, sir. I told Navrátil to get on and find Pluskal. That's doubly important now. And if he finds him he'll be making a major contribution to this case.'

'I could recall Doležal from his course. Ah! No need. Dvorník came back from leave yesterday. He could help you.'

'Dvorník does murders, sir. I sincerely hope this isn't one.'

'No, Josef, Dvorník does what I tell him. He's a competent officer.'

Lukas lowered his voice before qualifying his assessment.

'Not, perhaps, inspired, but certainly competent. More or less.'

'Very well, sir. If you insist.'

'I'll make plain to him that this is your inquiry. And I'll see who else is free to help you. Good luck, Josef. It's a horrible thing to have happened, but there's no-one better to have looking for her than you.'

'Except Samson.'

'Samson?'

'Dog I had as a boy, sir. He could sniff out a bone at the bottom of a coal mine.'

Lukas turned to walk away.

'Then get yourself some dogs, man. If she walked, she may have left a scent.'

Slonský took the stairs two at a time back down to the lobby.

'Mucha, where can I get some sniffer dogs?'

The van disgorged its contents. Slonský was unimpressed.

'What is that?'

'It's a kopov, sir.'

'A what?'

'A Slovakian hunting hound. These things trap wild boar, sir,' his handler proudly announced.

'Wild boar don't abduct police officers and make threatening phone calls, so some use this will be.'

'Trust me, sir, when Malý here gets a scent, he'll follow it to the end.'

'We'll see, Officer…?'

'Malý.'

'Malý? The dog's named after you?'

'Makes it easier, sir. His kennel club name is something awful.'

'Right, then, Malý. Let's see what Malý here can do.'

'Have you got something of hers, sir?'

'Navrátil says she was wearing this scarf on Sunday evening.'

'Very good, sir. Sniff! Not you, sir, I was talking to the dog.'

'I guessed you were.'

'He's got something, sir. It's been dry overnight, which helps. And I expect she was wearing some sort of scent.'

'I didn't notice, but then my nose isn't as sensitive as his, or I'd be on the end of your leash and he'd be redundant.'

The hound trotted along the pavement. So far so good — Slonský had seen her head this way. The dog also correctly spotted the point at which she had crossed the road. He led Officer Malý to the far side, then turned right and continued along the street to the next corner. Slonský followed close behind, but had to wait for a break in the traffic, so he was a little concerned that they might have slipped out of his sight.

When he caught up with them around twenty metres from the corner he found Malý turning circles at the kerb.

'Is he having a fit?'

'No, sir, the trail's ended here. She was snatched right at this spot.'

Slonský cursed. There were no cameras here, but he could put Dvorník onto looking at the nearest one to get a list of large vehicles that might have come past here just a few minutes after he dropped Peiperová the previous night.

'Well,' he said, 'we've got a place, and that tells me the time. I don't suppose Malý here can sniff a licence plate number?'

Lieutenant Dvorník's office was small anyway, but the man himself made it look even smaller. He was described by his wife as cuddly, an overly kind epithet but just about plausible if she had long arms. He had the same amount of furniture as

Slonský, but less area to accommodate it, so the free floor area was not great even when he was sitting down, and almost non-existent if he stood. A large number of the available surfaces were covered in photographs of his offspring.

Navrátil stated the obvious.

'He's not here, sir.'

'No, even on my worst days I can detect a Dvorník, and there isn't one here.'

'Are all those his children, sir? I thought you said he only had three.'

'He and his wife have been married before. He had two or three with his first wife, and I think his new partner had a couple, and then they've had three more since. I'm not sure of the running total, but it's high time he found some other hobby. At least when you look at his children there's no need for genetic testing. They all tend towards the fuller figure.'

'I'd better go look for him, sir.'

'No need. He'll be in the canteen. Come along.'

In fact, they met Dvorník in the corridor on his way back from the canteen. He had a coffee in his hand, upon which he had balanced a torpedo roll containing a substantial share of a pig. Slonský explained the job he wanted doing. Since it involved remaining seated, Dvorník was content, though still slightly resentful at playing second fiddle to another lieutenant.

'Now, lad,' Slonský continued, 'how are you going to find Pluskal?'

Navrátil felt obliged to sound decisive, though he had been wondering about that himself.

'Money, sir. Everyone needs money. He must use cash machines or credit cards.'

'Worth a try. But Griba's gang will deal largely in cash. They get lots in, and they can't bank it without questions being asked, so they work almost entirely in cash.'

'Driver's licence?'

'Well, we know he can drive, so he probably has one. Whether the address is up to date may be another matter, but give it a go.'

'I can see if any vehicles are registered to him while I'm at it.'

'I doubt it. He probably drives some of Griba's. Though of course there's one less now that he torched the Volkswagen.'

'Won't Griba be angry about that?'

'No,' Slonský answered with a touch of scorn. 'Griba probably told him to do it. So far as I know, Griba had no grudge with Holoubek, so he was probably paid handsomely to arrange it. He can stand the loss of an old Volkswagen van.'

'Who is this Griba, sir?'

'We don't know a lot about him. Griba is a nickname, and we don't know where it comes from. Someone told me it's a Hebrew word meaning wonderful, so perhaps he's Jewish. There's a synagogue somewhere called Griba. He just appeared in his late twenties and he's been a blight on Prague ever since.'

'Like Moriarty and Sherlock Holmes?'

'Not that high level. Griba doesn't bother with big, high-risk things, just a lot of protection rackets, prostitution, gambling, smuggling, probably some trafficking and plenty of drugs. That reminds me — let's find Mucha. I asked him to have a word with Colonel Tripka about Griba.'

'Nothing.'

'Nothing?'

'Nothing. Nada. Rien du tout,' asserted Mucha.

'But we know he has a finger in all those pies.'

'According to Tripka, they know it, but they can't prove it. Nobody will finger him and because he employs people with bad records, it'll stay that way.'

'Even by Tripka's standards, that's a stupid comment,' Slonský growled.

'He means that Griba takes on people who have every reason not to want to get back in front of a court. As witnesses against him, they'd be useless. A defence lawyer can shut them up very easily. They make a good living only because Griba helps them commit crimes they were too stupid to get away with themselves, so of course they're loyal.'

Slonský sighed. 'Like the Personnel Department.'

'That's right,' agreed Mucha.

'I don't understand,' protested Navrátil. 'What has our personnel department got to do with organised crime?'

'More than you'd think, except for the word "organised",' said Slonský, 'but I'm not talking about our personnel department. I'm talking about *The* Personnel Department. It was a setup from the early eighties. A disaffected underling in the Department of Justice hit on the brilliant idea of contacting criminals who had just left prison and couldn't get jobs. He'd offer them work in his scams. They got their instructions by telephone from "The Personnel Department", so they couldn't betray him because they didn't know who he was. Only one man knew, whose job it was to recruit them and hand over the wage packets. Working in the justice system meant the villain managed to screw up any number of investigations with fake alibis, lost statements and so on. Mind you, we could have done that ourselves in those days.'

'Yes,' added Mucha wistfully, 'those were the days. Do you remember that captain in Jihlava who took a statement from someone who'd been shot dead in a raid three days earlier?'

'Didn't even get disciplined. Just moved to a border post near Poland, which admittedly wasn't the best career move, not to mention being bloody cold in winter. So is Tripka even trying to nail this Griba character?'

'He says nothing would give him greater pleasure. He's convinced that Griba is probably behind one of Prague's biggest cocaine distribution networks; perhaps not the most valuable, but the widest reach. Of course, he says, his predecessor wasn't vigorous enough, which allowed Griba to get a toehold.'

'He would say that, wouldn't he? Everyone's predecessor was always too lax. It may be true in Tripka's case, but he hasn't exactly cranked up the action in the last couple of years since he's been there.'

'There was that big heroin seizure last winter.'

'Yes, but that had nothing to do with Tripka. The smugglers fell out and one of them snitched on the others. Even then, if he hadn't driven the van into the police station car park we'd probably never have found it.'

'You have to admit, Tripka falls on his feet. Luckiest officer I've ever known,' opined Mucha.

'I wonder how much is down to his father's reputation. Tripka himself is no great shakes.'

'But he's a colonel,' protested Navrátil. 'If he was an idiot they wouldn't have promoted him to colonel.'

'They would if they were bigger idiots,' Slonský pointed out. 'And rumour has it they wanted him out of ethics and internal affairs so when he applied for the leadership of the Drug Squad, everyone breathed a sigh of relief.'

'What did he do wrong in internal affairs?' asked Navrátil.

'He did nothing wrong because he did nothing at all, lad. No case ever seemed to have enough evidence to actually go anywhere.'

'To be fair to Colonel Tripka,' put in Mucha, 'he started unluckily when he charged a sergeant in the drug squad with graft and someone completely different turned up in Morocco with a large amount of cash. He took a lot of flak for that, but many of us thought he might well have had the right man. It made him ultra-cautious after that.'

Slonský was standing open-mouthed.

'What's the matter with you?' asked Mucha.

'I'm speechless,' said Slonský. 'I can't believe my own ears. "To be fair to Colonel Tripka"? When did we start being fair to people like Tripka?'

'I'm sorry,' muttered Mucha, 'I don't know what came over me.'

'I'm all for fair play and decency,' continued Slonský, 'but I never thought I'd live to see the day when you'd want to extend it to a nonentity like Tripka.'

Mucha took the hint.

'I'll go now.'

'I think you should,' agreed Slonský. 'I'll allow you to buy me a beer later to restore our friendship.'

'That's very good of you, sir,' said Mucha. 'Will I be allowed to stand in the same bar and watch Your Lordship drink it?'

'If you're good. Now, Navrátil and I have serious work to do. We've got to find Peiperová.'

'I'll send out an All Stations alert. Have we got a photo of her?'

'There's one in her personnel record.'

Navrátil fished in his inside breast pocket.

'This is a better one. Can I get it back?'

'Of course,' said Mucha.

'Excuse me,' Navrátil stuttered, and ran off along the corridor.

'Taking it hard,' Mucha commented.

'Yes. But it doesn't help find her. Let's get that alert out.'

'Right away. What's her first name?'

Slonský looked perplexed.

'Officer?' he offered.

Chapter 13

Navrátil looked miserable.

'We should be doing something,' he said.

'We are,' replied Slonský. 'We're having an early lunch so we can devote all our afternoon to finding Peiperová. Don't you want that?'

'No appetite.'

'Give it here, then. She'll be fine, lad. So long as we're looking for her, we're not working on the Holoubek case, and that's what the abductor wants. He has no reason to hurt her. If he does, he loses the only weapon he has.'

'How can you eat at a time like this?'

Slonský put Navrátil's sandwich down.

'If I don't eat that, how does that help find Peiperová?'

'It doesn't.'

'Thank you,' said Slonský, picking it up again. 'My point exactly. There's enough misery in this without letting good food go to waste.'

'I'll have to tell her parents.'

'Ah. Yes, we should.'

'We. Or me?'

'No, it's my job. Give me their number and I'll ring them.'

Navrátil tore a page from his notebook and copied the telephone number from his mobile phone.

'There.'

Slonský picked up his sandwich and his coffee.

'I'll do it now. You bend your mind to finding Pluskal. Wherever he is, she is.'

The phone rang. It was Valentin.

'I wondered what had happened to you,' said Slonský. 'I thought maybe you were too busy signing autographs to do the little favour you promised for me.'

'It wasn't a little favour. It was a thumping big mega-favour and it cost me a bomb in phone calls.'

'You'll get it back.'

'I certainly will. Where can we meet?'

'Is it important?'

'I think so. But since you never tell me anything, what do I know?'

'Where are you now?'

'Across the street.'

'Valentin, why don't you come in here?'

'No chance. I get a shiver up my spine every time I walk past that place, let alone go inside. When they've frogmarched you inside with a sack over your head and kicked you in the cellars you tend to get clammy about a place.'

'That sounds painful — a kick in the cellars.'

'It was. And when you've stopped the cheap innuendo at my expense, get yourself down here.'

Slonský's voice became grave.

'Someone has snatched Peiperová.'

'The blonde girl? Why?'

'To get me to lay off the Holoubek case.'

'Then I'm right. You will want to hear what I've found out. And so will Navrátil. I don't know if you've noticed, but his eyes light up whenever you mention her. I think he may have a soft spot for her.'

'Actually he has an extremely hard spot, and I've told him to take some cold showers to get over it. But I'll give him a call and get him back here. Meet me on the steps in half an hour.'

As it happened, Navrátil was already coming back. The search of driving licences had been fairly pointless, because Pluskal had not amended the address on his record. The new inhabitants of the flat, a young architect and his pregnant girlfriend, had never heard of Pluskal. Navrátil was finding it hard to think of any new lines of inquiry. There must be some, but he simply could not think straight.

He saw Valentin on the steps.

'What are you doing here?'

'Waiting for you,' said Valentin. 'Now you're here, Slonský may deign to talk to me.'

Before Navrátil could open the front door, Slonský erupted from it.

'I've been a bloody fool,' he announced, before striding past them and heading for the café on the corner. Pushing open the door, he entered and looked around. It was almost empty except for a few hardened drinkers, some of them police officers. Navrátil and Valentin walked towards the bar, only to notice that Slonský was not with them. He had taken a perch on a high stool in the middle of the room and was turning from side to side as if bewildered.

'Something wrong?' asked Valentin.

No answer came. Instead Slonský closed his eyes and slowly revolved on the stool. When he had completed a whole revolution, he opened his eyes.

'What'll you have, sir?' asked Navrátil.

'Hm? Oh, coffee,' replied Slonský abstractedly.

'Coffee?'

'Yes, Navrátil, coffee,' answered Slonský, as if no other answer had ever been possible.

'Pastry?'

'This is no time to eat, lad. Valentin, come and tell us your story.'

They sat at the adjoining table. Navrátil and Slonský had a coffee each, while Valentin tackled a small beer with a brandy chaser.

'You asked me to check the reports of the Válková death,' Valentin reminded Slonský.

'Well remembered. And did you?'

'Yes, I did. At least, I checked our files, both published and unpublished. Nothing much in the unpublished, of course. Nobody keeps papers for thirty years. But there was something that struck me as odd about the published stuff.'

'Go on, we're listening.'

Valentin took a lubricating mouthful before continuing.

'The murder was late on Friday night, so it's no surprise there was nothing in Saturday's edition. There was nothing on Sunday either. The first mention is a report on Monday, but with no by-line.'

'Which means?'

'Probably that it was written by the state news service and just printed verbatim. It tells you nothing you didn't already know, but I've brought you a photocopy. There's nothing much for a few more days, then eventually the announcement of the arrest of the Slovak boy. And that's it.'

Slonský glanced over the copies.

'A brutal murder in Prague and that's all the papers say?'

Valentin smirked.

'It's all the Czech papers say. But I was doing a bit of internet searching and I discovered a report had appeared on Monday in a Hungarian newspaper. It was dated Sunday. Now, the story was filed by a chap called Möller. I knew him. He was quite an old man when I started out, but he was a good reporter. He would have done his homework, so I thought I had better get that story. To cut a long story short, our man in Budapest managed to trace a copy and get it translated. You owe him a couple of bottles of something nice.'

'A couple?'

'One for him and one for the translator. On second thoughts, you don't want to look mean. Our man probably ought to have two for himself.'

'Mug me, why don't you, and have done with it.'

'Believe me, you won't begrudge a single crown of it. Wait till you hear what he discovered.'

'Stop spinning out your part and get on with it, you irritating prima donna.'

'Coming from you that's a bit rich. When Möller heard about the murder he went down to Ruzyně himself. Kopecký wouldn't talk to him — that was the neighbour who found the girl —'

'We remember. You've got thirty seconds to get to the bombshell or you've had your last brandy off me.'

'Okay, keep your hair on, while you still can. Kopecký wouldn't talk to him, but Hruška would. You see, Hruška was an old man, an ex-civil servant. But he joined the civil service during the First World War. In those days, they did all their business in German, so he was a fluent German speaker, and so was Möller, who had been brought up speaking it in Hungary.'

'But Hruška was stone deaf. Interviewing him had been a waste of time.'

'Deaf, yes. Daft, no. He hadn't heard anything, it's true. And he hadn't seen anyone leave. But none of the police had asked him the right question, and Möller did.'

'How?'

'He wrote it down and Hruška wrote out the answer. It worked perfectly well. Hruška didn't see anyone leave, but he had seen people come, and he said so.'

Slonský leaned forward eagerly.

'Who did he see?'

'He didn't give names, but look what he said.'

Valentin traced his finger over the translation of the report, indicating a sentence in the middle of the page.

Slonský read it and smiled triumphantly.

'Soldiers. He saw two soldiers.'

'That doesn't appear anywhere else, and in the subsequent days it disappears and they just become two men, before finally they are transformed into Bartoš and he is hanged for it. But at the time of the first Hungarian report, they're soldiers.'

Back in the office, Slonský kept his coat on and walked straight past his desk to Navrátil's, where he opened the drawer. It took Navrátil a few seconds to realise that Slonský was inspecting his academy passing-out photograph.

'I thought you were going to give this to your mum.'

'I am. I just want to get it framed first.'

'You're taking your time.'

'It's expensive,' Navrátil explained. 'The police don't pay me enough to do it properly, so I'm saving until I can.'

Slonský turned to face his young assistant. The smile on his face was reminiscent of a deranged cherub.

'Let me pay for it as a graduation present. I insist.'

'Why would you do that, sir?'

'Because you're about to solve this case for me, lad.' Slonský laid the photograph on Navrátil's desk. 'Who was your best friend at the academy, Navrátil?'

Navrátil responded at once. 'Him.'

'The one next to your right shoulder?'

'That's right. His name was…'

'I'm not interested in his name, lad,' replied Slonský, who was out of the door in the blink of an eye.

Slonský was feeling lucky. His enquiry at the Army Personnel Office had produced a list of names.

'Do you know where any of these men are now?' he asked.

'Certainly,' said the clerk. 'We all know that one.'

'Zelenka?'

'Major-General Zelenka. He's upstairs. He's our boss.'

'I need to see him.'

'I'm sorry…'

'You will be, if I don't see him today. I need two minutes with him, absolute maximum.'

'I'll ask.'

'You do that. If he says no, keep asking until he says yes. That usually works for me.'

But Zelenka did not say no. A dour, humourless man, utterly unremarkable apart from the two stars on each epaulette. He did not have a photograph of his national service class there, but given a name to conjure with, he remembered him well, though wondering whatever became of him, because he would never have made a soldier. Asked who the man's best friend was, he volunteered another name on Slonský's list.

'I probably have that photograph at home,' said Zelenka. 'I could send it on.'

'If you can, sir, that would be good. But all I need to know is whether those two are standing next to each other.'

'I'd be surprised if they weren't,' said Zelenka. 'They were like a man and his shadow. Big man, smaller shadow.'

And in that moment Slonský knew who had killed Jana Válková. Now all he had to do was prove it, thirty years later.

Chapter 14

Dvorník had scoured hours of video footage but had not seen a van that could definitely be identified as the one that collected Peiperová. However, being a man of a mathematical disposition, he unrolled a map of Prague, marked the kidnapping point, and then drew pencilled circles showing the distance that would be covered by a vehicle driving at 50 kilometres per hour, on the basis that anything faster might trigger a speeding fine. The first circle was set at around 1667 metres, the distance it might have covered in two minutes; the second was a further two minutes beyond that, and there was a third one two minutes further out. It was, of course, possible that the driver had doubled back or turned off, but Dvorník had a hunch that the driver would want to get out of the city centre by the most direct route. The van had probably been waiting for Peiperová, so there was no point in looking for the inward journey, but by knowing where the van could be expected to be on the way out of town he could narrow his search.

After a couple of hours of scanning video, he saw it. Not wishing to trust his line of thought he fetched Navrátil, explained what he was doing, and ran the footage again.

'You see there? At the end of the bridge, going along the river. That's around four minutes after Peiperová was snatched, if Slonský's timing is right. But the main reason for thinking this could be the one is what happens at the traffic light a little later.'

Navrátil watched closely. The video was apparently taken from an office building near the Hilton hotel. The van was about to enter an underpass and suddenly swerved between lanes.

'See that? That's a change of plan. If he hadn't done that he'd have been sitting at the red signal right opposite a police car. Instead he turned right, jumping the light to do it. And notice the back windows of the van are obscured.'

'Good enough for me,' said Navrátil. 'Can we get the registration number?'

'It's a bit blurry, but if we go through frame by frame we may get all the digits.'

They pieced together a registration and rang it through. A few minutes later their call was returned.

'Registered to the Silver Rings Gymnasium and Spa. Mean anything to you?'

'I think it's one of Griba's places,' said Dvorník. 'Tatty as hell outside but well set up within.'

'I'll get a message to the patrol cars to keep an eye out for it. Should we go to the gym, lieutenant?'

Dvorník thought for a moment.

'It's Slonský's case. I know what I'd do, but we'd better ask him.'

'I don't know where he is.'

'Neither do I. Stuff it, let's go.'

Slonský was reflecting on a successful day. If he was honest, he was finding Navrátil a bit of a trial at the moment. Granted, he had not yet found Peiperová, but there was no logical reason for anyone to harm her. Then again, criminals were not the most logical of people. Free from distractions, Slonský would do what he did best; drink and think.

A large beer before him, a plate of salami and bread and a selection of pickles at his right hand, his hat on the bar counter, Slonský began to piece together the jigsaw of clues. Like a master symphonist, he looked for themes.

First theme: Válková's death would be brought home to somebody — let's call them A and B for the moment — but who had stalled the investigation by pulling Holoubek off it? We know Válek's sister-in-law took the credit but in fact the conspirators must have been able to influence that somehow.

Second theme: Bartoš comes into the story. He had stolen some money from someone in high places who wanted revenge, and whoever it was knew where to find him because the nincompoop tried to flog an Order of Lenin or something similar in Olomouc, so he was a sitting duck. Already in jail, with a criminal record, he could be set up. And whoever it was who set him up did so either to get cheap revenge, or to distract from the real culprits, or both.

Third theme: Vaněček, who had been conned during the Válková investigation, and should have known it thanks to Holoubek, suddenly starts mouthing off about something that leads to his death in police custody. But what triggered that? He had kept his mouth shut for three years, so why blurt it out now? Was it just the compulsory retirement? Or did something happen that stirred even Vaněček into action? And who had the standing to order his arrest on pretty vague grounds?

Fourth theme: Old Holoubek, whose conscience was troubling him, is run down in broad daylight while crossing the road. We know who did this one — Roman Pluskal — but who put him up to it? Presumably somebody was scared of what Holoubek might know, but the events Holoubek knew about were thirty years old. Why leave him alive all that time, but kill him now? The obvious answer was because he was trying to get Slonský to reopen the case, but the killers cannot have known that Slonský would take it on, or that he would get anywhere if he did. The reason has to be fear. There must still be evidence out there that the killers know about but cannot secure, but what can that be?

Fifth theme: as a mark of respect to Slonský's investigative powers, they kidnap an assistant to get him to back off. Admittedly they seem to have thought she was a family member, but the principle holds true. But that's a sign of desperation. If they hurt her, they lose their hold on him, and earn his perpetual hatred which would, in due time, probably cost them a few broken ribs for starters. Against that, if he holds back for a while and they let her go, they must know that he would just start up again. After thirty years, waiting another year or two would not be an issue. And how would they know that he had backed off? He could tell them anything, if they bothered to contact him again, and he was not convinced that they would.

Sixth theme: what is the link between the killers and Griba? He seems prepared to do a lot for them, considering that he was not active in crime when the early events took place. Slonský tried to recall the crime history of Griba in his folder. He did not remember a contract killing. Certainly some enforcement, a lot of graft, some "teaching of lessons", but no killing; so why had Griba accepted this job? Was it just money? Pluskal would eventually go to jail and Griba could not prevent that, but until he brought Pluskal in he would never know who persuaded Griba, and how Griba persuaded Pluskal to risk a long sentence.

Slonský poured the last of his beer down his throat. It was time to find Pluskal. Do that, and all the rest would fall into place. Find Pluskal, and he explains what Griba was doing. Find Griba, and we discover just who has the clout to push him around. Find that person, and we have our murderer, and he will lead us to his mate.

Dvorník and Navrátil pushed open the swing doors and looked around the gymnasium. Seeing them standing there in their street clothes, including Dvorník's overcoat, since he felt the cold cruelly, a young woman in a vest top and tracksuit trousers marched towards them.

'Come to sign up?' she asked, tilting her head to one side as if well aware that the simple answer was no, but there might be a more interesting one.

'Never in a million years,' said Dvorník, who had instructed Navrátil to let him do the talking. 'We've come to collect Roman Pluskal.'

'Who?'

'Roman Pluskal.'

'I'm sorry, there must be some mistake. We don't have a Roman Pluskal, unless it's the name of one of these members.'

'No, love, he's staff.'

'Not here he isn't. And who are you anyway?'

Dvorník silently showed his badge.

'Police? Look, whatever this Pluskal character has done, it has nothing to do with us.'

'Really?'

Dvorník unfolded a piece of paper taken from his inside pocket.

'That's Pluskal driving the van. And that van is registered to this gym.'

The young woman inspected the photograph carefully, chewing her lip as a sign of perplexity.

'I didn't know we had a van. God knows I'd have used it to move equipment if I had. And I don't know this guy at all.'

Dvorník reclaimed the picture and folded it carefully before returning it to his jacket.

'You see, I'd like to believe you, but frankly I can't take the chance. This man snatched a policewoman and we want her back, unharmed and soon. So if you have a head office or a contact with Griba, you might pass the message to him that he had better do as we want.'

'Griba? Who is Griba?'

'Okay, have it your way. I'll give you the benefit of the doubt and assume that you really don't know anything about the drugs, protection rackets, sex trafficking, prostitution and illegal gambling that goes on in this organisation, because you're young and innocent. But if anyone asks what we wanted, you'll be able to tell them, won't you?'

Dvorník turned to leave and motioned Navrátil to follow. The woman watched them for a few metres, then walked away.

Slonský waved for a waiter to get refills for Navrátil and himself.

'Dvorník moves in dirty circles and he can take care of himself. They'll respect that. Of course, it means they'll shoot first and warn him later. I'm more concerned that if Pluskal didn't know we were on to him, he may now. And I hope she wasn't lying, because if Griba is under threat he may get nasty.'

The waiter was hovering, tray poised to remove the empties.

'I don't know what you put in my glass, but that horse isn't fit for work. We'll have two more from the barrel you opened last. Got any sausages?'

'We will have when the chef catches that horse,' said the waiter.

Slonský laughed and punched him playfully on the arm.

'You topped me,' he announced. 'But some sausage and bread would be good.'

Navrátil sat hunched and dejected.

'They could be doing terrible things to her and we're laughing and joking.'

'How many times do I have to tell you they have no reason to hurt her? And we're making headway. We just need them to make contact again so we can find anything we can about them. And don't forget every policeman in Prague is keeping an eye peeled for Pluskal. If he steps outside, we'll hear about it. Now, the best thing we can do is force down a bite to keep our strength up, keep well hydrated, and get a good night's sleep. Tomorrow could be a long day.'

'I'm off to bed then,' said Navrátil. 'I'll get in at six to get started right after dawn.'

Slonský sighed.

'And of course I'll do the same,' he replied reluctantly.

Chapter 15

Slonský's hand snaked out and batted the top of the alarm clock, but the ringing did not stop. A second clout knocked the clock on the floor, but the ringing continued brightly. It was only then that Slonský realised that it was the telephone.

'Slonský.'

'You want to be here, sir,' said Navrátil, who sounded feverish.

'You're wrong there, lad, that's the last place…'

'Peiperová rang you.'

Slonský sat up with a start.

'Rang me? How?'

'With a phone, I suppose.'

'But Ricka said her phone was out of service. What did she say?'

'She doesn't know where she is, but she left us a few clues. She rang your answerphone so the message is still there.'

'Right, lad, call Ricka and get the lout out of bed on my orders. I want to know where she called from and when. I'm on my way. Whatever Ricka says, do it. I want this particular lemon squeezed till we've got all the juice out.'

Ricka was strangely compliant. It seemed that he needed very little sleep, possibly because the most strenuous thing he did all day was to prise the top off his yogurt at lunchtime. He appeared in the office within fifteen minutes carrying a couple of laptops.

'This phone?' he barked.

Since it was the only one with a flashing red light, Navrátil saw no need to respond positively, but it was of no importance because Ricka started hooking up cables to the phone socket anyway. Before he had finished Slonský erupted into the room with the appearance of a man who had dressed himself by letting his wardrobe topple over onto him.

'Don't touch!' yelped Ricka. 'Just a minute more.' He produced a little silver box and connected it to one of the laptops. 'Got any more plug sockets?'

Navrátil pushed a waste paper basket aside to expose one by his desk.

'Great. We're away. First off, I'm going to play the message and record it so we can't lose it. Ready?'

The others nodded. Slonský had never been big on patience and he had already held his tongue longer than it had ever been held before in like circumstances. He rapped his fingertips impatiently on the filing cabinet. The message began to play and they could hear Peiperová's whispered voice.

'Sir? Sir? It's Kristýna.'

So that's her name, thought Slonský. Must try to remember that.

'They drove me about twenty minutes. I'm one floor up in what sounds like a warehouse. There's no activity inside but there's a bit of traffic noise. They took my phone but they stopped looking before they found the mobile you gave me. I'll turn it off to save the battery but I'll try to put it back on for a few minutes after eight o'clock. I can't see what the time is now — there's no light. I'm okay, they're treating me all right, but it's cold and my hands and feet are tied. I hope you get this. Don't know what else to say. Tell Navrátil I'm looking forward to seeing him soon. And you of course, sir. Oh, the window must face south because the sun comes in at midday. Right, I'll phone later if I can. Bye.'

They stood in silence until they were sure there was no more. Slonský gave a little cough.

'Load of waffle. She could have said that in half the time.'

Ricka was tapping at his keyboard like a deranged woodpecker.

'Okay, call made at 02:04. We've got the number she used but you probably already know that.'

'I didn't know she had a police mobile phone,' said Navrátil. 'I haven't.'

'This is no time for sulking, Navrátil. I'll get you one if it stops you pouting. What else can you tell us, Ricka?'

Ricka had switched to the second laptop. Around two-thirds of the screen was taken up with a map.

'Right, stage two,' he announced. 'The phone company will have strength of signal data for its masts. I'm going to suck those down and it will display on this map as circles of different sizes related to the signal strength centred on each mast. Where the circles intersect is where she was when she made the call. But it'll only be accurate to around fifty metres at best, so don't get too excited. It'll take me five minutes or so.'

'Fine,' said Slonský. 'Navrátil, go and get some coffees, rolls, whatever. Here's some cash. I'm going to call Captain Lukas and tell him what has happened.'

Navrátil reappeared with a tray. Either the canteen felt generous or it was unsold stuff from yesterday but it would do. Ricka was reciting a series of numbers to someone via his mobile phone and then the screen started to fill with pale blue circles. After a few moments a selection of them darkened and a couple began to expand.

'Just a moment,' said Ricka. 'We have to wait for them to stop pulsating.'

The images steadied.

'That's a bloody mess,' opined Slonský.

'We can tidy it up,' said Ricka. 'I'll take away the masts that had a minimal signal.'

One by one the circles disappeared until four were left.

'Now I can make them more transparent so we can see the map underneath,' he continued. 'And finally we enlarge the intersection like this.'

Slonský lent so far forward that neither of the others could see the whole screen.

'What's that big rectangle?'

'Switch to "aerial photograph" and we'll see,' said Ricka. 'There you are — you're in luck. It's one big building with a lot of space round it.'

'Certain that's the place?'

'Over 99.98% certain.'

'Can't you just say yes?'

Ricka raised his palms apologetically.

'That's south of the city, sir,' Navrátil observed.

'Yes. And what makes me feel happier about it is that it isn't too far from the place where Pluskal torched the Volkswagen. He knows his way round that district.'

Slonský pointed to a piece of wasteland. 'That's where the van went up. How far is that?'

Ricka measured the distance against his thumb and then laid the thumb on the scale.

'Perhaps six hundred metres, maybe a little more.'

Slonský clapped Ricka on the shoulder.

'Good work. Navrátil, let's go and get her back.'

'Shouldn't we get backup, sir?'

'Element of surprise, lad. Besides, they're all in their pits. I'll tell the desk sergeant what's happening and Dvorník can get some help on its way. We'll just get over there and keep watch. See if we can check that she's in there before we go in with guns blazing.'

'Guns? Isn't that dangerous?'

'It's a damn sight more dangerous if the bad guys have guns and you haven't. Can we leave you to tidy up, Ricka?'

'Sure. I'll print these out and leave them on your desk.'

'Fine. Can you spin your magic at eight o'clock when she switches it back on and phone me if anything has changed? Come on then, lad. Polish your shining armour and let's go rescue the damsel.'

It was surprising how fast Slonský could walk, thought Navrátil, finding it difficult to keep up despite breaking into a trot.

'One thing, lad; how did you know it was Peiperová?'

'Sixth sense, sir. That, and she told me the code to your voicemail.'

Slonský stood still, hands on hips and a scowl on his face.

'Does everybody know that damn code except me?'

On Slonský's orders, they parked the car a block away from the warehouse and continued on foot. The removal of any markings made identification of the building difficult, but where the letters of the sign had been removed the paint was a darker green, allowing them to make out a word that could well have been "turbine". The building was broadly rectangular with a large double door in the nearer short side. There was a forecourt of around twenty metres between the door and the road. Navrátil made for the main door, but Slonský grabbed his arm and dragged him to one side.

'Keep in the shadows, lad. When we open the door, don't stand behind it. You'll be silhouetted against the light and make an easy target. If she's here, she's probably at the far end of the upper floor.'

'How do you know that?'

'She said the sun came in at midday, and that's the south end. Are you happy you know the plan?'

'What plan, sir?'

'Breathtakingly simple. We open the door, sneak in, rescue her, arrest Pluskal, and live happily ever after.'

'I thought we were going to wait for backup.'

'We are, but if I know Dvorník he'll arrive with all the sirens going and all hell will break loose. We need to be in position when that happens. Come on. Keep it quiet, and when we get inside head for the darkest corner.'

They crept to the door and Slonský gently rotated the handle. It was locked.

'Damn!'

Navrátil dropped to his knees and squinted under the door. He selected the corkscrew attachment on his knife, spotted a piece of cardboard and slipped it under the door, and jabbed the corkscrew into the keyhole. There was a gentle clink as the key dropped on the card and Navrátil pulled it back under the door. He smiled triumphantly at Slonský.

'Beginners' luck,' whispered the older man. He turned the key and they slipped inside, bearing to the left to get under the east windows where light was dribbling in half-heartedly.

'Let your eyes get used to the gloom,' said Slonský.

There was a staircase that started about a third of the way into the building and ran upwards along the west wall. At the far end there was a second staircase that doubled back on itself in a tight spiral.

'Okay,' hissed Slonský, 'you're quicker than me. Can you get to the far end and position yourself on the stairs to block anyone running away? Keep your head down. I don't think there are lots of them — they couldn't stay this quiet. If you're sure it's safe, start creeping up the stairs. If you spot anyone at this end, don't shoot. It'll probably be me.'

Navrátil nodded and slid along the wall. It was necessary because the nearer part of the upper floor was in the form of an atrium, so someone at the top of the stairs or on the gangway might have seen him. He relaxed as he passed halfway and found his way to the foot of the rear stairs. It was difficult to see Slonský, who had secreted himself in the shadow at the far side of the staircase, but Slonský must have been able to see him, because he waved his gun and started to climb the stairs slowly. Navrátil tried to keep pace, but it was tricky to judge how quickly to climb given that he had to keep looking upwards to watch for Pluskal or another of Griba's goons.

Navrátil reached the top of the stairs and gingerly raised his head. He was looking at a large room, almost square. The wall furthest from him did not exist; what he had taken to be a companion-way was simply the edge of the upper storey. The stairs met it at the left side and there was a double safety rail from there to the wall on the right. Peiperová was sitting against the wall to his right on a grubby mattress, her hands and feet tied with duct tape and cable ties and she had another piece of tape across her mouth. Navrátil briefly wondered how she had made the call, but then decided to puzzle that out later. He ducked his head again and found his penknife, extending the blade in readiness to cut the tape. His chief concern was that he could see no sign of Pluskal or anyone else, but he was sure that someone must be there.

Slonský had climbed two-thirds of the way up the stairs when hell was unleashed. So far as Navrátil could make out, it began when Slonský's mobile phone rang. Slonský fumbled in his pocket for it, just having time to register that it was Ricka before Pluskal erupted from a pile of blankets that Navrátil had mistaken for rags. Pluskal dived down the stairs and Slonský's gun was jarred out of his hand. Navrátil was torn between helping Slonský and rescuing Peiperová, but there was no real contest, so he fell to his knees and began sawing at the tape and ties with his penknife. Once her hands were free, he pulled off the tape over her mouth and gave her the knife to finish the job. Navrátil decided that the best plan would be to get back downstairs and form a second line of defence behind Slonský, so he plunged down the stairs again and started running the length of the building. To his horror, he could see an elderly tourist silhouetted in the doorway. He was wearing a backpack and was consulting a map, apparently unaware of the danger he was in. It meant that Navrátil did not dare to use his gun.

Pluskal had barged past Slonský and despite a ragged tussle on the stairs, he had managed to free himself. He raced for the doorway with Navrátil about twenty-five metres behind him, and made to push past the hiker. As he sprinted through the doorway the old man took a step to the side and jabbed his walking pole into Pluskal's ankle, causing him to tumble to the ground. With an inelegant flop, the man finished up sitting on Pluskal's back, and Navrátil was able to throw himself on top of the criminal to pin him down. It was only then that Navrátil realised that he was looking at Captain Lukas.

'Quick, man, your cuffs!' Lukas barked. 'There are spares in the rucksack.'

Navrátil unzipped the rucksack to discover a clanking mass of ironware. In addition to half a dozen revolvers, there were several pairs of handcuffs, a baton or two and a coil of fine rope. It was a surprise that Lukas could walk with it on.

Slonský arrived, panting heavily and bleeding from the knuckles of his right hand. He applied another pair of cuffs to Pluskal's ankles and took the opportunity to give him a sly kick in the ribs while he was lying on the ground.

'Perhaps you would help me to my feet,' said Lukas.

'Of course, sir. Thank you, sir,' said Slonský. 'Navrátil, help the captain up.'

Peiperová had limped down the stairs and was walking towards them, her legs still numb from the binding. She was dishevelled, in need of a good wash and rather embarrassed because she knew she smelled of urine.

Lukas straightened his clothing. He was wearing a gaudy tropical shirt such as nobody would have believed that he might own.

'Don't stare,' he snapped. 'I got it from the lost property box. Now, Slonský, perhaps you would explain to me why you didn't wait for back-up?'

'We were just conducting a reconnaissance when my phone went off, sir. Ricka is a genius but has no common sense. The ringing alerted Pluskal and it all happened from there.'

'I see,' said Lukas, apparently unconvinced. 'It's as well that the desk sergeant gave me your message instead of Dvorník, so I gathered together a few guns just in case and threw them in this malodorous backpack, thus showing, if I may say so, considerably more foresight than you.'

'Yes, sir,' replied Slonský, who had divined that a display of abject contrition was his best policy. 'But you were taking a chance, sir. You put yourself in great danger.'

'Not really,' said Lukas, and swept his arm behind him. Now that he drew their attention to it, Slonský and Navrátil could see the detachment of four police marksmen with their rifles trained on the doorway.

Peiperová had reached them, and threw herself against Navrátil's shoulder. She cried quietly for a few moments as he stroked her hair, and then she pulled away and looked at Pluskal lying face down on the concrete.

'Has he been arrested, sir?' she asked.

'Not yet,' said Slonský. 'But it's a fine distinction.'

Peiperová nodded, then kicked Pluskal at the side of the knee. He yelped with pain.

'That'll teach him to resist arrest,' said Slonský.

Lukas looked away.

'I'm glad I didn't see anything,' he said, 'but I'm sure you will treat the prisoner with respect henceforth. Now pick him up and get him over to the cells before his masters realise what has happened.'

As Lukas had noted, there was a certain urgency in getting information out of Pluskal before the villains realised that Peiperová had been freed, so Slonský was prepared to forego his usual degree of delicacy during the questioning.

'Here's the thing,' he said. 'I've got evidence proving that you were driving the van that killed Holoubek.'

'As if,' Pluskal said scornfully.

'Please yourself,' said Slonský. 'Navrátil, show him the steering wheel from the Volkswagen with his prints on it. Now, we can link this van to the killing of Holoubek and I have two eye-witnesses who can identify you. Wriggle all you like, but you're looking at forty years inside. Courts take a dim view of killing old age pensioners and policemen, and

Holoubek was both, so you're doubly stuffed. They'll probably give you great medical care to make sure you stay alive for every day of your sentence. You'll be an old man when you get out. *If* you get out, that is.'

Pluskal snorted. Slonský took two large strides towards him, grabbed him by the front of his sweater and hoisted him to his feet. It was an inelegant move because Pluskal was handcuffed to the chair, but eventually he was upright and Slonský was undoing the handcuffs and refixing one end to his own wrist.

'Come along!' he growled, and dragged Pluskal into the courtyard at the back of the cells.

'Navrátil, cuff him to those window bars,' said Slonský. When that was done Slonský unfastened his own cuffs and put them back in his pocket.

He stood in front of Pluskal and lifted the prisoner's chin so he could glower into his eyes.

'Forty years. Have you got any idea what forty years in jail will be like? Look up. Go on, look up!'

Slonský yanked Pluskal's head back.

'See that blue stuff? Last time until 2046. You'll be — what? Seventy-nine? Make the most of it. Breathe in the fresh air. It may never happen again. In fact, maybe forty years is too few. Perhaps we'll ask for forty-five. What's an extra five years between friends? Of course, if you helped us I could get five years off for you. Thirty-five instead of forty. What difference will five years make, you wonder? Ask yourself again when you've served thirty-four and a half. There may not be much between thirty-five and forty, but there's a world of difference between six months more and five and a half years more. You're not looking at the sky.'

Pluskal felt his head being pulled back again.

'Got kids? They'll be middle-aged when you next hug them. You won't have to pay for a daughter's wedding, because you won't have done a quarter of your sentence by then. If she has kids, you won't see them till they're adults.'

Slonský grabbed Pluskal by the chin and squeezed his cheeks.

'My only regret is that I'd have to make it to a hundred to enjoy every last day of your imprisonment. But if I can, I'd love to. It would be worth the effort.'

Pluskal made the mistake of smiling.

'Then we've got kidnapping a police officer to add in,' continued Slonský. 'That should be good for an extra fifteen years. Consecutive, of course. There'd be no fun in a concurrent sentence. And maybe we can add some more.' He gripped Pluskal firmly by the ears so he could maintain fierce eye contact. 'Did you touch her? Did you?' His voice was quiet, conspiratorial, menacing. Pluskal tried to pull away. 'I bet you did. Pretty girl like that all tied up, how could you resist? Cop a quick feel, did you?'

Slonský was taken by surprise by the punch. And even more by the second, third, fourth and fifth punches. He grabbed Navrátil by the upper arms and wheeled him away. Navrátil's baby face was contorted with anger.

'It's his skin I'm trying to get under, not yours,' bellowed Slonský.

'If he did … if he laid a finger…'

Slonský trapped Navrátil against the wall and lowered his voice.

'Look, she didn't mention it, did she? If he'd molested her, she would have said.'

'She kicked his knee pretty hard.'

'Yes, she did,' agreed Slonský, 'but she's a well brought up Czech girl. If he'd groped her, she'd have rammed her knee in his groin.'

'Yeah, I suppose...'

'Go and see how she is. She won't want to be alone when she wakes up. Take her to get some new clothes, have a hairdo or some other treat. If she wants to talk, you can listen. Now go. You can give me a call later and we'll make plans for tomorrow.'

Navrátil nodded and went back inside. Slonský straightened his jacket and took a couple of deep breaths to get back into inquisitorial mode.

'Sorry about that,' he said to Pluskal. 'Now, where were we? Ah, I remember. We were calculating the length of your sentence.'

Pluskal chuckled. 'Your maths is bad. I'll be out long before that.'

Slonský sat on the windowsill.

'Now, that's where we disagree. I know you'll be gone much longer than you think, and actually you know it too. This is all just bravado. It's a shame Navrátil has gone. It stops us playing good cop, bad cop with you, though actually we're more bad cop, bad cop. As you saw, Navrátil believes in direct action, while I'm hot on sarcasm and humiliation. We're a good team.' He fished in his pocket for something. 'Did you ever play rock, scissors, paper as a boy?' he asked.

'Yes.'

'Me too. I have my own version we could play. It's called testicles, cheese wire, confession. Cheese wire cuts testicles; confession stops cheese wire.'

'I'll go cheese wire.'

'That's where my version is different.' He opened his hand to show what he had taken from his pocket. 'You see, I always have the cheese wire in this game. The only choice you have is between offering testicles or a confession.'

'You wouldn't dare. They'd lock you up too.'

'I don't care. I promised Holoubek I'd finish his work, and if that's what it takes to get what I want off you, it's a small price to pay. I'm getting on and I'm on my own. At least in prison I won't have to pay for heating, it's dry and I'll get my meals provided. And anyway, some consolation it would be to you. I'll be sitting in jail but you will too, and only one of us will still have balls. Have a think.'

Slonský walked inside and left Pluskal chained to the window bars. It was just starting to rain.

The young soldier was standing so rigidly that Slonský thought his spine might snap.

'Are you waiting for me to tell you to stand easy?' he asked.

'I'm to invite you to make a copy and then to take the photograph back to the general, sir.'

There was a barrier to the successful completion of that task. Slonský had no idea how to use the new photocopier, but he had no intention of letting the soldier know that.

'Come with me, young man,' he ordered, and marched him down to the front desk, where he handed the photograph to Mucha.

'Make some copies of this,' he said, 'then give the original back to the Good Soldier Švejk here.'

'Certainly, O Master,' replied Mucha. 'And where would you like me to put the copies?'

Slonský told him, and walked away.

Pluskal was unhappy, and let Slonský know it.

'I'm soaked. I'll catch my death.'

'That'll shorten your sentence, then. They turf you out of your cell when you die. At least now your family gets your body back. In the old days, they cremated you and used the ashes to melt the snow on the roads.'

Pluskal dried his hair with the towel Mucha had brought.

'Five years, you say?'

Slonský understood, though Mucha looked puzzled.

'Yes, I reckon I can get you five off if you co-operate.'

'I can get my throat cut too.'

'Not by us. And I'm not asking you to be a witness. I just need a link.'

'What good is that without testimony?'

'I'm not stupid, Pluskal. I know nobody is going to finger Griba unless they know he's going behind bars.'

'Griba? Forget it.'

'You know him. I'm pretty sure that he ordered you to run Holoubek down. I just don't know why.'

'I don't know why. Griba doesn't tell you why.'

'Only a handful of people see Griba, I'm told. Everyone else deals through intermediaries. You're one of the privileged few, aren't you? That's because you do some of his bodyguarding.'

'I'm saying nothing.'

'All right,' said Slonský. 'Let's try it another way. You don't have to say anything. I'll tell you, and you can tell me if I'm right.'

Pluskal made no reply, but watched as Slonský unrolled the sheet of paper. He carefully placed his finger on it, then moved a fraction to the left. Pluskal nodded once, briefly, and Slonský rolled it up again and smiled.

'Five years, remember?'

'I'm feeling generous. If this comes off, I'll give you ten and settle for thirty.'

Outside Mucha was curious.

'Are you really going to ask for thirty years?'

'Yes,' said Slonský. 'I'll tell the prosecutor I've agreed it with the suspect. It'll come as a shock, because he was only planning to ask for twenty-five.'

Major Klinger, head of the fraud squad, scrutinised the photograph closely without touching it.

'I don't know why I'm doing this, Slonský. I have no idea what Griba looks like.'

'But the fraud office came closest to building a case against him, didn't it?'

'It's still live, but we're running up against the time limit for action.'

'We've got an identification.'

'Have you, by Jove? Well, that's a great leap forward.'

'Navrátil arrested one of Griba's bodyguards this morning, and he's prepared to identify Griba in exchange for a reduction in his sentence.'

'Sentence? For what, pray?'

'Murder and kidnapping a police officer.'

'That young woman of yours? I heard about that. It's obviously a risky business working for you. High time you handed that bright young chap of yours over to me. He's made for financial work. He's meticulous, you see. You'll ruin him if he isn't separated from your influence soon.'

'If Navrátil wants to go, I can't stop him, but he's only been in the criminal division for three months.'

'That's long enough to suffer your supervision. Goodness knows what he'll be like after a whole year.'

'Look, I want to pool what we know about Griba. Every little helps.'

Klinger produced a folder from his filing cabinet. Like all his folders, it was immaculate, with coloured stickers on some of the pages. The manila cover was unblemished, primarily because Klinger threw them out if they became creased.

'He first came to our notice in the late eighties. You'll recall that the Albanians appeared around then. When the Wall came down, the Albanian mafia became really active. There are numerous tales of sex trafficking, drug running, prostitution and arms trading in which they were involved. We had some CIA people here for a while helping us clear them out.'

'I remember.'

'Griba arrived sometime then and was initially a very minor player, but it seems likely that at some point he executed a remarkable double cross and eliminated one of the key Albanian leaders. Of course, the Albanians are still around, but they don't cross Griba who, incidentally, speaks Albanian and Czech fluently. He can be ruthless if he needs to be.'

'Is he still running all the businesses?'

'That's the interesting thing. He still trades in drugs and prostitution, but we're told he no longer touches arms. I assume his supply dried up when the fighting in the Balkans ended. Now, why am I looking at your old National Service picture?'

'Because, if our prisoner downstairs is to be believed, that man there is Griba.'

Klinger stared intently at the picture.

'So he speaks fluent Czech because he is Czech.'

'Precisely. Not an Albanian at all. Though, as an hour in the library told me, Griba is an Albanian word meaning rake or comb. It's a nickname he acquired at some time. And thanks to Major-General Zelenka, I now know his Czech name.'

Chapter 16

Navrátil ran up the stairs as quickly as he could, straightened his tie, and knocked on the office door.

'Come!' commanded Lukas.

Navrátil was not a great reader of facial expressions, but he knew relief when he saw it, and he saw it now on Lukas' face. Peiperová's parents were sitting in front of the desk and turned to see who was entering. Mrs Peiperová gave a slight smile of recognition when she saw Navrátil, whom she vaguely recalled having been told about when he was in Kladno though Peiperová refused to bring him home for tea. Mr Peiper had never been one for small talk or bothering to remember people, so he shook Navrátil's hand with the formal movement of a first encounter. There was no antagonism; it was just that you meet a lot of people in a lifetime and it stretches the brain a bit to try to recall them all.

Navrátil had forgotten that Slonský had telephoned them to tell them of Peiperová's kidnapping, so he had not mentioned it to Peiperová, who assumed that her parents knew nothing of her adventure.

'Navrátil, I believe you've just come from Officer Peiperová's barracks. I hope she is getting some rest.'

'Yes, thank you, sir. She's sleeping. I said I would be there when she woke up, if you don't mind.'

Lukas glanced quickly at her parents. Mrs Peiperová had tensed slightly until she realised that there was more than one construction that Navrátil's words would bear.

'Yes, indeed. It's very good of you to provide support for her after her ordeal. Has the doctor examined her yet?'

'I believe so, sir, before I got there. She has some minor cuts on her arms where she was tied, and a few bruises, but no other physical injuries. It's mainly the stress and shock. And of course, she didn't sleep well.'

'Of course. I wonder, would you be kind enough to take Mr and Mrs Peiper to see their daughter? I have promised them that she will be given time to recover before she returns to duty.'

Navrátil agreed, though now he was concerned that they would take her back to Kladno and she might never return to Prague again.

He held the door open and invited them to follow him to his car. They were happy to walk, partly because they wanted to see where she was kidnapped.

'Imagine!' Mrs Peiperová said. 'What a place Prague must be! They snatched her there in broad daylight.'

Navrátil resisted the temptation to point out that ten minutes to ten at night was hardly broad daylight, but hastened to assure her that such kidnappings were extremely rare. It was then that he had the misfortune to meet Slonský who was returning from Klinger's office with a jaunty air.

'Heigh-ho, Navrátil,' he boomed, 'and what have you arrested this pair for?'

Navrátil winced inside.

'These are Officer Peiperová's parents, sir. Mr and Mrs Peiper, may I introduce our boss, Lieutenant Slonský.'

Without a missed beat, Slonský took each by the hand and expressed his delight with their daughter's performance since she had been under his tutelage, and his firm conviction that she might well be the first female Director of Police.

'That's as may be,' said Peiper, 'but not if it puts her in danger like this. It's not worth it.'

Despite nearly four months with Slonský, Navrátil had no idea how the old detective would overcome this observation, particularly since he had said the same thing himself on more than one occasion. To his surprise, Slonský dealt with the objection with a flamboyant impatience.

'I can understand that view, sir, but I'm sure that if you ask your daughter she will tell you that we who serve the public do not worry about the dangers. It's a measure of the helplessness to which we have reduced the criminals that they felt compelled to try something this desperate. They intended your daughter no harm, of course. Any mishap to her would have wrecked their last chance of avoiding imprisonment. Your daughter willingly allowed herself to be abducted, having cleverly concealed a second telephone about her person which she used to contact me on the night after they fell into our trap.'

'A trap? So this was planned?'

Slonský carefully avoided answering the question.

'When dealing with the criminal mind, you can't plan like you can with ordinary people, but we made it possible for them to take this rash step. It's greatly to Officer Peiperová's credit that she came up with such a daring idea. I shouldn't be surprised if an official commendation came her way.'

'But you sounded so concerned when you rang us,' protested Mrs Peiperová.

Slonský gathered them in so that he could speak quietly.

'As will become clear in a few days, there was a good reason to give that impression. I can say no more until further arrests are made.'

'Further arrests?' said Mr Peiper. 'Then someone has been arrested?'

'Certainly,' said Slonský. 'Captain Lukas and young Navrátil here fearlessly captured the kidnapper at the scene. He has implicated others, but I'm afraid I can say nothing about that at the moment.'

Evidently not even to me, thought Navrátil, since I haven't a clue what you're talking about. And I bet you haven't either.

Mrs Peiperová pointed at the bandage on Slonský's grazed knuckles.

'You were injured too.'

'A mere flesh wound,' he replied with the air of someone downplaying a serious incident, whereas to describe it as a flesh wound was itself hyperbolic. 'A week or two and it should be back to normal. I'm very lucky,' he added with an attempt at a brave smile as he ushered them towards the canteen. 'Let me give you a coffee and describe this morning's events more fully while Navrátil runs ahead to tell your daughter the good news that you're coming to see her. It'll give her a minute or two to tidy herself up, then I'll take you there personally.'

'Are you sure you can spare the time?' asked Mrs Peiperová.

'Tsk!' replied Slonský. 'What is more important than my staff's families?' He looked steadily at Navrátil. 'No doubt Navrátil will bring dear Kristýna up to date with developments,' he added meaningfully.

Navrátil could hardly believe his ears. A few hours ago, Slonský didn't know her name, and now he was speaking of her like a child of his own. The poor benighted parents were ready to sign up to the Slonský fan club, while he was left to explain to Peiperová that while she may have thought she was being kidnapped, in fact it was all a cunning plan that she had sprung with herself as bait.

To his surprise, she was more than happy to adopt this account, since it offered the best chance of being allowed to stay in Prague. Although part of her was worried about the possibility that this might happen again, she could not face having to return to Kladno and listening to all her mother's friends telling her that they had told her so. Besides, if Slonský meant what he said about a commendation, that was not to be sniffed at.

'If you're sure…' said Navrátil in tones betraying his own uncertainty.

'I am,' Peiperová said. 'When all is said and done, my parents still have their child, which is more than can be said for poor old Mrs Bartošová. I'll have a shower and we'll put on a brave face for Mum and Dad.'

Navrátil was unconvinced that she could recover as quickly as that, but if she wanted to try, he would go along with it. But he could not help feeling that it was lucky he was around to keep an eye on her, and it was in her interests if he set about making that a permanent arrangement.

Slonský had taken the Peipers to the barracks and then excused himself by saying that no doubt they would want some family time together. Navrátil showed every inclination to stay until Slonský announced loudly that they had a witness to interview, and then announced even more loudly that they would do so together.

'Who is the witness?' asked Navrátil, 'or was this a subtle way of getting me out of there?'

'Well, a bit of both. We have got a witness to speak to, and there's no point in delaying if it helps to get the villains behind bars. On top of that, we don't pay you to sit around gawping at young women.'

'I'm not gawping. I'm supporting her after a really frightening ordeal.'

'Of course you are, but the two aren't mutually exclusive, as you've just been proving. I saw the look on your face. Look, I'm not knocking it. Just saying you can't shield her from the world forever.'

'Maybe not forever, but I was hoping for more than six hours.'

'Her family are with her now, and that's as it should be. She'll need you again when they're gone.'

'That reminds me, sir, where did this masterplan to get Kristýna kidnapped come from?'

'It's Officer Peiperová to you during working hours, lad. It set her parents' hearts at rest and it didn't do her self-esteem any harm. Who is hurt by it?'

'The truth comes to mind as a victim.'

'I seem to remember that someone important once asked "What is truth?" and shot off without waiting for an answer.'

'Pontius Pilate, I think.'

'I rest my case. What kind of policeman was he? He only had one case and he fluffed it.'

'Which way now?'

'Out to Ruzyně again. We're going to see Mr Kopecký.'

The old man was wearing a particularly startling pullover of his wife's devising with red and white diamonds on the front and back and a zigzag design down each sleeve.

'You could get migraine looking at that,' whispered Slonský as they waited for Mrs Kopecká to return with coffee and sufficient cakes and pastries for six ordinary people and place them in front of Navrátil who, she thought, might have lost a little weight since he was last there.

When they were all provided for Slonský unfolded the paper he had brought and explained their purpose.

'I want you to think back to the day Jana Válková died.'

'We talked about that,' said Mr Kopecký.

'Indeed we did, and you said you saw a couple of men running away. I know you only caught a brief glimpse, but we think they may be in this photograph. Take your time, and see if you can identify them. It doesn't matter if you can't.'

Kopecký hunched over the photograph and inspected each figure in turn. Finally he stabbed at a man near the right edge.

'That's the big one who got in the front seat,' he said. 'The littler one who got in the back may have been this one beside him. It's a bit hard with a black and white photograph, but if his hair is fair, I'd say he was the one.'

Slonský smiled. 'Excellent. Navrátil will just put that into a statement that you can sign, if you will.'

'Did I pick the right ones?'

'You must pick the people you think were there, sir. It's not for me to say whom you should point out. But those were the two I thought it would be. It's a shame your neighbour isn't around to confirm it, because he got a better view in daylight.'

'Mr Hruška?' said Mrs Kopecká. 'He never said.'

'Nobody asked him properly. The chances are that they found his deafness too much of a barrier or that he didn't hear the question properly.'

'That's very likely,' said Mrs Kopecká. 'When I took food in to him, we had a conversation of sorts, but I never felt he knew what I'd said. I think he just answered the question he expected you to ask.'

'A reporter conducted an interview with him by writing down the questions. Mr Hruška said he saw two boys arrive. He thought they were soldiers.'

Kopecký took a sudden interest.

'Do you know, I believe he's right. I thought they might have been policemen, but they may have been in fatigues.'

Slonský understood. In the dark there had not been much difference between the uniforms in those days.

'And of course, it was a police car they got into,' added Kopecký.

Slonský came close to taking a bite out of his cup.

'A police car? You didn't mention that.'

'Didn't I?' said Kopecký. 'I must have forgotten. I do, you know. It's my age.'

'No, I mean you didn't mention it at the time.'

'I'm sure I did. I don't mean it was one of the green and white things. It was like a staff car. You know the kind. The ones they come to take you away in.'

'An StB car?'

Kopecký became agitated. 'Keep your voice down! We don't want to upset them.'

'But those cars were unmarked. How did you know it was a police car?'

'Well, because the man who got out was in police uniform. I was surprised he drove himself, because he had a fair amount of decoration on his jacket.'

Slonský needed to get this straight. 'Who got out, and when?'

'The car came into the road and turned round with a big loop at the end of the cul-de-sac before it pulled up by the Váleks' house. It was on the wrong side of the road by then, facing back to town. The driver opened the door and started to run towards the house, but the two boys must have seen him and ran out. The stocky one got in the front so the little one got in the back. The driver was an older man. He put his cap on as he got out but I could see he was quite grey.'

Slonský understood now. He had already guessed that this must have happened, but he was surprised that the driver had come in person, at some risk to himself. Navrátil had written out a statement which Kopecký signed, then they took their leave, Navrátil politely declining a bag of buns.

Mrs Kopecká saw them to the door.

'Mr Válek visited the other day. He's not well, the poor man, but it was good to see him. I don't think he'll come again. It upset him too much to see his old house. Bad memories, I suppose.'

'You could meet up in town,' suggested Slonský.

Mrs Kopecká shook her head. 'I doubt it. My husband doesn't go out much. But perhaps when he has a hospital appointment in town we could see what is possible.'

They sat in the car in silence for a few moments.

'Surely if he'd mentioned a police car…' said Navrátil.

'I think he did. He mentioned it to someone who didn't want to hear. When Holoubek visited he didn't think he needed to say it again because it would already be in the file, but whoever it was mentioned to didn't make a note. And I bet that wasn't an accident.'

Navrátil started the engine.

'Now where, sir?'

Slonský lifted his hat and scratched his head.

'I suppose we may as well go and arrest the killers.'

Chapter 17

'You know who they are?'

Both men exhibited surprise, Navrátil had no idea that an arrest was imminent, and Slonský had not realised that their identity was not as blindingly obvious to Navrátil as it was to him.

'You really don't know?'

'Not a clue.'

'Are you pulling my leg?'

'No, sir. How long have you known?'

'I knew one of them almost from the start. The other one, I wasn't certain about until I saw Zelenka's photograph. There's just one little bit I'm having to guess. Never mind, I'll explain when we get there. In the meantime, put your foot down. I want to arrest him at work.'

'It would help if you told me where we were going, sir.'

'What? Oh, park the car at our station. We'll go the rest of the way on foot.'

On arrival, Slonský instructed Navrátil to see to the most pressing matter on their agenda by fetching two coffees and any non-toxic edible material that the canteen might be stocking, with a stern warning that Slonský did not regard any kind of vegetation as fit food for human beings. Fortunately, there was still some sausage left, so the kindly canteen lady piled some into a roll and wrapped it with care once she knew it was for Slonský. Although Slonský had never been one for flattering any authority figure, he laid it on with a trowel where the canteen ladies were concerned since, in his view, the canteen was the hub of the Czech police force and it was impossible to detect on an empty stomach; or, indeed, a stomach filled with lettuce, which was more or less the same thing. In this opinion, he was at one with Dumpy Anna, who believed that men need meat and that a lot of the young officers she served were much too fussy about their diets. She exempted Dvorník from this criticism, since he was prepared to eat any part of an animal that did not have hair on it and had a particular fondness for tripe stewed with onions, as she did herself.

Slonský had closeted himself with Lukas. When the door opened and both men emerged, Lukas looked very grave.

'I'll make some calls to explain the situation,' he said. 'Don't assume they'll come quietly. Put your vests on.'

Slonský agreed to do so, though he hated wearing the bulletproof vests, since he hated being shot too. He ate his roll in silence and with an intensity in his gaze that Navrátil found intimidating.

'Ready?' barked Slonský.

'Yes, sir.'

Navrátil reached for his coat.

'You won't need that,' said Slonský, and led them down to the front desk, where he exchanged a brief word with Mucha.

'I think cell 7 is available at present,' Mucha confirmed. 'Will sir be requiring it for just the one night?'

'Probably a few. We'd better remove any of the frills and extras in there.'

'Of course,' replied Mucha. 'I've got a leaky slops bucket if that suits.'

'Excellent. And don't give him the wooden seat for the top. Don't stand with your mouth open, Navrátil, people will think the police are employing simpletons.'

'We do,' protested Mucha.

'Yes,' agreed Slonský, 'but not usually at Navrátil's rank.'

'That's true,' Mucha agreed. 'You need a lot of experience to be truly clueless.'

Slonský marched across the foyer to the double doors leading into the other wing of the building and climbed the stairs with vigour, Navrátil trying to keep up despite his shorter legs. On the upper floor, they passed through the swing doors into a corridor equipped with a thick carpet. Navrátil could not help noticing that the office doors were polished hardwood and had name plaques on them. Slonský pushed one of these open and marched past the secretary's desk.

'Is he in?' he asked, without waiting for an answer.

'You can't…' she began to reply, but stopped when Slonský turned to face her and she saw the fire behind his eyes.

'Isn't it your coffee break?' he asked.

Without a word, she slipped from the room, and Navrátil heard her begin to run as she left them. Slonský stared after her then, when he was sure she was not going to turn back, he jerked the handle of the inner office and entered.

Colonel Tripka was signing papers and looked up only briefly.

'Don't you knock?' he asked.

'Not when I'm arresting people, no,' replied Slonský.

You had to admit that Tripka was impressive, thought Navrátil. He carefully replaced the cap on his fountain pen, laid it on his blotter, and fixed his eyes firmly on Slonský's.

'You had better explain yourself,' he said, without inviting them to sit.

Slonský sat anyway.

'It's really quite simple. Me good guy, you bad guy. Good guy puts bad guy in jail.'

'On what charges, pray?'

'Conspiracy to murder, corruption, conspiracy to kidnap, dereliction of duty in a public official and probably a few miscellaneous other bits we'll find out as we go along.'

'That's ridiculous,' snorted Tripka. 'Now get out of my office before I get annoyed and stop treating this like the joke it is.'

Slonský grabbed Tripka's arm and turned it palm upwards.

'Lesson eighty-six, Navrátil. You can't control your nervous system. See the sweaty palm. The Colonel — or should I say, soon-to-be ex-colonel — is under stress.'

'This is a career-ending move you're making,' Tripka snapped.

'It certainly is,' agreed Slonský, 'but not for my career. This all starts when Holoubek came to see me. He wanted to reopen a case from 1976, the murder of Jana Válková. Remember her?'

'Is there any reason that I should?'

'Actually, a lot of reasons. The simplest is that you'd met her. Her father remembers thinking you'd be a good catch for her when you came to her birthday party in February. He didn't think you'd shown any interest so when he was asked about boyfriends he didn't mention you. But he'd have been delighted. After all, your father was an officer, if not quite a gentleman. And you were destined for high things. You just had to get your national service out of the way, like we all did, by which time Jana would be old enough to get engaged. Then you'd start your long climb up the greasy pole that would elevate you to your current status. He wasn't wrong, was he? You'd have been a good catch for Jana. In some ways, that is.'

Tripka was clearly furious. His fists were clenched and the knuckles were showing white.

'Anyway, Holoubek had investigated her murder and had proof — absolute proof — that the wrong man had been hanged. Not only that, but people in the police had known he was the wrong man before the life was choked out of him. It wasn't much of a life, Tripka, but it was the only one he had and he was entitled to keep it. Normally I'm opposed to the death penalty but I would be willing to make an exception in your case.'

Navrátil tensed, hoping that Slonský was not going to produce a gun, but he seemed content simply to talk.

'Holoubek returned to see me, and the same day he was creamed by a van driven by a thug called Pluskal. We've got Pluskal downstairs by the way. He doesn't have much of a brain but he does have eyes and ears, and I don't doubt he'll tell us a few juicy snippets once we've loosened his tongue. Pluskal is employed by Griba, and don't tell me you don't know who Griba is.'

'No, I know who he is. One of Prague's foremost criminals.'

'That's right. A man you're paid to try to stop. After all, you're in charge of our anti-drug efforts, and he sells drugs. It sounds like a good fit. And yet although everyone knows what Griba does, our attempts to stop him have been remarkably ineffective. I wonder why?'

'That's an offensive insinuation.'

'Hold on to it. I have plenty more. So, who knew Holoubek had been to see me? You see, Pluskal was waiting for the tram. A brighter villain would have followed Holoubek and killed him in his flat, but Pluskal's orders were to make it look like an accident. Fortunately, he has no idea what an accident should look like. He also left his fingerprints all over the van and some were retrieved before he set fire to it. He's going to plead guilty to the murder of Holoubek, I believe, but he may try to reduce his sentence by being very cooperative about naming others. Needless to say, he doesn't know many others, because Griba likes to keep his secrets, but as a personal bodyguard Pluskal knows a few things others might not know. Things like who Griba meets, for example. Oh, and to answer my own question, there's one person we know for sure knew that Holoubek was here. He asked me what you were doing now, because he'd seen you downstairs. I thought perhaps his son had let the news of his father's visit slip out, but Ondřej only knew about the first visit. He didn't know his father had come back, so he could hardly have told anyone. In the time Holoubek was here, someone organised his death. There's barely time for an outsider to do that, is there?'

Slonský paused and draped one leg negligently across the other so his ankle rested on his knee before continuing.

'Let's go back to Jana Válková. Her parents were going out for the evening. You knew that, because your father had been involved in the security arrangements for the banquet, so you'd seen the guest list. It was Friday night, so you got yourself some passes and made your plans. You'd take some food and a lot of drink and have some fun with Jana. You liked her, she liked you. It could have been a good evening. The snag was that you didn't go alone. I have an eye-witness who has identified you and your companion leaving the Válek house on that evening.'

'Surely it was thirty years ago? You'd never get a conviction based on digging up someone who thinks they might have seen me thirty years ago.'

'We'd have to let a court decide that. But he's a good witness. His memory is stuck. He doesn't remember many new things, but he doesn't forget many old ones either. Memory can work like that. You wanted people to forget, and he can't forget. He doesn't know it was thirty years ago, but he knows it was you. And he has also identified your friend Sedláček.'

Tripka could not conceal his surprise. There was an involuntary stiffening of his shoulders that showed that the name meant something to him.

'I see you know who I mean. Not that you could deny it. Just as Navrátil here is standing next to his best friend in his class photo, so you're next to Sedláček in your national service group photo, which Major-General Zelenka was kind enough to lend us. And he remembers the two of you as best buddies — or are you going to tell me the Major-General is feeble-minded too?'

'No, Sedláček was my best friend. But it was a long time ago.'

'Strange how you never really know someone, isn't it? I suppose if you'd known about the stuff Sedláček had in his pockets you might not have taken him. Because it was Sedláček who started it all, wasn't it? He took his drugs and turned nasty, didn't he? He raped Jana and started torturing her. And you didn't stop him.'

The statement was greeted with silence.

'I said you didn't stop him, did you?'

Tripka reached for the telephone.

'I think I'd like my lawyer here now.'

Slonský threw it on the floor.

'All in due time. All the lawyers you want. You can fill your cell with lawyers. But first I'm going to tell you what a spineless little worm you were. You tried to stop her bleeding with a towel. But it had already been going on a long time by then. You'd enjoyed it at first. You'd even joined in. The forensic report tells us that two different hands had done the stabbing. Did you take the drugs too? Or were you perfectly sober when you sliced into her arms and belly? You were sober enough to ring Daddy for help, weren't you? The telephone record vanished but you rang the hotel where the banquet was taking place, and your father came to fetch you. You were seen arriving by the old man across the road, and another witness saw you climb into a car driven by a senior policeman. Just to convince you he knows what he saw, I'll tell you Sedláček climbed into the front and you rode in the back. I don't know if Jana was actually dead by then. Can you tell me?'

'I want a lawyer,' Tripka croaked.

'No, you want a long pointy stake up your backside with plenty of splinters sticking out. But all in due time. Let's go on with the story. It was your great good fortune that Válek's wife wanted a senior officer to take over the case, so they replaced Holoubek, who might have discovered the truth, with Vaněček, who wouldn't have seen the truth if it was painted on a buffalo and paraded through Prague. He was floundering, and then a colleague gave him a bit of help. He produced a ready-made confession from Ľubomir Bartoš. Bartoš was in jail in Olomouc after trying to flog a Soviet medal, so Vaněček didn't even have to find him. What wasn't said, and Vaněček didn't ask about, was that Bartoš had been in jail at the time of the murder, which is usually reckoned to be a pretty good alibi. Even in those days, we didn't let prisoners out to commit murder and then let them back in again afterwards. Now, here's the bit that was a stumbling block for a while. I can understand the need for a scapegoat, but why Bartoš? What had he done that put him in the frame? The man was a cat burglar with no record of violence at all, but someone went to a lot of trouble to frame him.'

Slonský retrieved a bundle of papers from his pocket, selected one, and unfolded it so Tripka could read it.

'There's your answer. The list of houses Bartoš burgled during a spree in Prague. Your dad helped to compile it by driving him around town, but your father was only really interested in one. Your old house is on it. But even that isn't much of a reason to see someone hanged. However, when you add to it with his mother's testimony it becomes clearer. Bartoš stole some money, but not Czechoslovak money. It was dollars. Quite a bundle of dollars. And in those days ordinary people couldn't get dollars. It wasn't even allowed for most people in high places to hold dollars, but your father had access to them. He'd sneaked a few here and there and built a little stash, and now it was gone. No wonder he was mad. He couldn't report them as stolen because he wasn't supposed to have them in the first place, so if he couldn't have redress, he'd have revenge. And that's why Bartoš hanged. Your father went to Olomouc, persuaded him to sign a confession — which, by the way, he couldn't read — and dumped him in court to face the music. I can't prove it but I suspect he squared the judge to throw Bartoš in the cells and proceed in his absence so he couldn't deny anything. Poor Bartoš didn't know what had happened, but he did give us one good clue. He told the chaplain that the police officer who took his confession knew Mandy.'

Tripka tried to remain stone-faced, though the strain was showing.

'That had me foxed for a while,' Slonský admitted. 'I couldn't think of anyone called Mandy who featured in the case. I thought the priest must have misheard. Perhaps it was Mandl and we were looking for someone Jewish. Then my dear ex-wife, God rot her soul, came to visit me and the light dawned. We weren't looking for a person. Bartoš had been talking about a song. We didn't get to hear a lot of American music then, but somehow this policeman had picked up all the words of the song and could sing it in English. You'd have to listen to it quite a few times to do that, wouldn't you? It's the kind of thing someone who worked at a counter-espionage listening station near Český Krumlov from 1972 to the end of 1974 might have done, don't you think? I got that from your dad's personnel record, by the way. Bartoš couldn't read, but he had a good memory for a tune. It was the only way he could identify your father, the man who stitched him up. There have been four killings in this case and I can't decide which is the most revolting. What do you think — slicing Jana Válková to death slowly like you did, or hanging an innocent half-wit who stole what you stole, like your dad did? Or perhaps it was having a ninety-year-old man run over, like you did, as opposed to kicking a fellow policeman to death like your dad did? The score is two each, but you're still active and unfortunately, your father isn't. That's a shame, because we don't get many father and son murder trials. The public gallery would have been packed with geneticists wanting to run tests on such a pair of psychopaths. Now you'll have to stand there on your own, which is a shame. It's good for a father and son to have a shared interest, provided it isn't mindless violence.'

Tripka winced. His former bluster had seeped away under Slonský's angry onslaught.

'Let's come on to Vaněček. I'm not going to pretend he was a great policeman. In fact, he was a walking disaster area. Forcing him into retirement was possibly a great blessing for us all. Of course, he was furious. Your father had him thrown out and despite Vaněček's contacts he couldn't prevent it. He lost his nice house and finished up in a small place in Zdiby, brooding in his garden and waiting for a chance to take his revenge. And he thought he'd got it, didn't he? That's why he wouldn't go quietly. He'd found new information and thought that it would see him reinstated and your father retired or worse. But that was Vaněček's weakness, wasn't it? He wasn't ruthless enough. He said his piece to the wrong people, and your father had it characterized as a piece of vicious gossip. Vaněček was taken in for questioning and kicked to death. There wasn't even the spurious dignity of its being labelled as an unfortunate accident. No pretence at all — just a series of boots in the ribs until he died. It was all so panicky and rushed that they didn't even construct a good cover story. He was alleged to have fallen on a fence post, except that his garden didn't have one. They had to deliver a fence post when they took the body back. And his neighbour, who was, after all, a policeman, thought it was suspicious, but he knew better than to raise his head above the parapet. Look where it got Vaněček. I wonder, by the way, what that new information was? I haven't been able to check that out, but I'm struck by the coincidence that Sedláček hurriedly left Czechoslovakia in 1979, just before Vaněček was murdered. Did Vaněček recognise the method in another killing? We'll never know, unless you tell us. No, I didn't think you would.'

Tripka unfastened his jacket and ran a finger around his collar.

'Let's come to your first big mistake — other than being born, that is. That mysterious phone call I received when Peiperová was kidnapped. Why would anyone think she was my niece? Then I remembered an incident on her first day. We were in the place on the corner of the street and for some reason I said to her that Uncle Josef would look after her. You remember that, Navrátil?'

'Yes. And she gave you a hug.'

'And that's the only time anyone has ever done that to me. So whoever thought she was my niece was there. And when I close my eyes and picture the scene, lo and behold you're sitting reading your newspaper at the round table by the pillar about four metres away.'

Navrátil was astonished. He was no student of body language, but even he noticed that Tripka was shrinking in his seat.

'Arranging for Peiperová to be snatched wasn't too difficult. She didn't work here in the intervening period so your mistake wasn't obvious. I thought Pluskal was watching the station, but in fact he tells me he was keeping an eye on the bar because that was the only place they thought she might turn up. Griba told him to pick the girl up and take her somewhere safe. Then he had to phone me with the message, but how did he know when to phone? I arrived at work early and within a few minutes the phone rang. If it had been a bit later, when we were all there, I could have understood it, but somebody must have told him I'd arrived. In fact, an eye witness said Pluskal was phoned and then phoned me. So, who phoned Pluskal? It must have been someone watching this building. Someone who was so panicked by my inquiry that they didn't dare leave me an hour in case I made a breakthrough. They wanted me warned off as soon as I arrived. So much so that they took a big risk. They used their own mobile phone to ring Pluskal, as his account records show. I don't remember the whole number but it ends one-six-five. Oh, look, so does yours! I don't know why I feign surprise, because I checked it beforehand. You saw me arrive, and you rang Pluskal. Navrátil, meet the man who kidnapped your girlfriend. Feel free to give him a sound thrashing.'

'I'd like to, sir, but it's against the rules.'

'I'm sure I saw him attempting to resist arrest.'

'Well, in that case, sir…'

Navrátil landed a beauty on Tripka's cheek before wheeling away to hold his fist in pain.

'There's a water cooler in the outer office, lad. Run it over your hand. Don't worry about getting the carpet wet, they'll be burning it all anyway in a few days to eradicate all traces of the previous occupant. Now, are there any loose ends? We've explained how you murdered Jana Válková, how your dad set up Ľubomir Bartoš to take the rap for that, how he had a former colleague kicked to death when it looked like it would all be reopened, and how you asked Griba to have Holoubek killed when he was trying to do the same thing. Ah, yes — why would Griba, a hardened criminal and one of our most wanted villains, do a favour for you, the head of the anti-drug office, given that you're trying to shut him down? Except, of course, that you aren't really trying, are you? He's pretty immune. Evidence goes missing, witnesses are bumped off, and if anyone inside his circle tries to betray him word somehow gets back to him. Pluskal is very voluble on the subject. He didn't know who the police informant was but he was sure that there must be one, and if even someone like Pluskal with the IQ of a retarded amoeba has come to that conclusion there must be something in it, wouldn't you say? Griba has the best possible insurance policy, hasn't he? He has the head of the anti-drugs squad by the short and curlies because on a July evening in 1976 they murdered a girl together.'

Tripka closed his eyes and pinched the bridge of his nose.

'Griba and Sedláček are one and the same, aren't they? He escaped in 1979 and made his way to Albania. In the mountains, he was safe because the government couldn't make its writ run up there. He was a good shot and he made a first class bandit. That's what Vaněček discovered, I think. There were intelligence reports from Yugoslavia that mentioned a Czech working with the Albanians who raided over the mountains into Kosovo. When the Albanian mafia started muscling in on Prague, Sedláček was the ideal front man. He just needed a new identity, and he got himself one. Just to keep the pressure on you, he picked a good one. He passed himself off as your brother. You couldn't refuse to acknowledge him, or he would bring you down, so to those who know him he's your little brother Vladimir who has been so lucky in his property dealings. Mind you, I only discovered that when I saw a photo of him taken by the fraud squad. They have an innate suspicion of recluses, you see. Give Klinger his due, he's a good fraud officer. When I said I was investigating you, he volunteered the opinion that it must be difficult for you to live in the shadow of such a successful brother and told me all about little Vladimir. He's lost a kilo or five, but he's still the cheeky little chappie in Zelenka's photograph. I don't suppose I need to tell you that I wasn't surprised that your father made no mention of having two sons in his personnel record, or that your mother would have been astonished to discover that she'd given birth to two sons just four months apart. You see, Griba kept his real date of birth when he had his new papers forged. It's easier to remember then, isn't it? The fewer lies you have to remember the easier it all is.'

Slonský reached across the desk and gave Tripka a slap.

'Resisting arrest again, eh? Did you see that, Navrátil?'

'Yes, sir.'

'Let's get the cuffs on him and take him down to the cells, lad.'

Tripka straightened his collar and brushed his jacket with his hand.

'Perhaps you'd give me a minute or two to put my personal effects in order.'

Slonský dived forward and slammed the desk drawer shut.

'No, you don't. There's no easy way out for you. Navrátil, put the cuffs on him and I'll take his gun from the drawer. Tripka, I won't be satisfied with anything other than your complete and utter humiliation. I want you to be treated with universal contumely. I want Prague mothers to substitute your name for the bogeyman's when they're telling their children off. I want to watch as they rip your epaulettes off and write you out of the police service's history. And I want to see you taken down after your trial. Just think how warm a welcome a one-time police colonel is going to get in prison. I'll have to make sure they know I'll take it amiss if anyone kills you too quickly. Navrátil, hold the door open, please.'

Slonský marched Tripka to the door. The secretary had crept back to her desk and was watching goggle-eyed as her boss was led away in handcuffs. In the corridor Slonský was surprised to come face to face with Captain Lukas, who was in full uniform. He ignored Slonský and addressed Tripka.

'I came to tell you in person,' he said, 'that I think you're a complete shit.' He seemed to have run out of things to say, and simply muttered 'Pardon my language' before returning to his office.

Slonský and Navrátil had never heard Lukas use a word like that before. They looked at each other for confirmation that they had not dreamed it.

'It's impressive,' said Slonský, 'how sometimes a man is able, in a few short words, to sum up the thoughts of his entire nation.'

Chapter 18

Tripka was a picture of misery. Slonský had insisted on removing his uniform, leaving him sitting in a bright orange jumpsuit with one leg chained to the table. His rank had vanished too, leading to his being addressed as Prisoner Tripka, and in a further flourish his wife had been telephoned to be told that he was under arrest and was unlikely to be returning home. She arrived at the station to speak to him and instead found herself sitting opposite Slonský.

'Surely there is some mistake,' she protested.

'Certainly,' replied Slonský, 'and your husband made it. He is being charged with one count of murder, one of conspiracy to murder, one of kidnapping, one of obstructing a public official in the execution of their duties — need I go on?'

Mrs Tripková dabbed at her tearful eyes.

'But he's a good man,' she cried.

'He's good at having people killed, I'll give him that. And apparently he's good at pulling the wool over your eyes for thirty years. All the time you've known him, he's had a guilty secret. He murdered his first girlfriend.'

'I refuse to believe that,' she shouted. 'Let me speak to him.'

'I'm afraid we're still questioning him. I can't allow you more than a few minutes and one of us will have to stay in the room.'

He led Mrs Tripková down to the interview room, which was what they called cell 8 when they wanted to impress people. Tripka was led in, and his wife tried to embrace him, but Slonský and Mucha intervened.

'No touching, I'm afraid, madam,' said Mucha.

Mrs Tripková attempted to make eye contact with her husband, but he found it too painful.

'Tell me it isn't true,' she pleaded.

Slonský decided to be helpful.

'You're not under oath,' he said. 'You can lie and tell her you didn't do it, if you've got the brass neck.'

Tripka remained silent. His lip was quivering and he looked ashen.

'Perhaps you'd like to tell Mrs Tripková about your brother,' Slonský suggested.

'He hasn't got a brother,' she replied.

'No, but he lets people think he has, when it suits him. Isn't that right?'

'What's going to happen to him?'

'Hard to say,' Slonský answered. 'If he gets a lenient judge he could be out in twenty-five to thirty years. Of course, prison is a difficult place for ex-policemen. There are a lot of inmates with scores to settle. There may even be some that he put away. I doubt it, because he hasn't actually solved much crime for years, but you never know.'

Tripka's head dropped. He was openly sobbing now.

'You'll have to think carefully about whether to let the children visit,' Slonský added, in what he hoped was a concerned tone. 'It can be very distressing for them.'

'What have you done to us?' his wife screamed.

Tripka just shook his head and continued to cry.

'Technically, he's only suspended at present,' said Slonský, 'so there'll be some money this month. I don't know how long it will take for his wages to stop but at least you've got some time to adjust to your new standard of living.'

'Are you enjoying this, you monster?' spat Mrs Tripková.

'I wish it had never happened,' replied Slonský, 'but your husband made his bed and now he has to lie in it. All we're doing is turning the sheets down.'

Lukas received an unexpected phone call.

'I have Dr Pilik on the line for you,' announced a sepulchral voice. Instinctively Lukas combed his hair and straightened his tie before sitting to attention to take the call.

The minister was delighted. He must have been, because he said it at least four times.

'I shall look forward to these villains appearing before the court. Of course, one is above revenge, but I can't forget that they have caused me some personal embarrassment in the matter of Bartoš.'

Lukas was confused as to whether the minister realised that the identification of Bartoš as the murderer was the work of old Tripka rather than the one in custody, but he let it pass.

'I shall have a word with the prosecutor's office,' Pilik continued. 'We must not show any weakness in dealing with errant police officers.'

'Certainly not,' agreed Lukas.

'There must be exemplary sentences.'

'Certainly.'

'Are you likely to arrest the other conspirator soon?'

'We have identified him, minister. He will take some finding.'

'If you need extra resources, please ask the Director of Police. I shall instruct him accordingly.'

'Thank you, minister. At present we are building our case methodically,' Lukas responded, hoping that it was actually true.

The difficulty with putting the pressure on Tripka was that he had collapsed mentally and was proving impossible to interrogate because he would not stop crying. Eventually the police surgeon was called to give him a sedative.

'I hope it's a placebo,' muttered Mucha.

'I just hope it's painful,' replied Slonský. 'We're not going to get any more out of him. We'll have to make our move soon before Griba knows what has happened.'

'I wouldn't be surprised if he knows already. You know what this place is like for gossip.'

'Yes,' agreed Slonský, 'but you and I start most of it and I haven't said a word.'

'Me neither.'

'It should all be fine, then. Peiperová says she wants to be in on the arrest seeing as Griba ordered her kidnapping.'

'Is she up to it?'

'She's a tough girl. Besides, I wouldn't want to try telling her she can't. She needs it to wrap the whole thing up in her head.'

'Griba was at Tripka's beck and call just as much as the other way round, wasn't he? Tripka was the one person who could lead the police to him.'

'Yes. When Tripka said it was necessary to kill Holoubek, Griba didn't argue. He just did what he was told. He only had an hour or so to arrange it.'

'Do we know where to find Griba?'

'Yes, now that we know he's Tripka's so-called brother. But it's a high security site and it's going to be difficult to get in.'

'So do we wait until he comes out?'

'The trouble is he could land a helicopter in his garden and escape us. I toyed with arresting him at night, just for old times' sake really, but the best bet is to walk calmly up the drive at breakfast time. I've got a rifle squad having a look round for points of entry.'

'So what now, old friend?'

'Now? The only fixed points in a changing world — a beer, some sausages and a good night's sleep.'

It was 06:30 and Slonský, Dvorník, Navrátil and Peiperová were in their car. Navrátil was driving.

'The gate is under CCTV so we'll all have to enter together and just hope nobody is paying it much attention. Navrátil and I will go to the front, while you two make your way to cover the back. Watch out for dogs or security guards. If you meet any you're entitled to disarm them. Security guards, that is — never try to disarm a dog. So far as we know, he and his wife live alone here. There'll be staff around but they don't live in. Any questions?'

'Do you want him taken alive?' asked Dvorník.

'Ideally. But don't put yourself at risk. I've divided us this way so there's one experienced officer in each pair. If anything happens to me, Dvorník takes charge.'

'What about if something happens to you and Dvorník?' asked Navrátil.

'Then you'd better run like hell, because you'll be in real trouble,' Slonský told him.

They could hear a deep rumbling sound not too far away.

'What's that?' asked Peiperová.

'That,' replied Slonský, 'is as subtle as a spade round the back of the head. That's an armoured car moving into position. If a gunfight starts they'll take out a chunk of the perimeter wall and the army boys will move in. If that happens, we all come back here and sit in the car. No point in heroics.'

They climbed out and wrapped their coats around themselves in the chill morning air. It was bright, but in the lee of the trees there was a definite coldness and their breath fogged in front of them.

'Best leave the car unlocked,' said Slonský. 'We don't want to be unable to get into it if we have to run back.'

'Should I leave the keys in the ignition?' asked Navrátil.

'Better not. There may be criminals about who would steal it, and how stupid would we look then? Tuck them in the glove compartment.'

Navrátil obeyed. Slonský asked each of them to show their gun and check it was loaded, just in case. He also suggested that they should verify that the safety catch was on, now that Novák had shown him how easy it was to disengage it. In fact, it was so easy that Slonský was very careful as he put it back in his holster in case he shot himself in the foot.

'Right. On we go.'

At the gate, Slonský pressed the buzzer. A voice asked who he was.

'Detective Lieutenant Slonský and Officer Navrátil. We'd like a word with Mr Tripka away from his office, please.'

The gate opened and all four walked through. Dvorník and Peiperová slipped off to the left behind some bushes and made their way round the perimeter, hoping there were no cameras watching them. Meanwhile Slonský and Navrátil marched boldly up the drive, and were met at the front door, where they showed their badges.

Griba was still a square man, perhaps not as nakedly powerful as in his youth, but nevertheless quite impressive. He wore his hair in a steel grey crewcut and was dressed for a day at the office.

'What can I do for you?'

'I'm afraid there is some embarrassing family business,' said Slonský. 'Your brother has been arrested for corruption and he has mentioned your name several times in questioning.'

Griba did not flinch or twitch. He chewed something slowly and finally responded.

'I'm sorry to hear that. What has he been saying?'

'He says that he did some of the things we discovered because you put pressure on him.'

'That's nonsense. What pressure could I possibly put on my big brother?'

'Well, that's what we thought,' said Slonský, 'but you can understand that we had to ask.'

'Of course.'

Griba's wife appeared in the hallway.

'What is it, darling?' she asked.

Griba answered without looking at her.

'It seems my brother is suspected of taking bribes or something of the sort.'

'Never! I don't believe it.'

'Neither do I,' Griba said, 'but these gentlemen wouldn't be here unless something needed explaining. I hope he's able to satisfy them.'

Slonský smiled his simplest village idiot smile.

'He's certainly being very talkative. I don't doubt he'll tell us everything in the end. For example, he has already told us you're not his brother, Mr Sedláček, and implicated you in a murder you jointly committed. Not to mention fingering you for another murder and a kidnapping.'

Griba tried to shut the door but Slonský had jammed his foot in the way. Springing back, the criminal seized his wife by the shoulders and held her in front of him as a shield.

'Get back,' he said. 'Retreat down the path. We're going to walk calmly to our car and drive away and no-one gets hurt.'

To illustrate how someone might get hurt, he flourished a flick-knife he drew from his pocket.

'I don't think so,' said Slonský, drawing his gun and levelling it at Griba. 'We seem to have reached a bit of an impasse. If you cut her throat, that just adds another to your catalogue of victims. It's no skin off our nose.'

Griba's wife was whimpering. It sounded as if she was on the verge of an asthma attack.

'I think your wife is finding this a bit stressful,' Slonský commented. 'It must be difficult to discover your husband has an assumed name and you've been living for twenty years with a murderer. Since I may not get the chance to ask her later, do you mind if I ask her whether you've carved a cross on her nipples too?'

'You're very cocky, Mr Detective, but I only have to wait a minute or two, and then my men will be here to even up the fight.'

Griba opened his left hand to show a panic button.

'They're on their way even now,' he gloated.

Suddenly there was a loud noise and Griba's wife slid to the floor, blood running from her shoulder. Griba let her slip and stood stunned as his white shirt sleeve reddened. Navrátil kicked the knife from his grasp and pushed him against the wall as Slonský stood transfixed and uncomprehending, until he was able to see past Griba and saw Dvorník and Peiperová in the kitchen doorway. Dvorník's gun was levelled and smoking.

Slonský showed his gratitude in his usual way.

'You could have bloody killed us,' he growled.

'Could have, but I didn't,' said Dvorník.

'You shot his wife.'

'Just a flesh wound, I expect. The bullet went through his arm and smacked her in the shoulder. Small price to pay if you ask me. Better than getting your throat cut, anyway.'

Slonský paced to the kitchen door, completely ignoring the scuffle as Navrátil and Peiperová subdued Griba and tried to get handcuffs on him.

'You had a lot of confidence in your aim, I'll give you that.'

'Belong to a gun club,' Dvorník smirked. 'If I can't hit an arm at ten metres, there's something wrong.'

'Sir,' Navrátil interrupted, 'shouldn't we tell the boys outside what's happening and warn them that a bunch of armed guards may be coming?'

Slonský sighed.

'I suppose so. Don't want the health and safety people onto me.'

Chapter 19

'Of course, there'll have to be an enquiry,' Captain Lukas announced.

'I don't see why,' replied Slonský. 'Dvorník didn't shoot at Mrs Tripková. He just happened to hit her after he hit her husband. You could argue that it was her husband's fault for not stopping the bullet properly.'

Lukas was having none of it.

'You know as well as I do that there is an enquiry every time someone is shot by the police. The mere fact that there is an enquiry does not imply guilt. It means that we have nothing to hide.'

'We have plenty to hide,' argued Slonský, 'but not involving bullets. The amount the fraud squad spends on disinfectant thanks to Klinger's obsession with cleanliness comes to mind. And doesn't the fact that we're charging the head of the anti-drug centre with murder suggest that we have nothing to hide?'

Lukas became grave. 'I hope we can get a conviction. A confession would be helpful, but I rather fear he's going to claim that he isn't fit to stand trial.'

'So he was fit to head the drugs squad at half past three, but by four o'clock he wasn't fit to be held to account for what he did thirty years ago? Of course, there are some of us who believed he was out of his tree for much of the intervening thirty years, but that's just prejudice, not a psychiatric evaluation.'

'What about Griba? Do we have enough on him?'

'Pluskal began to sing like a lark once he heard that Griba was in the cell across the way. I explained to him that he had a free choice whether to grass on Griba or not, but since Griba was going to believe that he'd informed on him anyway, Pluskal had every reason to make sure Griba stayed behind bars for the sake of his own future safety.'

'And he bought that argument?'

'He isn't very bright, but he understands a threat.'

'He can't be bright if he doesn't realise Griba isn't there.'

'That's because I've let him believe Griba is. We threw a blanket over Dvorník and kicked up a bit of a fuss as we locked him up.'

'And how is Griba?'

'Sore arm, no doubt. Being shot does that for you. But the surgeons sorted the wound and gave him enough sedative to keep an ox docile, so as soon as they give us the nod we'll throw a blanket over his head and repeat the manoeuvre.'

'There's no danger that he'll be liberated from the hospital?'

'I've got four marksmen standing guard and we've manacled one of his legs to his bed frame.'

Lukas indicated the chair and motioned Slonský to sit. The word "retirement" began to form in Slonský's mind.

'How is Peiperová?'

'Better for having come back to work, I think. Navrátil is good for her. I don't know why, because some days he irritates the hell out of me, but she seems to enjoy his company.'

Lukas made a steeple from his fingers and held it to his lips for a few moments.

'I'll reach retirement age around the same time as you. There'll be a captain's job going. If you wanted, I'd go before you so that you can get the rank for a few months and bump your pension up. Not that I can guarantee you'd get the job,' he added hurriedly.

'Thank you, sir, but I don't think I'm captain material. I'm happy being a lieutenant.'

Lukas would normally have approached this objection obliquely, but since Slonský did not appear able to understand anything less subtle than a simple declarative sentence, he tried the more direct approach.

'If you don't take it, it will probably go to Doležal.'

Slonský twitched. It was just a reflex, he told himself, something that he would learn to control.

'In that event, perhaps I've been too hasty, sir. I'll give it some thought.'

'You do that, Josef. You do just that.'

Tripka sat on his cot, rocking slowly and cuddling the pillow in front of him.

Slonský opened the door, closed it behind him, and leaned against the wall.

'How are you enjoying your stay? The food is hardly cordon bleu, but then you're getting it for free. And I managed to wangle you your own cell. Not much of a view but better than Griba has across the corridor.'

Tripka did not respond, so Slonský straddled the chair facing him. This allowed Slonský to slouch forward, but also protected his genitals in case Tripka had a fit of the habdabs.

'He's not many metres away. Would you prefer to share?'

Tripka's eyes widened.

'Ah, you understand. You see, we're always short of space here. In your wing you've got that big cell because it doesn't matter if you put twenty whores or junkies in together. If we did that, there'd just be a few bones left in the morning. But there would be a certain poetic justice in locking you up in your old department's cells, because then we could put Griba and Pluskal in with you. It would be like a reunion, just like old times. What more could a man want than to die surrounded by his friends?'

Tripka refused to speak, but his eyes betrayed his fear.

'If you want to stay on your own, you'd better start talking. In the normal run of things, I would regard you as the grubbiest, nastiest, most despicable, loathsome lowlife we've ever had in here, and believe me we've had some who would give you a good run for that title. There was that chap who liked beheading nuns, for example. And then there was the one who stabbed a teenage girl so she bled to death slowly. Oh, no, hang on — that was you. Scrub that example, then; I'll find a better one. The key is that I'm coming under pressure from others to get you a bit off your sentence if you ensure that Griba stays in jail so long he'll leave in a cherrywood urn. Can we do business? Don't dither too long, or I may take the offer across the corridor and see what Griba is prepared to offer to keep you inside for the rest of your days. Personally I'd prefer that. He's a mere sex trafficking drug dealing pimp, extortionist, kidnapper and multiple murderer, whereas you're a corrupt policeman. The distinction is that if you were both on fire, I would be prepared to pee on him to put him out. But if you were to make a clean breast of the whole thing, save us a lot of police time and ensure that Griba is taken off these mean streets, I can be magnanimous. So here's a pencil and paper. Get writing. An hour from now I take them away and give them to Griba instead.'

Navrátil opened the door in response to Slonský's knock. As they walked back to the main desk, Navrátil asked a question that had been puzzling him.

'You know you talked about mean streets. Does Prague have mean streets, then?'

'Oh, yes,' replied Slonský. 'Not to mention some tight corners and some really stingy alleyways.'

Dvorník was ecstatic. Slonský no longer needed him, and he was restored to his normal freedom of action. On top of that, he was the man who had shot the fearsome Griba, and he would be the recipient of many a free drink over the next few weeks on the strength of that. Admittedly he was also the man who had shot Griba's wife, but you can't have everything, and she was recovering well in hospital. The surgeon had spoken to Lukas and assured him that her shoulder blade would be good as new, if you overlooked the hole in it which he might try to fill with some mashed up bone and cement. Despite Lukas' scepticism it appeared that this was perfectly respectable medical practice, according to Dr Novák, and not a species of mumbo-jumbo akin to chicken entrail inspection.

'It was a good job, there's no denying it,' said Slonský to him. 'Should I have heard a warning?'

'Of course not,' said Dvorník. 'A warning would only … well, warn him.'

'That clarifies things,' said Slonský. 'I wondered why standing orders said we had to shout a warning before we shoot someone, but now I see that the idea is that he won't get a nasty surprise when the bullet hits him.'

'Next time I'll let him cut her throat, shall I?'

'No, no need to get defensive. I'm not judging you. Given half a chance I'd have done the same myself. I just want to sort out what we're going to say to the investigation team.'

'How about "It happened. No regrets. Get over it."?'

'Perfect.'

Slonský breezed into the cell. Tripka pushed the paper wordlessly towards him.

'Let's have a read of this, then,' said Slonský. 'Nice handwriting.'

I, Bohuslav Tripka, make the following statement voluntarily.

I first met Jana Válková at a camp organised by the Pioneer movement. She was about eighteen months younger than me but I was immediately drawn to her. However, she was too young to show an interest. On the occasion of her seventeenth birthday, which I believe was in February 1976, I was surprised to receive an invitation to her party. I had not realised that this invitation was extended to a number of those she had met at the camp, as well as schoolfriends. As a consequence, I knew very few people there and I found myself talking to her mother, Mrs Válková. Although I believe that she did not know my father personally, she knew of him and asked me a number of questions about him. She said she hoped they would see me there again when the house was less crowded. From these remarks I deduced that she approved of me as boyfriend for her daughter.

However, no further invitations arrived. We met briefly at another camp and Jana was friendly and remembered me by name. When the time came for me to do my national service I found myself doing my initial training not too far from her house — we lived in the centre of Prague at the time.

My best friend in the army was called Sedláček. He was physically bigger than me and boasted of his success with girls. When we came to know each other well, I asked him for some advice and told him about Jana. He suggested that we went to see her together and he would put in a good word for me. He said that she would know I was respectable and safe, but that young women wanted adventure and danger, and that was why bad boys like him had so much success with girls. I should show her that I knew how to have fun.

At my parents' house, I discovered a guest list for a banquet and saw that Jana's parents were invited. Since it was a Friday night, I was able to obtain a pass to go out of barracks and Sedláček and I took a bus out to Ruzyně. He had some beer and some food in a canvas bag. I did not know that he also had some illicit drugs. To this day, I do not know exactly what it was. It may have been cocaine, because after we had some drinks, he opened the bag and put some crystals on his hand so he could sniff it like snuff. He then rubbed some on his gums, after which he became louder and more aggressive. He wanted us to try some. I used a little but the powder made me sneeze so I think I absorbed very little. My nose tingled but I cannot say that I noticed any other effects. Jana at first refused to try any, but after some coaxing from Sedláček she agreed to place a little on her tongue and lips. After a while she said her lips were numb. Sedláček told her he did not believe her, and kissed her before asking if she could feel it. After that we took it in turns to kiss her. Sedláček used more of the powder and he became rougher. At one point I noticed he had pushed his hand inside her top and she was telling him to stop, though she did not really seem annoyed.

We had some more beer, then Sedláček passed round his powder again. This time Jana seemed disorientated or intoxicated and she made no protest when Sedláček started to undo her clothes. She slipped off the sofa onto the floor and Sedláček told me to hold her shoulders so she would not keep moving. I did not realise what he had in mind, but soon he was raping her. She started to shout so he turned the music up then pushed her jumper into her mouth and slapped her. She stopped protesting after she was hit. I remember Sedláček telling her she was one of those girls who liked being bullied. She disagreed, but he hit her until she agreed to say that she liked him doing it. He told her she would like pain, and she agreed, probably because she thought he would hit her again if she didn't.

He produced a penknife and prodded her arm. He didn't pierce it, but it dented the skin. He repeated this several times, but on the fifth or sixth occasion he drew blood. He gave me the knife and told me to see how hard

I could push before I penetrated the skin. Next he tried throwing the knife to see if it stuck in. Finally he started slicing into her skin. He said he wanted to see how many cuts she could tolerate before she passed out.

Suddenly I became aware that her arm was bleeding badly. I told Sedláček we needed to give her first aid and together we carried her to the bathroom, where we tried to stop the blood with towels and a curtain. I tried to make a tourniquet but Sedláček just kept giggling and when I finally got the bleeding from her right arm to stop, he laughed "That was fun. let's make another one" and cut into her left biceps and armpit. There was a lot of blood and I wanted to send for help but Sedláček said we could fix it.

I don't know when I realised that she was dying. I felt completely sober and I was shaking Sedláček to make him stop playing his silly games. He punched me quite hard and I knew then that I could not stop this by myself.

I rang the hotel where my father was at the banquet and asked to speak to him. When he came to the phone he told me to calm down and he would come over at once to sort things out. I don't know how long he took. It seemed to be hours. By the time he came Jana was dead and Sedláček was less aggressive. We ran out to the car and father drove off. He took us to his house and made us shower and change our clothes, then he returned us to the barracks and ordered someone to issue us with some new kit. Although he was in police uniform, he was a major and the quartermaster felt he should obey his orders.

Father told us to say nothing to anyone, and not even to discuss it ourselves in case anyone overheard. After a few days he said that he did not think we were likely to be arrested because the investigation had run out of steam and in any event an incompetent officer had been placed in charge, but he said the best way of ensuring our safety would be if someone else had been convicted of the murder. I did not realise that he was going to make that happen.

I knew that our house had been burgled earlier in the summer and I remember father being very angry because something had been taken and he could not recover it. I heard him say to mother that even if it was found, he could not claim it was his. I heard later that he found the culprit and decided to make an example of him. I knew nothing of this until a Slovak man was hanged for the murder of Jana Válková.

After that I tried to forget the whole episode. Sedláček said we would have to watch out for each other and that this would make us even better friends now that we had a shared secret.

A couple of years later I had completed my service and joined the police. Father told Sedláček that he wasn't suitable, and suggested that he should stay in the army. He used his influence to have him accepted in a commando unit. I had occasional letters from him telling me how much he enjoyed it. He especially liked mountain training and camping outdoors. I don't know exactly when it happened, but within a couple of months there were two serious developments.

First, we heard that the police officer who had investigated the murder had discovered proof that the wrong person had been hanged. Father was worried because this officer, whose name I have forgotten, was blaming him for having provided evidence against this Slovak which had now been shown to be false. Fortunately the officer had left the police and he confronted my father personally. My father was able to use his influence to have the officer neutralised before questions were asked.

After that, Sedláček got into trouble with the army. He wounded an officer in a quarrel and I do not know if he was discharged or just ran away. He made his way to Albania where he found a welcome amongst the mountain people who prize a good fighter. He stayed there for over ten years and made a number of firm friendships. I did not hear from him during this time.

When Communism collapsed, he heard that Albanian gangsters were coming to Prague to set up various illegal operations and offered his services as an interpreter and guide. He returned covertly to the Czech Republic and obtained new papers. I did not know that he had created a new identity as my half-brother. He claimed that we had the same father but that his mother had been my father's mistress. This explained how he was almost the same age and why nobody had previously known of him. By this time, my father was dead and unable to disprove the story.

Over a period of time he took over a large part of the illegal Albanian activity, masquerading under the codename Griba. The Albanians had given him this name because he was skilled at finding and defusing mines, so they called him "The Rake", like the garden tool.

From time to time our paths crossed, and Sedláček would remind me that he had not forgotten our past, and if I wanted to keep our secret I must ensure that he knew if the police were planning to move against him. When his staff threatened to leak information to the police I would let him know, and he would take whatever action was needed to keep them quiet. In this way he remained immune from prosecution. I admit now that I gave him this information.

However, I did not protect him as has been alleged. I wanted nothing more than to have him arrested. I did not fear this because once he was in prison he would no longer torment me. If he had tried to tell anyone what had happened to Jana Válková, I would have argued that it was fantasy with no evidence and it would have been my word as a police officer against that of a known criminal and fugitive. In my view, I had nothing to fear from his arrest.

This changed when Holoubek began to interest the police in reopening the case. We knew that Holoubek had some information, but despite burgling his flat we could not find it and did not know exactly what it was. As a result of Holoubek's meddling, we were no longer secure.

I discovered that he had been to see Lt Slonský. I also determined that Lt Slonský had requested some relevant files from the archives. I had been able to remove a few incriminating pages in the past without being noticed but I worried that Lt Slonský might still find something that I had overlooked. I therefore suggested to Sedláček that we should take steps to get the case dropped.

I did not realise that Holoubek would be killed, particularly in so brutal and public a manner. When I heard what had happened I felt quite sick. It was also counter- productive, because it encouraged the said Lt Slonský to investigate more thoroughly, and he is a more formidable adversary.

Sedláček suggested that we had to find some way of deterring Slonský personally. Since we knew nothing dishonourable about him and we did not think that we had any credible threat against him personally, we did not at first know how to do this. Then I remembered that he had brought a young woman to a bar, and that this young woman had addressed him as "Uncle Josef". Since Slonský has no other family and very few friends, we thought a threat to this woman might deter him. We did not realise that in fact she was a member of the police force newly arrived from some other city.

I wish to state that I made it very clear to Sedláček and his men that this woman was not to be harmed and that she should be held only until Slonský dropped the case.

I am prepared to co-operate to the full with any enquiry.

Slonský put the papers down and looked at Tripka, who was waiting apprehensively for Slonský's comments.

'I should put your name down for a creative writing course when you get to prison. You have a definite talent. Of course, I doubt you can string it out for thirty years, but it'll give you an interest. That said, I'm afraid I can only grade this as a B minus. You haven't really put the effort in, you see. For a start, there's no mention of the fact that you stabbed Jana Válková too. If you didn't rape her it can only have been because you weren't up to it. Remember we have forensic evidence that two different people did the stabbing, and it was more than just testing to see how hard you could push before the skin popped open. You participated to the full, didn't you? You're not giving yourself credit for the part you played. That's why there was a cross on her nipple, wasn't it? Sedláček made one cut and you made the other.

'Then there's the choice of language. The officer was neutralised, was he? It sounds like you took him to a vet. He wasn't "neutralised"; he was kicked to death in cold blood. And it's very good of you to feel sick about the killing of a senior citizen and former colleague. Do you know what a body looks like when a van runs over it at high speed? But the bit that really offends me is that nowhere in this self-justifying trash is there the word "sorry". Nowhere is there any acceptance of any responsibility for what happened. Jana was killed because you took some drugs and were too spaced out to realise what had happened, then you were too weak to intervene. How many times do you say that you didn't realise, you didn't know, you didn't approve? Actually the thing you didn't do was give a toss. That nasty Sedláček put you up to all this, did he? Your father could sort all the rest out for you — a scandalous misuse of his office and rank, by the way — but he couldn't sort out Sedláček? Tell me, where is your father's headstone? I may want to relieve myself later.'

Tripka had taken refuge in tears again.

'You've got some paper left. I'll sharpen your pencil, and you can start from scratch. And if you don't tell me the truth I'll put you in Sedláček's cell and show him this account in your handwriting that lays all the blame on him. You know him better than I do — how do you think he'll take it? Laugh it off, will he? I can picture that winning smile of his as he gouges your eyes out. Now, start writing and this time tell the whole story.'

'You're sure you want to do this?' asked Lukas doubtfully.

Slonský merely nodded.

'It'll surprise a lot of people,' Lukas went on. 'It's been a shock to me.'

'Things change,' Slonský shrugged. 'Ideas you used to be certain about become less definite and then you find yourself thinking exactly the opposite.'

'That's obvious. Well, if you're absolutely sure this is what you want I'll put the wheels in motion. But once I've done it, you realise there's no going back. You can't have thought about this for long.'

'I'm going with my gut feeling,' Slonský explained. 'It's rarely let me down over the years.'

Lukas looked into Slonský's eyes for any sign of doubt, then, seeing none, he reached for his pen, uncapped it, and signed the sheet of paper.

'I'll keep it in my desk until the morning in case you change your mind,' he said.

'I won't,' replied Slonský, 'but thanks for the thought.'

From his adolescence, Navrátil had pictured what happened when you got engaged. He had replayed the scene many times in his head. He would take his intended for a quiet dinner, the best he could afford. Afterwards they would walk in the woods or along the river, just the two of them, ignoring anyone else who came near their space, and at some point he would invite her to sit on a tree stump or a bench, kneel in front of her and announce his undying love, simultaneously producing a ring from his pocket. He had even practised removing a ring box from his jacket and talking at the same time, just to prove this particular act of multitasking would not be beyond him. If she said yes, he would give her a passionate yet chaste kiss. If she said no, he would give serious thought to romantically heaving himself in the river, because that was how you showed your disappointment.

Peiperová wanted to go to the cinema, to lose herself in another world for an hour or two. The movie was not the sort he would have chosen, since it seemed to consist mainly of young women in their pyjamas talking a lot and he wanted to shout at the screen that the best way of finding out if the journalist loved the blonde one was simply to ask him instead of talking about it to her friends for eighty minutes. It was too late for dinner when they came out, but Peiperová said she would like a *párek* so Navrátil bought a pair at a stall.

'Slonský would be proud of you,' he said. 'His world revolves around sausages.'

'And pastries.'

'And beer. Especially beer.'

'Do you think he'll see his wife again?'

'There's a lot of anger there for him to overcome. I can't see it. He's getting on and he won't change now. He's a nice man, a good man, but I fear he's going to finish up living in one room on his own. When they eventually kick him out, that is, because he'll never retire voluntarily.'

Peiperová nodded. 'We're like a family, aren't we? It's one of those discussions my parents used to have — "what are we going to do about granddad?"'

'I feel a responsibility towards him, and I've only known him four months or so.'

'So do I, and I've only been here a fortnight. The most exciting fortnight of my life! What more can possibly happen?'

'Marry me,' Navrátil blurted out.

Peiperová froze, the sausage halfway to her mouth.

'What did you say?' she asked.

'Marry me. I hadn't planned to ask like that, and I haven't got a ring, and I've probably messed it all up now. You haven't even met my mum yet and I should have told her about you but it's just that when I saw you hogtied like that…'

'I hope you're not one of those boys who gets turned on by tying up women.'

'Certainly not! I only meant that I realised I wanted to take care of you forever.'

'We've only known each other a short while. Are you sure?'

'I'm sorry, it was a dumb question, forget I asked. I—'

'Yes.'

'Yes what?'

'Yes, it was a dumb question. But yes, I think I'll marry you. Not yet, but I will.'

'When?' asked Navrátil, his voice breaking with excitement.

'Can I finish my sausage first?'

'Not really,' said Navrátil. 'It dropped out of your bun when I asked you.'

Slonský had a few glasses in front of him, while Valentin looked more like the disreputable and dishevelled specimen he used to be before dreams of television stardom induced him to comb his hair more than once a week and wear matching socks.

'It worked out all right, old friend,' said Valentin.

'We've got Tripka. And I think there's enough to nail Sedláček too. A confession would be good, but I doubt he'll be that obliging. I just need to get Tripka to own up to what he did so the judge doesn't think he put the blame on his mate to save his own skin.'

'But he did.'

'That's why I need him to rewrite his confession. At the moment you'd think the pair of them were Adolf Hitler and Mother Teresa. I'm hungry. Do you think they'll have any sausages left?'

Slonský was in luck. The waiter soon returned with a plate of sausages, sauerkraut and onions. While these last two were technically vegetables, Slonský was prepared to eat them as necessary accoutrements to a good sausage, provided he had enough beer to wash them down.

'When did you know it was Tripka?'

'I was sure it was a policeman when Holoubek was killed so soon after seeing me. I settled on Tripka after Peiperová was kidnapped.'

'But the other one had been around Prague for ages. Didn't anyone recognise him as Sedláček?'

'It had been over ten years when he came back, and it was a few more years before he started making serious money. He'd gone grey and lost a bit of muscle.'

'So what put you on to him?'

'That newspaper story you found. I'd been trying to find one killer for all the victims, but then it struck me that it didn't have to be the same one. The fact that Hruška saw soldiers confirmed the way I was thinking. I'd realised that when Válková was killed young Tripka would have been doing his national service. And I'd also realised that the dislike between old Tripka and Vaněček was such that Tripka could well have engineered Vaněček's killing. I just couldn't see who would have helped Vaněček by framing Bartoš. Of course, if you want to get off a charge, finding someone else to carry the can is a good move, but I couldn't see why it had to be Bartoš until his mother mentioned the money. After that it was clear in my head. Young Tripka had to be involved in the killing of Jana

Válková, and the old man had covered it up and found a scapegoat. I started by believing that the spat with Vaněček three years later must have been about something else, and that eventually Tripka had eliminated him, but why take the risk of killing someone who had lost anyway? Then it dawned on me that it must be fear that the case was going to be blown open. That would cause a killing, because it was the only way the Tripkas would ever be safe. The Mandy thing was a confirmatory detail — plenty of us listened secretly to Western radio, but only an StB agent would sing American tunes publicly. I still need one or two more things ironing out, but we're almost there now.'

'A job well done, Josef. You must be very pleased.'

'Actually, old friend, I'm feeling flat, dejected, tired, old, you name it. Get your thesaurus out, because I've run out of adjectives. Young Tripka had done all this and he was still one of the police force's top men. Why hadn't we spotted him? How many others are there in high places with dirty pasts? When Communism fell I thought we'd clear all these villains out and I'd see a proper, honest police force doing what I joined the police to do — to sort out crime and keep people safe. Here I am, coming up to retirement and we haven't finished the job. Thank God for the likes of Navrátil and Peiperová who may just be good enough to complete the spring cleaning.'

'They're bright kids.'

'They're the future, and I'm ancient history. Come on, old friend, I'm getting maudlin. Put me on the night bus and let's go home.'

Chapter 20

The morning dawned bright and cheerful, and the sun slanted down on a police headquarters that was missing Josef Slonský. During the night an idea had occurred to him, and he was therefore moving from office to office collecting signatures and permits. It might have been helpful if he had communicated his intentions to his increasingly frantic boss, who was unsure whether to tear up the paper in his top drawer, or go ahead with it. It also crossed his mind that Slonský might have been seized by Griba's men with a view to swapping him for the criminal. If that happened the official policy of the government was that the captors would be told that no deal was possible and they must do their worst. Lukas would have felt very uneasy about condemning Slonský to death in that way, the only mitigating factor being that Slonský would undoubtedly have done the same if the roles were reversed. Indeed, if a deal were to be done, Slonský himself would probably repudiate it. But that did not make it any easier for his bemused superior.

If he had only thought to ask Mucha, his mind might have been set at rest, because Slonský had consulted the desk sergeant before beginning his quest, and a small smile was flickering across Mucha's lips even now as he stood arranging the staff roster for the next month. Its cause was not the thought of giving himself a weekend shift when his wife's sister was coming to stay, nor even of the pleasure he would derive from making that slimy little toad Bureš work on his birthday, but of the lengths Slonský was prepared to go to in order to ensure a conviction. His plan might not work, but you had to admire the fact that he was even bothering to try.

Tripka looked up as Slonský and Navrátil entered the interview room. Slonský sat opposite the disgraced policeman and placed a box on the table. Removing the lid, he carefully lifted the contents out and stood it in front of him.

'Recognise this? I thought you'd like to see your dad again.'

'What do you mean by digging him up? What has this to do with him?'

'I've brought him in for questioning in connection with a very serious offence that he may have committed. He's just as guilty as you, so this way you both get to spend thirty years behind bars. I admit it probably won't worry him as much as it will you, but you'll enjoy each other's company. Unless you'd prefer me to scatter him in the exercise yard?'

'No! You can't do this. It's inhuman.'

'Inhuman? That's rich coming from someone who held a teenage girl down while his mate raped and slashed her. What's inhuman about scattering ashes? It happens all the time. What would be inhuman would be if I took this urn and emptied the contents down the toilet, but fortunately you have an hour to prevent that.'

'You wouldn't dare.'

'Wouldn't I? Now that's where you're wrong, because I've done a lot of stupid things as dares in the past. Running across the railway line when the express was coming, skiing over a blind jump, eating sushi — this would just be another in a long line. Now, you give a fresh statement to Navrátil while I go and pick the wax seal off the lid of the urn.'

'You're a monster, Slonský. We're the same vintage. We've worked together for years. You know what the old days were

270

like. Why couldn't you just let me take the best way out, for old times' sake?'

Slonský leaned menacingly over the table and spoke slowly but with passion.

'Because you're an ordinary criminal, and ordinary criminals don't get to avoid a trial by shooting themselves. Because we were never that close anyway and I've despised you for many years. It was probably unfair of me because I disliked you because of what your father was, but that's how I felt. Because Jana Válková and Edvard Holoubek deserve to be avenged for what you did to them. They weren't offered a clean, quick death with a pistol. Because if I don't put you in the dock I'm as bad as you are, and I have enough on my conscience already without doing anything else that I shouldn't.'

Tripka closed his eyes and seemed to be composing himself.

'I didn't go to Jana's house intending her any harm. If I'd known what Sedláček was going to do I'd never, ever have taken him. I let my loyalty to a friend get in the way of what I should have done. You have to remember I was very young.'

'Young, but not an idiot. You knew right from wrong.'

'Yes, and it was wrong. There, I've said it. I did wrong. I should have stopped him. I should have owned up. I didn't know what my father would say when I phoned him. I suppose I hoped he'd stay with me while I was being questioned. It honestly didn't occur to me that he would cover it all up. Even if he'd wanted to, I didn't think he could. If he'd been caught he'd have been disciplined and disgraced.'

'He'll be disgraced now. Like father, like son, eh?'

'I accept that I bear some of the blame for what happened to Jana. I also regret what happened to Holoubek. I didn't really know what I thought Sedláček would do when I asked him to stop Holoubek asking for the case to be reopened. I can't say it didn't cross my mind that he might kill him, because nothing crossed my mind. I panicked, and I didn't think. I was wrong and I deserve some of the blame. What proportion of the guilt is mine, I leave to others to decide.'

'The greater the share Sedláček has to carry, the less there is for you. For what it's worth, I believe you when you say you didn't plan to hurt Jana. You liked her too much. And if Holoubek had left well alone you'd have left him alone. But he didn't and you didn't. Now, the last chance you have to redeem a bit of honour for yourself is to tell the whole story, stop Sedláček getting off and take your punishment like a man.'

Tripka took a deep breath and inspected his hands for some time. When he spoke, his voice was barely above a whisper.

'In my house, there's a crawlspace in the eaves alongside the guest bedroom. In there, there's a metal toolbox. It's painted blue. If you lift the top tray out you'll find a bundle of letters from Sedláček that he wrote while he was in the army here. In a couple of them he talks about what happened to Jana. He says he enjoyed it and wanted to do it again. He recalls how she tried to shake him off her despite having her hands tied. I kept them so that if he ever tried to incriminate me I could turn the tables.'

'You're not very trusting, are you?'

Tripka raised his head, and his sad brown eyes met Slonský's.

'Only a fool trusts Sedláček. I may be a fool, but even I'm not that stupid.'

Slonský acknowledged the truth of this statement with a cursory nod.

'We'll go and get the letters. If you're right, we can start talking about mitigating your sentence.' He started to walk to the door, then turned back, picked up the urn, and handed it to Tripka. 'Villain or not, he's still your dad. Take care of him.'

Slonský was no psychologist, but he could detect a certain amount of latent hostility in Sedláček's attitude to him. For a start, the hoodlum was slightly put out that he had been shot.

'When I get out, you'll regret that,' he said.

'When you get out, I'll be sitting on a cloud with wings,' Slonský corrected him, 'or I'll be over ninety. I suppose you'll run me over like Holoubek, now that you've got your eye in and you know exactly how to take out old age pensioners with a van.'

'I'm not going inside. What sort of evidence have you got that would hold me?' Sedláček asked scornfully.

'I'm sorry,' said Slonský, 'I'm not allowed to discuss whatever evidence we have in detail. But I can tell you that Tripka will tie you to the murder of Válková, Pluskal will say you ordered the killing of Holoubek and the kidnapping of Peiperová, and some Albanian acquaintances of yours have been queueing up to give us evidence on a range of other events in recent years.'

'Losing rivals can't be trusted to tell the truth,' Sedláček replied.

'That's fair comment, but I don't think they're too worried about whether it's the truth, so long as it puts you away for a long time. Come to think of it, I agree with them. Whatever they're fabricating, I hope it stands up in court.'

Back at the office, Navrátil voiced their shared concern.

'Have we got enough to hold him?'

'The prosecutor says so. He reckons he'll get convictions on the murder of Holoubek and the abduction of Peiperová without much difficulty. The murder of Válková is more problematic, but we've got an eye-witness, Sedláček's letters and a conspirator's sworn statement. Either way, you'll be close to retirement when he gets out.'

Peiperová and Navrátil came to stand in front of Slonský's desk. As their shadow blotted out the feeble light from the bulb overhead, he looked up to see them standing side by side to attention.

'May we have a word, sir?' Navrátil began.

'If I say no?'

'I'll ask instead, sir,' Peiperová explained.

'I take it the use of the word "we" is significant, in view of my warning that there mustn't be a "we".'

'It is, sir. We've become a "we",' Navrátil explained.

'Congratulations. Are you still standing there because you're expecting a present?'

'No, sir,' Peiperová interjected. 'We're wondering what happens to me now. Plainly I can't stay here if Navrátil and I are engaged, and I'm only with you temporarily anyway.'

'Not so fast, young lady. How do you know I won't keep you and give Romeo here the elbow?'

Peiperová looked anxiously at Navrátil, who was definitely flustered by this turn of events. His face was reddening and he had the facial expression of a frog with dyspepsia.

'Because that wouldn't be fair to Navrátil, and you're a fair man, sir.'

'If you believe that you're a shocking judge of character, my girl. I think there's something you should both know.'

'Sir?' they chorused.

'I went to see Captain Lukas yesterday to talk about my future. Let's go and find him so he can tell you what he has decided.'

If Lukas' office had possessed a back door, he might well have disappeared when he saw the three of them approach, but he was trapped. He invited them all to sit.

'Now,' he asked, adopting his most avuncular manner, 'what's all this about?'

Slonský motioned Navrátil to speak.

'The thing is, sir, that Officer Peiperová and I—'

'How are you, Peiperová? Recovering well?'

'Yes, thank you, sir.'

'Good. First class. Sorry, Navrátil, you were saying?'

'Well, sir, when Officer Peiperová was kidnapped, it made me think that perhaps, in the fullness of time, she might possibly not be averse—'

'We're engaged, sir,' Peiperová interrupted.

'Excellent,' Lukas responded. 'I'm pleased for you both.'

'Thank you, sir. However, we're aware that there are rules about couples working together and we weren't clear how separate we have to be. For example, can we work in the same department under different lieutenants?'

'Ah, yes. Very good question.'

They sat in silence for a moment or two, until it dawned on Lukas that the only one who could answer that very good question was him.

'There is a difficulty. Undoubtedly, having married — or even engaged — people working together can be tricky for their colleagues and is therefore frowned upon, but in the present circumstances I don't have anywhere else to assign you. Dvorník and Doležal both have assistants already.' He paused and looked squarely at Slonský. 'You haven't changed your mind, Lieutenant?'

'No, sir,' said Slonský stiffly.

'Very well. We must deal with matters as we find them. Lieutenant Slonský has decided that if I am prepared to grant permission, he would like to have two trainees to look after.

He says that he will not find that your relationship causes him any concern. Is that right, Slonský?'

'Yes, sir, because I'm going to ignore it completely. In the event of untoward canoodling by either party, I shall put some bromide in Navrátil's coffee or describe my prostate operation. Either of these steps should suffice to cool their ardour.'

Lukas did not reply at first, since he was contemplating his own prostate's performance and his doctor's plans for it, and feeling more than a little uncomfortable as a result.

'I've signed the forms,' he finally announced. 'Officer Peiperová, you are now formally attached to Lieutenant Slonský.'

'Though not in any physical sense,' Slonský quickly added.

'This calls for a celebration drink,' Slonský announced. 'We can raise a glass to your future at the same time as we celebrate a job well done in putting Sedláček and Tripka behind bars for years to come.'

'I thought you'd be anti-marriage, sir,' said Navrátil.

'Me? No, marriage is a fine institution. For everyone else, that is.'

'Forgive my asking, sir, but did you call Mrs Slonská as you promised?'

'Ah, now, the thing is, I lost the number.'

'No problem, sir. I found it. Here it is.' He handed Slonský the crumpled napkin.

'Maybe I'll call later.'

Navrátil handed him his mobile.

'Be my guest, sir. We'll be at the bar.'

A NOTE TO THE READER

Dear Reader,

I wanted to thank you for spending your time reading about Josef Slonský and his colleagues. If this is your introduction to them, you may want to read *Lying and Dying* in which they first appeared. If you've already read that, thank you for your loyalty and perseverance, and I'll look forward to welcoming you to book 3, *Death on Duty*.

This story came about when I read an account of a trial of a man who was alleged to have been a concentration camp guard. The witnesses were, perforce, very elderly, and it seemed to me that there was a dilemma here; they were entitled to justice for their suffering, but increasing age and the passage of time meant that the chances of a successful conviction were declining. It seemed to me that, to a greater or lesser extent, this must be true of all cold cases. There will come a point at which a conviction just is not possible.

This led to the idea of a crime committed under the old regime being investigated many years later. The previous book was set in 2006, so that established a time for this one; going back thirty years would make all the witnesses sufficiently elderly.

As for Edvard Holoubek, he came into my mind when I was watching a documentary about Erich Honecker, the former leader of East Germany. Their shared initials are either coincidental or some deep subconscious thing I cannot explain. In my mind's eye, Holoubek had the look of a Honecker in his old age.

In reality, the dividing line between the police and the army in Communist Czechoslovakia was not as clear as I describe here. They formed a state internal security service and people could move between them. However, many of the staff saw themselves as either police or army and spoke about them in that way. I will also admit to having simplified the system of ranks of police officers.

If you have enjoyed this novel I'd be really grateful if you would leave a review on **Amazon** and **Goodreads**. I love to hear from readers, so please keep in touch through **Facebook** or **Twitter**, or leave a message on my **website**.

Všechno nejlepší!

Graham Brack

Sapere Books is an exciting new publisher of brilliant fiction and popular history.

To find out more about our latest releases and our monthly bargain books visit our website:
saperebooks.com

Printed in Great Britain
by Amazon

82421128R00161